Date: 1/29/20

A KILLER CAROL

 This Large Print Book carries the Seal of Approval of N.A.V.H.

A KILLER CAROL

LAURA BRADFORD

THORNDIKE PRESS
A part of Gale, a Cengage Company

Farmington Hills, Mich • San Francisco • New York • Waterville, Maine
Meriden, Conn • Mason, Ohio • Chicago

Copyright © 2019 by Laura Bradford.
An Amish Mystery.
Thorndike Press, a part of Gale, a Cengage Company.

Thorndike Press® Large Print Mystery.
The text of this Large Print edition is unabridged.
Other aspects of the book may vary from the original edition.
Set in 16 pt. Plantin.

LIBRARY OF CONGRESS CIP DATA ON FILE.
CATALOGUING IN PUBLICATION FOR THIS BOOK
IS AVAILABLE FROM THE LIBRARY OF CONGRESS

ISBN-13: 978-1-4328-6809-3 (hardcover alk. paper)

Published in 2019 by arrangement with Berkley, an imprint of Penguin Publishing Group, a division of Penguin Random House, LLC

Printed in Mexico
1 2 3 4 5 6 7 23 22 21 20 19

For my family.

ACKNOWLEDGMENTS

This is always one of my favorite parts of the book publishing process — getting to say thank you to the people who have helped make this book happen in one way or another. For this go-round, I'd like to thank my cover artist, Mary Ann Lasher. Every cover in this series has been amazing, truly. But this one? Wow. She absolutely outdid herself.

I'd also like to thank my editor, Michelle Vega, and the whole Berkley Prime Crime team for their faith in me as a writer. Thanks are in order, too, for you, my readers — you are why this book, and this series, continues. Keep spreading the word so I can keep writing these stories!

And last but not least, a huge thank-you to my family. Their patience when I'm writing (and oftentimes zoning out) is invaluable to me.

If you enjoy this book, and this series,

come see what else I write at laurabradford
.com.

CHAPTER 1

Claire Weatherly backed away from the butcher block paper, her thoughts, her gaze, riveted on the single taunting question mark she'd underlined a half-dozen times over the past hour. Every detail she'd painstakingly planned for Heavenly's first ever Christmas festival was right there in front of her in red and green marker.

The Living Nativity was all set now, thanks to Esther and Eli Miller's promise of three sheep . . .

Santa Claus was secured for a five P.M. arrival atop Heavenly's sparkly new firetruck . . .

The horse-drawn sleigh that would transport festival-goers from one end of Lighted Way to the other had been located and rented . . .

Annie's friends had agreed to sing Christmas carols by the gazebo . . .

The Amish teen tasked with manning the

open fire so folks could roast their own chestnuts had confirmed his participation . . .

The flyers she'd created the previous weekend were already posted on every shopkeeper's door, and buzz was growing . . .

The —

"That is a lot of things for one person to keep track of."

Slanting her attention toward the open doorway, Claire smiled at the Amish woman standing just a few feet away, studying the paper with a mixture of curiosity and confusion. "Ruth Miller — I mean, *Yoder*! How long have you been standing there?"

"Long enough to know you have been working very hard on your plans." Ruth stepped forward, collected her hug, and then reclaimed their original distance to study Claire from head to toe. "But not quite long enough to know why you look so worried."

Claire opened her mouth to protest her friend's assessment but instead perched against the edge of her simple metal desk and allowed her shoulders the sag she could no longer hold back. "It's just that I want One Heavenly Night to be perfect. For everyone. I mean, I know there will be things that work and things that don't. It's new, so mistakes will be made. But it's my first real sizable contribution as a Lighted Way business owner, and I want it to be the best it can be."

"And you do not think it will be?" Ruth asked, her naturally arched brows inching upward toward the snippet of blond hair peeking out around the edges of her white prayer kapp.

Claire looked again at the paper. "It's missing something. It's not something big, or probably even all that important, really, but whatever it is, I feel like it'll tie the proverbial bow on everything."

"If you need another cow, Samuel can bring over Nettie or Nellie. And if it is a goat, he could bring over Gussy."

"No, the animal portion of the Living Nativity is all set, although I'll keep that in mind should one of your brother's cows or goats come down with a case of stage fright."

"A cow is just a cow," Ruth said, drawing back, her startlingly blue eyes momentarily dull. "And a goat is just a goat. They do not get stage fright."

Claire's answering laugh filled the tiny work space. "Technically, I was kidding. But it's the unexpected stuff that tends to throw a monkey wrench into stuff like" — she swept her hand toward the papered wall — *"this."*

"I saw Esther today," Ruth said, stepping all the way into the office. "She is very excited for your festival, too. *Everyone* in our district is."

"I'm glad." And she was. Really. It was just tempered, quite heavily, by a healthy case of nerves she couldn't quite get under control . . .

"What do you think it is missing?"

Claire swung her gaze back to her plans and shrugged. "I don't know. One final touch that will put a smile on everyone's face."

"Perhaps this" — Ruth held out her hand to reveal a small rectangular piece of candy wrapped in green wax paper and tied at each end with red ribbon — "will put a smile on *your* face while you figure it out."

Claire's stomach rumbled in response as she took the treat. "What is this? It looks so festive."

"It is one of Hannah's caramel candies wrapped for the holiday."

"One of Hannah's caramels?" she echoed, untying both ribbons. "Ooooh, I love Hannah's caramels."

"Then I am glad I brought you one."

"I am, too." She folded back the top edge of the green waxed paper, took a bite of the candy, and gave in to the moan of pleasure the first bite always demanded. "Oh. Wow. So, so good."

Ruth nodded knowingly. "Yah. People still buy my apple pies, but it is Hannah's caramels that are the favorite now."

"Trust me, it's not a reflection on your pies," Claire said between chews. "It's just that the newbies to Lighted Way aren't getting lured up the steps by their smells the way they did when you worked there. Now I think it's more about what kind of treat they're hankering for when they go into the bake shop on their own accord. Maybe they want caramels, maybe they want brownies, maybe they want cookies . . . But if they opt for a piece of your apple pie, I have no doubt they'll be every bit as addicted as your unending allegiance of fans."

Shyness drove Ruth's gaze toward the floor while hunger pulled Claire's attention back to the remaining candy in her hand. "I love this wrapper . . ."

"It was what you said to Samuel and the other shopkeepers that made me think of such wrappers," Ruth said, looking up.

"What *I* said?"

"Yah. Samuel said it was when you spoke

of" — Ruth gestured toward the papered wall again — "your special night."

Claire waved at the woman's words with her candy-holding hand. "It's not *my* special night, Ruth. It's for everyone who lives in Heavenly. It's for the grown-ups and the kids and everyone in between. If the holiday window displays in front of Glick's Tools 'n More, and Shoo Fly Bake Shoppe, and Glorious Books, and Heavenly Brews, and Taste of Heaven(ly), and your Samuel's furniture shop lull people back to shop along Lighted Way the next day, that's wonderful. But the real fun, the real memories, the real reason for doing this, will be happening outside — on the sidewalk and by the gazebo, and down in the park area. *That's* where people will be celebrating the season and visiting with their neighbors. Assuming, of course, people even come . . ."

"You do not think people will come?" Ruth asked, stepping back.

"I can't know for sure. Not yet, anyway." Claire finished the last bite of caramel and then carefully folded the green paper in her hand. "It's the first time doing this. There's no precedent."

"It is all Esther and I talked about this morning."

"So then you'll both be there? With Samuel and Eli, too?"

"Yah. Many Amish will be there. They have said so when Samuel and I have been visiting."

She peeked at Ruth, her thoughts tilting between her friend and the festival. "You and Samuel have not finished your post-wedding visits yet?"

"Sunday we will finish. With Mary and Daniel Esch." Ruth leaned her slender frame against the wall, her eyes, if not her thoughts, returning to the paper and Claire's notes. "When we learned Samuel's hope would not be so, I wished we had visited them first. But he is a good man. He understands God's will and does not question."

She knew Ruth was talking, even knew it was something she probably wanted to hear, but at that moment all she could really focus on was the green wrapper, the red ribbons, and —

"Wait . . . Oh my gosh — Ruth! This is it! The missing piece!" Holding up the wrapper and ribbons, Claire unleashed her growing smile on Ruth. "These candies! Wrapped up just like this! Can Hannah make more? For us . . . for *this*?" She jerked her chin and Ruth's attention back to the board as the elusive last detail finally clicked into place. "It — it doesn't even have to be just caramels. It could be peppermints, or — or brownies, or wait — no, I've got it! We'll do cookies . . . shaped ones. Maybe a snowman or a reindeer or something like that. And they could be decorated really sweetly, so they look extra special when the kids untie these red ribbons and pull off this green paper!"

Ruth furrowed her brow. "I would need to cut the wrappers larger for a shaped cookie . . ."

"You cut this wrapper yourself?" she asked, looking down at the wrapper and ribbons once again. "You didn't buy these?"

"I bought the paper and the ribbons, but I cut them to the right size, just as I do with the white paper the caramels are usually wrapped in."

"I can help cut them during quiet times here, and maybe Hannah could do the same at the bake shop. And I'm sure, if we needed more help, Esther would lend a hand, especially if we timed it to when the baby is sleeping. And maybe, after each cookie is wrapped up, we could stick on one of those little Shoo Fly Bake Shoppe stickers you always used on your pie boxes."

Ruth reached out, touched the wrapper, and then pulled her hand back, the hint of

16

a smile lifting her already high cheekbones even higher. "Would you need many cookies?"

"I don't know . . . maybe a hundred, maybe . . ." Turning back toward her desk, Claire grabbed her festival notebook and flipped to the second page. "Yeah, I'm thinking you'll need to make more like a hundred and fifty just to be safe. I'd rather have some leftovers than not have enough for every child who comes. If we have a surplus, I could always take the leftovers to the police station, or some of the Amish schools around town, or even the library, for that matter."

"One hundred and fifty is a lot of cookies and a lot of wrappers," Ruth said.

Rising up on the toes of her ankle-length boots, Claire closed the notebook, hugged it to her chest, and let loose a tiny squeal. "I'd be willing to help bake so it wouldn't take too much of your time from Samuel. And as for Benjamin and Eli, it's not like Shoo Fly Bake Shoppe would be donating these cookies at its own expense. The Lighted Way Business Association would pay you for the cookies just like we're paying to rent the sled and the horse and the chestnuts and everything else we need to pull this thing off."

17

"They would *buy* them?"

"Absolutely. Just tell me what you would've charged for them when you were working at the bake shop, and we'll pay the same amount."

"A hundred and fifty cookies, you say?" Ruth asked.

"That's right."

"For *one night . . .*"

Claire swapped the notebook for the red marker, pulled off the cap, and held it to the butcher block paper. "That's right, one night — *One Heavenly Night,* to be exact . . . So? What do you say? Do you think Samuel will be okay letting Shoo Fly Bake Shoppe borrow his new wife for however long it'll take to make, decorate, and wrap a hundred and fifty Christmas cookies?"

"It would only take a few hours," Ruth mused, tapping her finger to her chin. "And it would certainly help with . . ." Waving away the rest of her sentence, Ruth nodded at Claire and the marker. "Yah. I think a hundred and fifty cookies will please Samuel very much."

CHAPTER 2

Claire lowered the red and white porcelain mug to her lap and sagged back against the wooden swing, defeated. "For a moment there, I'd actually dared to hope the steam was playing tricks with my eyes, but it's not. The gap is there, the gap is real."

"Gap?" Aunt Diane tucked her chin inside the turned-up collar of her down coat.

"In the lights. See?" Claire pointed at the colorfully lit spruce tree just beyond Sleep Heavenly's front porch. "It's about midway up, and then slightly to the right."

"Midway up, slightly to the right, and" — Diane dismissed her visual tour with a flick of her hand — "I don't see any sort of gap."

"No, it's there. *Squint,*" she said, demonstrating. "You'll see it."

Diane looked back at Claire. "Why? Who walks around squinting?"

"You don't do it because people walk around that way, Aunt Diane. You do it *just in case.* So you can know it's perfect."

"Seems to me the only thing your squint test does each year is drive you batty."

"There's that, yes. But it works!" she protested.

The sixty-three-year-old innkeeper rolled her eyes. "Remind me again, dear, who taught you this silly squint test? Because I'd like to remove them from my Christmas card list if they're on it, or add them just so I can remove them if they're not."

With one last look at the strands of lights she'd spent the better part of two hours arranging, Claire pulled the mug to her chest and breathed in the limited warmth that remained. "I'm not sure exactly. Probably someone in New York — an old co-worker, or someone I met through Peter, maybe?"

"Then consider whoever it was to be on and" — Aunt Diane brushed her gloved palms against each other — "now *off* my list. And you — you need to just see that tree the way I see it."

Lifting the mug to her lips, Claire refrained from taking a sip in favor of smiling at her father's only sister. "Okay, so tell me how *you* see it, then . . ."

"Beautiful. Elegant. Charming. Magical. And most definitely spirit-igniting."

"Spirit-igniting?" she echoed, cocking an

eyebrow.

Aunt Diane nodded. "I could see you from the kitchen window while you were stringing those lights."

"And?"

"I left the soup simmering while I went up into the attic and brought down my Christmas decorations for the kitchen." Aunt Diane unburied her chin just long enough to take a sip of her own drink. "Those Santa canister covers we bought at that outdoor market over the summer look even more darling on my countertops than I imagined. Ditto for the Rudolph spoon rest."

"Ooooh, I must see them." Claire dropped her slipper-clad feet onto the floor, stilling the swing's answering sway with the tip of one foot. "Martha brought in some canister covers with snowflakes embroidered on them for the store. I'm sure they're going to fly off the shelf, like everything else she makes does."

Aunt Diane's chin rose above her collar once again, her warm brown eyes landing on Claire. "Actually, dear, could we hold off on looking at the kitchen for a few moments? Maybe talk for a little while instead?"

"Sure," she said, leaning forward. "Is

everything okay?"

When there was no response beyond a loss of eye contact, Claire scooted across the swing's bench, reducing the space between them to little more than the length of her leg. "Aunt Diane? Are you not feeling well?"

"No, no, it's nothing like that, dear. I'm fine. Just . . . I don't know. I guess I'm feeling a little nostalgic, is all."

"But nostalgia usually makes you *happy*," Claire reminded her.

"And I *am* happy. I really am. But even the best of changes are still changes."

Depositing her mug beside her feet, Claire reached across the divide between their seats and enveloped Diane's hand with her own. "Is this about including Bill and Jakob in our Christmas traditions this year? Because if it is, it's going to be wonderful. They're going to love it — all of it. Guaranteed."

Diane's eyes dropped to her own mug still clenched in her free hand. "It's just that Christmas is such a special time of year. Everyone has their own traditions, their own way of doing things. And I don't want to let anyone down, least of all you."

"*Me?* Are you kidding? I love the way we do Christmas — the special ornaments for each other, the candlelight service on

Christmas Eve, the dessert buffet we have when we get back, the matching pajamas we wear to bed, writing silly riddles for your presents and reading the ones you've written for mine, watching an old Christmas movie in the middle of the afternoon, and Christmas dinner on Grandma's fancy china. It's"— she released a happy sigh — "the best. All of it."

"You're right. It is." Diane slid her hand out from under Claire's, set her drink on her armrest, and stood, her focus shifting to the moon-drenched fields of their Amish neighbors in the distance.

Claire, too, stood, and trailed her aunt over to the porch railing, the rapidly plummeting temperature eliciting a shiver from between her lips. "R-r-remember that first day after Ruth and Samuel's wedding last month? When it really hit me that Ruth wouldn't be filling the alleyway between her bakery and my shop with all those wonderful smells any longer? And how I went on and on about how much I'd miss her sunny greeting when we were sweeping our front porches at the same time?"

Diane nodded.

"You told me the most important stuff wouldn't change all that much." Claire pivoted until her back was flush with the railing and her focus was locked on Diane's. "And you know what? You were right. Ruth Miller becoming Ruth Yoder didn't change the stuff that matters. Sure, I don't see her every day like I did before the wedding, but I still *see* her — like I did yesterday. And between the pies Ruth still sends into the shop each day via Samuel or one of her brothers, and the homemade toffees and candy Hannah King has added to the old menu, the smells are still there. Do I still think *Annie* should have thrown her hat into the ring for Ruth's job? Sure. The stuff Annie bakes and brings in for me to try on occasion is nothing short of mind blowing. But as far as Shoo Fly Bake Shoppe, and Ruth not being there every day . . . it's all worked out. Like you said it would."

"But it's still different, yes?"

Claire considered her answer as she watched her breath turn the air white. "It is. A little, I suppose. But it's okay. Good, even. Because now, in addition to having Ruth as a friend, I'm growing closer to Hannah, too. And in the process, I've discovered I have a real penchant for butterscotch toffee."

As Diane's answering laugh trailed away, Claire reached for her hand once again, this time adding a reassuring squeeze. "Will our

24

Christmas traditions be exactly the same with two more people there? Maybe, maybe not. But seeing as how those two people happen to mean the world to both of us, I'm willing to bet their presence will make this year's Christmas the best yet. For you. For me. For all of us."

Flipping her hand inside Claire's, Diane pulled her niece in for a quick hug. "Thank you, dear. I don't know what I'd do without you sometimes."

"I feel the same about you. A million times over."

Diane stepped back, gesturing over her shoulder toward the front door. "I suppose we should head inside before we both end up catching colds and having to spend the holiday in bed."

"I'll be in in a few minutes. I just need to fill *that*" — she pointed toward the tree — "gap. If I don't, I'll be squinting at it from my bedroom window all night long."

"You're incorrigible, dear."

"I love Christmas, you know that."

"And you have since you were a little bit of a thing," Diane mused. "Which is why I know that trying to get you to wait until tomorrow to fix those lights would be futile."

"You know me so well." Claire kissed her

aunt's forehead and then crossed to the stairs, glancing back as she reached the top step. "Do me a favor? Don't tell Jakob about this little issue I have, okay? Especially now, with him being so . . . off, so hard to figure out."

Diane held up her hand. "Whoa. Stop right there."

"I really should get to those lights," she protested.

"And you will. After you tell me what you mean by Jakob being off and hard to figure out. Since when?"

Claire cut short her mental chastising in favor of a labored shrug. "I don't know, maybe as much as a week."

"Off? Off, how?"

Oh, how she wished she could answer that. If she could, then maybe the trio of restless nights she'd had wouldn't balloon into a fourth. Then again, it was the nervous energy sparked by his odd behavior that had her ahead of schedule on her weekly tasks at both the shop and her aunt's inn . . .

"Off, how?" Diane repeated, waiting.

"Distant. Removed. Like . . . like he's keeping something from me."

"Have you asked him about it?"

"I haven't really had a chance. Every time we've seen each other these past few days, he gets a call or a text that has him cutting our visit or our conversation short. But when I ask him about it afterward, he either pretends he doesn't remember what I'm talking about or he changes the subject to something completely unrelated."

"I'm sure it's nothing to worry about, dear. Detective Jakob Fisher is a straight shooter who happens to be head over heels in love with —"

A siren from the direction of town cut short the rest of Diane's reassurance and sent their collective attention down the stairs, across the driveway, and toward Lighted Way. Bobbing her head to the left, Claire took advantage of the leafless maple trees bordering the northwestern edge of the inn's property to note the lone gas-powered streetlamp visible from her vantage point. The light, she knew, was the one nearest the mouth of the quaint thoroughfare, a few footsteps from Glick's Tools 'n More and just two shops away from her own. On a clear, cloudless day, she could make out the front corner of the popular hardware shop if she stepped a bit more to the left and added a jump, but the clouds passing in front of the moon at that moment kept her feet, if not her thoughts, rooted to the porch. "It's too early in the season for a

Christmas tree fire," Claire mused aloud. "Maybe a space heater?"

"I don't think it's a fire, dear," Diane said, her voice hushed. "Those look like *police* lights to me."

Claire glanced back at her aunt, only to be distracted away by intermittent slices of red and blue racing around the same bends and over the same hills she so often walked after work during the summer months. Only instead of the leisurely pace she preferred, the pulsing lights moved at a speed that didn't fit with the quiet Amish countryside or its people. Sucking in a shallow breath, she silently ticked off each farm in the patrol car's path — King, Lapp, Stoltzfus, Lehman, Beiler — then sighed in relief as it sped past each and every one. Just beyond the first of three mailboxes she knew bore the name of Miller, the lights broke left, headed south for a few heartbeats, and came to an abrupt stop. Before she could fully process the where in relation with a who, a second set of red and blue lights hijacked her attention, speeding past the same driveways, the same fields, the same farmhouses . . .

"What on earth do you think is going on down there, Aunt —"

"Claire, it's Annie."

Her mouth ran dry as she stared into the distance, her mind's eye swapping the almost melodic rhythm of the lights for a fully formed image of Annie Hershberger, the now seventeen-year-old Amish girl Claire employed at her gift shop, Heavenly Treasures.

The wide-set brown eyes . . .

The curious nature . . .

The infectious smile . . .

The desire to please . . .

Raw fear ripped through her body as the second set of lights drew to a stop behind the first, flashing and spinning in sync with one another. "It can't be Annie . . . The bishop's farm is the other way, isn't —"

"She sounds upset, dear."

Sounds?

Confused, she turned to find her phone clutched tightly in Diane's outstretched hand.

"Wait. You mean she's — oh thank God . . ." Relief overtook her and she sagged backward down the last step. "I . . . I didn't hear it ring."

"I heard it vibrating against the swing and picked it up."

Shaking her head, Claire jogged back up the stairs and took the phone from her aunt. "Annie, sweetie? Are you okay?"

Answering sniffles gave way to a heart-breaking cry that sent shivers down Claire's spine.

"What's going on?" Diane whispered.

Shrugging, Claire tilted the phone so her aunt could hear, too. "Are you hurt? Is it your dat?"

"N-no. It is not Dat."

With that ruled out, Claire moved on, her thoughts rewinding to the moment they'd gone their separate ways after closing the shop the previous evening. "I thought you were caroling tonight. With Henry and your other friends from youth group."

"I am. I mean, I *was.*"

"Did something happen?"

"Yah."

She looked again at the emergency lights shattering the quiet darkness of the night and willed herself to breathe. "Talk to me, kiddo."

Another round of sniffles gave way to a cough and, finally, a full sentence, albeit one peppered by brief pauses and even a hiccup. "Henry and I got there first. But it was not by much. Maybe a few minutes."

"Got where?"

"To Daniel and Mary's farm."

"Daniel and Mary?"

Annie's breath hitched once, twice, in her

ear. "Esch."

Something about the name tugged at Claire's memory, and she tried to place it among the many Amish faces she'd come to know since moving to Heavenly two years earlier, but she came up empty.

"You know them, dear. They're one of Nancy Warren's regular customers. Brings them into town a few times a month," Aunt Diane whispered, only to grow quiet as Annie began to speak once again.

"Since it is Sunday, and there are no Englishers there, Daniel's buggy was outside the barn and his horse inside, I am sure. When the rest of our friends came in their buggies, we began to sing. But the curtain did not move. That is when I waved to everyone to sing louder in case Daniel and Mary could not hear." Annie's inhale echoed in Claire's ear. "Sometimes at church, Dat asks me to sit next to Mary and be her ears. And later, after church, I fill Daniel's plate with the things he likes to eat because *he* cannot *see* very well anymore."

"Wait." Two kind faces emerged, fully formed, in Claire's thoughts. "I think I know who you're talking about. They're elderly, aren't they? In their mid-eighties, maybe? Mary has white hair, right? Big

31

round cheeks? And pretty blue eyes that seem to laugh when she smiles?"

"Yah, that is Mary."

"And Daniel . . . He's tall and slender? Gets around on a cane? Long gray beard that reaches nearly to the top of his pants?"

"Yah, that is Daniel."

"Ruth mentioned something about them when we last spoke but the names didn't ring any bells at the time. But now, talking to you, I realize I've seen them going into Gussmann's General Store on occasion — usually with Nancy Warren in tow to help carry their groceries." Claire leaned against the closest upright, her eyes on the flashing lights, her thoughts rewinding back a few weeks. "In fact, if I'm picturing the right people, I spoke with them a little at Ruth and Samuel's wedding last month. I found them to be very warm and welcoming — especially Mary."

"When my mamm died, it was Mary Esch who let me cry without saying it was God's will. When I could not cry anymore, she told me to look and look until I found things to make me happy. She said the sadness would not go away, but happy things would make it a little lighter." Annie exhaled a breath into the phone. "That is why I wanted everyone to sing louder. Because I knew the carols would be a happy thing for Mary."

"Okay . . ."

Annie's breath hitched again. "But still they did not come to the window. When I stepped closer, I saw that it was open."

"The window?" At Annie's strangled yes, Claire added, "But it's cold and the temperature is only dropping."

"That is what I thought, too. So I showed Henry and he walked up to the window with me while the others continued to sing. When he bent down to pick up a worker's glove, I called to Daniel and then to Mary through the open part of the window. But they did not answer. That is when Henry handed me the glove to hold while he got the lantern from his buggy and shined it inside. At first we did not see anything but a chair that was tipped over, and a dish. It was on the floor. Chicken and potatoes, too. Henry said it was a good thing that Mary and Daniel did not have a cat or it would be big and fat because of such food on the floor."

A glance at her aunt yielded a visual of the growing fear she felt snaking up her own spine. When Diane's eyes traveled back to the flashing lights in the distance, Claire closed her own and waited.

"It is then that I saw her foot. And soon,

his boots . . . and his legs. Henry climbed in. He looked at Daniel and then moved the pillow to see Mary. It is then that he knew they were" — Annie's voice broke — "dead."

Diane's gasp echoed Claire's. Before either could speak, though, Annie continued. "Henry told one of the other boys to run to the phone on the other side of the Dienners' farm and call for help. Soon there were many lights — blue lights and red lights, spinning and spinning."

Again, Claire looked at the flashing lights, one set belonging to a patrol car, the other surely to —

"Your Jakob is here," Annie said as if reading Claire's thoughts. "The lights from his car make it so I can see him and the other policeman through the window. He has been looking at Mary and Daniel a long time. But I wish he did not have to. I wish he could be drinking hot chocolate with you at Heavenly Brews, and I wish Mary and Daniel could have heard us sing. They would have liked that very much, I think."

Slowly Claire shifted her focus to the evergreen tree just beyond the porch railing, the lights she'd intended to fix just moments earlier no longer quite so pressing. An elderly couple was dead, Annie was traumatized by the discovery of their bodies, and Jakob was now tasked with notifying the couple's next of kin.

The sniffling in her ear segued into a raspy whisper. "Claire?"

"Yes, yes, sweetie, I'm still here."

"I know it is late, and I know it is wrong to ask when you must get up early in the morning, but if Henry and the others do not mind, could we sing a Christmas carol for you tonight? Outside your aunt's inn? You — you don't have to come outside, or even stand at the window if you are too tired. I just want . . ." Annie paused, then made a sort of dismissive noise that echoed in Claire's ear. "Pay me no mind. My question is . . . silly."

Was it?

Maybe.

Then again, maybe not. Maybe —

"Sometimes at church, Dat asks me to sit next to Mary and be her ears."

Sliding her hand over the phone, Claire leaned closer to her aunt. "Do we happen to have some cookies, by any chance?"

Diane cocked her left eyebrow. "Is that a question you even need to ask, dear?"

"Any of the Christmas-y ones left from the other day?" she clarified.

At the nod she sought, Claire removed her

hand. "Annie, come. Please. I think we could all use a little pick-me-up right about now, don't you?"

CHAPTER 3

She'd just finished tacking up the final piece of garland across the back wall when the jingle of the door-mounted bell alerted her to the arrival of a customer. Stepping down onto the carpet, Claire double-checked the greenery's evenness in relation to the red bow she'd affixed to the center and then nudged the step stool out of tripping range. "Welcome to Heavenly Treasures," she said, turning. "I'm Claire, and I'm happy to help if —"

"There was never a day I did not enjoy working here with you. Spring, summer, fall, it did not matter. But this time of year was always my most favorite."

"*Esther?* Is that you?"

Claire's former employee-turned-best-friend stepped fully into view, her sweet grin brightening the room more than any holiday decoration ever could. "Yah, it is me, and" — Esther's sparkling eyes dropped to the

carefully bundled mound in her arms —
"Sarah."

Squealing, Claire fast-stepped her way to
the door, her gaze ricocheting between Esther and the sleeping infant. "Ohhhh, sweet,
sweet little Sarah . . . I can't tell you how
happy I am to see you today . . ."

"It was not so long ago that you would
smile because *I* came for a visit," Esther
said, relinquishing her infant daughter into
Claire's ready arms. "Now, it is Sarah who
you are happy to see."

Claire planted a gentle kiss on the baby's
softly puckered cheeks and then fixed her
attention on the child's young mother.
"Now, now, Esther Miller. I still get every
bit as excited to see you. It's just that . . .
Well . . ." Her cheeks warming, she peeked
again at the baby. "I mean, look at her. She's
just so cute. And soft. And . . . wonderful."

Mindful of the pride she should not voice,
Esther nibbled back her answering smile
and, instead, cast the amber-flecked eyes
she shared with her uncle Jakob toward the
toes of her black lace-up boots. After a beat
or two of silence, she returned her gaze to
Claire's and the shop around them. "It all
looks so pretty," Esther said, sweeping her
hands toward the garland. "It will bring
many customers, I am sure."

38

"I hope so. I haven't started on the ornament tree yet, but now that the garland is on the counter and across the back wall, that's really all that's left to do."

Esther cocked her ear toward the back hallway and listened for a moment. "Are you working alone today?"

"Annie will be here at noon."

"That will give you time to do the rest."

Claire shrugged. "If I didn't have work to do back in the office, yes. But since I do, I'm taking advantage of the intermittent lull in customers to do as much of the decorating as I can now." Sliding her glance back to the garland, she smiled. "And it's coming along if I do say so myself. Now, if only *the tree* will go as well . . ."

"It will, *if* you do not do that silly thing you do with your eyes."

Sarah stirred at Claire's quiet laugh. "You sound like my aunt Diane."

"Because it is true."

"I know, I know. But I can't seem to stop myself. That's why I moved the tree to the last thing on my to-do list."

"So you will not squint?" Esther asked.

"No, so I *can.*"

Esther's eyebrows rose nearly to the patch of hair just barely visible along the front edge of her kapp. "I do not understand why

39

you do such a thing when it makes you so . . . so . . ."

"Crazy?"

"Yah."

"Well, as infuriating as it can be at times, I *like* to do the squint test. It makes the tree prettier, which, in turn, makes me happier. But I have a feeling even *that* won't shake off the sadness that's come from — oh . . . Esther . . . I'm so sorry. I shouldn't be talking about trees and decorating, or any of that stuff." She stopped, pulled her right hand out from under the baby, and gently squeezed Esther's forearm. "How are you and Eli holding up? Did you know them well?"

Confusion traded places with understanding as Esther removed her mittens and set them on the counter. "You speak of Daniel and Mary Esch, yah?"

At Claire's nod, Esther wiggled out of her coat to reveal an aproned emerald green dress. "Eli told me of their passing this morning. Bishop Hershberger stopped by with the news as Eli was filling the water troughs."

"Did you know them well?" Claire pointed toward the pair of stools on the other side of the counter and, when Esther sat, took the vacant one for herself and the baby.

40

"I remember them as kind when I was growing up. Mary always took time to ask about my quilts, and Daniel was helpful to my dat and many of the others in our district. Even though he was not a farmer, he knew many things. When Eli and I married, Daniel gave us a wagon he did not use anymore. It was a blessing, of course, but so, too, was the time we spent with them, listening and learning." Esther leaned back against the counter's edge and pursed her lips through a long, drawn-out exhale. "At first, when Eli told me they'd gone to be with God, I was sad. I could not picture a church service without them. But it was God's will for Mary and Daniel to go together, and I think that is the way they would have wanted it to be."

Claire let Esther's words sink in, the image they created sending her thoughts far beyond the confines of her shop. "Wow. I hadn't thought about it that way, I guess. I just thought how sad it was for their family to lose them at the same time. But what you just said? About them going together? It's hard not to see that as a little bit comforting, as well."

"Yah, I hope that will bring Ruth and Samuel comfort, too."

A memory she couldn't quite grab on to

41

retreated as fast as it had come, and she snapped her focus back to her friend. "Ruth and Samuel? They were close to Mary and Daniel?"

"I am sure it was for them the way it is for Eli and me. The wedding gift is helpful, of course, but so, too, is the learning you get when you visit."

"I think that's why I've always enjoyed spending time with the guests at the inn. Many of them are older, and you learn so much about life when you simply listen to them speak," Claire mused.

"Yah." Esther reached up and fingered an errant strand of brown hair back inside her kapp. "It was while sharing pie and cookies with so many in their homes during the visits after our wedding that we got to know friends in ways we did not know when we were younger. And we learned things — helpful things from everyone. Especially Daniel and Mary Esch."

"How so?"

"It is because of Daniel that Eli thought to get a sturdier buggy horse before Sarah was born. It is because of Mary that I take Sarah for a walk before she is to nap — she naps longer when I do."

Sure enough, when Claire looked down at Sarah, the child showed no signs of waking.

"I have to admit, I kind of wish she'd wake up just so I can hear her gurgle and coo the way she does."

Esther grinned. "But it is when she naps that I get my inside chores done. If she did not nap, I would get nothing done."

"A small price to pay."

"Yah. But Eli would have no dinner, and we would not have clean clothes to wear." Esther parted company with the edge of the counter, kissed her daughter's soft skin, and stood, her boots taking her around the shop in much the way they had when she, rather than Annie, had been in Claire's employ. "I know how close I felt to Mary and Daniel after Eli and I visited. I am sure Ruth felt the same way after her visit. But our visit was last year. Hers was" — Esther stopped midway across the room and turned back to Claire — "yesterday."

"Yesterday?" she echoed, only to roll her eyes upward. "Oh, that's right! I'd forgotten."

Esther nodded. "Daniel and Mary must have gone to the Lord not long after Ruth and Samuel headed back home in their bug —"

The quick jingle of the front door brought Claire to her feet in anticipation of the tourist or group of tourists she expected to see.

Instead, Jakob Fisher stepped inside, breathed into his fisted hands, and then dropped them to his side as his gaze slipped from Claire's to the baby in her arms. "Is that who I think it is?" he asked, stepping forward.

Before she could answer or even nod, the handsome detective closed the gap between them, the troubled expression she'd managed to register within seconds of his arrival bowing just as quickly to the smile now spreading across his face. "Well, hello, my sweet girl," he whispered. "It's your great uncle . . . Jakob."

Claire followed his gaze to the baby before meeting it, once again, with her own. "You look tired, Jakob. Are you okay?"

"It's been a long night." He took in the baby one more time and then pulled Claire in for a one-armed hug and a lingering kiss to her temple. "You should have told me you were babysitting. I'd have found a way to get over here sooner."

She noted the bloodshot eyes, the disheveled hair, the uncharacteristic stubble along his jawline . . . "Not babysitting. Just soaking her up while I visit with her beautiful mamm here . . ."

"Her beautiful —" Jakob swallowed the rest of his words as, guided by Claire's chin, he glanced to the left. "Esther! Hello! I'm sorry, I didn't see you standing there just now. How are you? How's Eli? How . . ." He stopped, cleared his throat, and strode over to his niece. "How's my sister taking the news about Mary and Daniel Esch? Like me, she grew up knowing them. Unlike me, however, she'd been able to maintain contact in the years since."

The familiar red tint that always accompanied the first few moments of contact between Esther and her once Amish uncle disappeared from her cheeks with a few deep breaths and a sweeping glance out the shop's front window. When she was sure no one from her church district was visible, she spoke. "Eli and I stopped by with the baby to see her after Bishop Hershberger's visit. Mamm and Dat were sad to hear such news, of course, but they, too, know it is God's will."

Jakob started to speak but stopped, his mouth tight.

"Jakob?" Claire prodded. "Is everything okay? You —"

"I'm sorry I didn't call last night." He raked a hand through his sandy blond hair, finding a smile — albeit a forced one — as he did. "Things were a little crazy."

"I understand. Aunt Diane and I were on

the porch last night. We saw the police lights." She closed the gap between them and, at Esther's nod of encouragement, placed the still sleeping child in the detective's arms. "Then Annie called and told us what was going on, so I knew you'd be tied up for a while."

His face softened as he took in his great niece. "Still am, actually," he said, his voice hushed. "According to what we know from the medical examiner's initial assessment, time of death was around four o'clock — about three hours before Annie and her friends showed up to carol."

"Is that for Mary or for Daniel?"

Lifting his gaze, he pinned Claire's. "Both."

"Wow . . . So what you see in the movies and read in books sometimes is actually true? People who spend a lifetime at each other's side really can go within minutes of each other?" She rubbed her arms against a sudden and unexpected chill. "That's both heartbreaking and beautiful all at the same —"

"Poor Ruth," Esther said from behind her hand. "Now she will really wonder if there was something she could have done to help them."

Jakob's chin snapped to the left, putting

his niece in his sights. "Did you say *Ruth*?"

"Yah."

"As in Ruth *Miller*?"

"She is Ruth Yoder now," Esther reminded.

He seemed to weigh the information in his head before handing the baby back to his niece. "Why would Ruth think she could have done something to help Daniel and Mary? Were they close?"

"She and Samuel were at Daniel and Mary's farm yesterday. Visiting."

He stared at Esther. "Yesterday?"

"Yah. To receive their wedding present."

"Do you know when — what time?" he asked, his voice sharp.

"It was yesterday."

"I get that. But . . ." His words petered out briefly as he paused to take in Esther's. "Yesterday was Sunday."

Clearly confused by Jakob's attitude shift, Esther's arms tightened around her daughter. "Bishop Hershberger was at his other district, so it was our visiting Sunday."

"Did you see Samuel's buggy at the Esch farm?"

"No. But I know they were to go there," Esther said. "Ruth told me so when I saw her on Saturday morning. She stopped by with a pie and to see the baby."

Jakob reached inside his front shirt pocket and extracted the tiny notebook he often kept tucked inside. "Do you know when, exactly, Ruth and Samuel would have been at the Esch farm?"

Esther traded glances with Claire. "I . . . I cannot say for sure. Only that Ruth was bringing a pie when she went — an *apple* pie because she said it was Mary's favorite."

"So maybe lunchtime or shortly thereafter?"

"Jakob?" Claire set her hand atop his arm. "What's this about? These questions . . ."

"Knowing the time of their visit would be something" — he waved his hand toward Esther — "to go on . . . a starting point."

The familiar fingers of dread began to make their way up Claire's spine. "*Starting point?* Starting point for what?"

"My investigation."

Her ensuing gasp, a few beats before Esther's, echoed around the shop, officially waking Sarah from her peaceful slumber. "Your investigation?" Claire echoed. "Into what?"

"Into the murders of Daniel and Mary Esch."

CHAPTER 4

"Claire?"

Pausing her index finger atop the minus sign, Claire redirected her attention toward her office doorway and the Amish teenager standing rather uncertainly inside it. "What's up, kiddo?"

"I am sorry to bother you, but Benjamin is here, and I think perhaps he would like to speak with you?"

"Ben's here? In the shop?" At Annie's nod, Claire pushed aside the calculator and stretched her arms above her head. "Absolutely. Just send him on back."

"I think he wants you to come inside the shop."

Stopping, mid-yawn, she stared at the girl. "Is there something wrong?"

Annie glanced over her shoulder before modulating her voice to a level only Claire could hear. "I do not know. When he came in a little while ago, he asked after you. I

49

told him that you are in here and that you are working on the consignment envelopes. I asked if he wanted me to get you, but he said no."

"Okay . . ."

Again, Annie peeked in the direction she'd come. "For twenty minutes now he has walked back and forth in many areas, whispering things to himself. But when I ask if I can help, it is as if he does not hear me."

"Is he alone?"

"Yah." Annie gestured toward the two distinct stacks of envelopes on Claire's desk. "I did not want to disturb you when I know you have much work to do. But I thought maybe, if you ask to help, he will answer."

The chair creaked as she stood. "You did the right thing, Annie. This stuff" — she waved at the envelopes still waiting to be filled with money — "can wait a little while. Friends can't."

"I knew you would say such a thing." Turning, Annie led the way out of the office, only to stop and gesture toward the broom resting against the wall. "Perhaps it would be a good time for me to sweep the front porch."

Claire started to protest, but after a quick glance at the hatted man slowly pacing around her shop, she reached inside her front pocket, extracted a five-dollar bill, and pressed it into Annie's hand. "When you're done, why don't you poke your head in next door and get us a couple of cookies — your choice. I've got a headache brewing and I could use the sugar boost."

"I will get chocolate chip. Those make you smile most."

"You think so, huh?"

"I know so." Grinning, Annie grabbed her simple black coat from the hook, slipped it on, and ducked outside, broom in tow.

For a moment, Claire simply stood there, watching as the girl methodically swept each step before disappearing toward the front of the shop to tackle the front porch and its own set of stairs. From where she stood, she could just make out the side of Shoo Fly Bake Shoppe, the Amish bakery that served as the opposing bookend to their shared alleyway. Prior to Ruth's wedding to Samuel, Ruth had run the popular tourist stop almost entirely on her own save for the several-times-a-day visit from either her twin brother and Esther's husband, Eli, or her older brother Benjamin. Since her wedding, Eli and Benjamin still stopped by periodically to make sure things were running smoothly at the family-owned business, but now it was Esther's younger sister, Hannah, who baked the majority of the offerings and manned the counter during shop hours.

As Esther had been when she'd worked for Claire, Hannah was determined to do her best at all times. She'd spent hours working with Ruth before the wedding, learning to bake many of the shop's most sought-after desserts. When those had been mastered, the teenager had added in a few of her own specialties, like toffees, homemade sucking candies, and hand-dipped caramels.

All in all, the transition from Ruth to Hannah had been relatively seamless insofar as the products. Now it was really just about getting the tourists — in particular, the ones who'd been coming to Heavenly for years — to realize the change in face behind the counter didn't mean Shoo Fly Bake Shoppe had gone the way of the dogs.

A string of murmurings cut through her woolgathering and yanked her eyes back to the front room in time to see Benjamin Miller walk toward the table of holiday place mats and then turn and head toward the snowflake candle-holders she'd arranged across a shelf on the opposite wall. With careful hands, the widower picked up the holder, turned it from side to side, and with a labored sigh set it back on the shelf, his shoulders sagging.

"You know she'll love anything you pick out simply because it's from you, right?"

Whirling around, Ben pinned his ocean blue eyes on her with first surprise and then relief. "Claire!"

Striding all the way into the room, she stopped, pointed to the candleholder, added a raised thumb, and then rose up on tiptoes to kiss the man's clean-shaven cheek. "Annie told me you were out here."

His gaze dropped to the floor, where it remained long enough to clear his throat. "I did not want her to interrupt you from your work."

"You are never an interruption, Benjamin Miller." She drank in his strong jaw, his dark eyebrows, and the way the skin crinkled around his eyes as he redirected his attention back to the candleholders. "I'm guessing you're wanting to buy a Christmas gift for Rebeccah?"

He tucked his thumbs inside his suspenders. "I know Christmas is not to be about expensive gifts, but in my home we have always given little things to one another on Second Christmas. Ruth would make everyone's favorite pie, my mamm would make a new dress or shirt for each of us, and Eli and I would work together on a new stool for Mamm and a tool holder or something else for the barn for Dat. Such gifts would always bring a big smile. That is why I would like to give Rebeccah *something* from me."

"So it's still going well? Between the two of you?"

The crinkles widened with his shy smile just before they disappeared from view via the brim of his hat. "Yah. It is . . . good."

"I'm glad." And she was. Ben deserved happiness. His wife's death just months after their marriage more than a decade earlier had left him living alone for far too long. His determination to turn away from his baptismal vows in order to have a life with Claire shortly after her arrival in Heavenly had been touching but not right for either of them. Now, she had Jakob, and Ben was courting the younger sister of a local Amish widow — a woman who clearly made the man happy if the sparkle in his eyes at the mere mention of their budding relationship was any indication.

Reaching out, Claire fingered the snowflake pattern dusted onto the glass candleholder and then dropped her hand to her side. "Tell me what you're thinking. You know, what you're wanting to say with this gift?"

His dark brows furrowed. "I do not understand."

She wandered over to the shelves dedicated to kitchens and fished a place mat with a manger scene from the bin.

"Like *this*. It's the kind of gift I might give to Aunt Diane for the counter in the kitchen. It'd be something festive for a spot we often sit at together after the guests have had their dinner in the dining room, or on the rare occasion there are no guests at all.

"And *this*?" She swapped the place mat for a set of napkin rings with a snowman motif. "This is pretty, and would make a nice gift, but it's not special."

Shrugging, he pointed at the candleholders. "These are pretty."

"Thank you. I made them this past weekend. But they're not special enough, either." She crossed to the trio of quilt racks situated closer to the back wall and ran her fingertips across the intricate snowflake pattern Benjamin's sister-in-law, Esther, had created. "Now, if *Esther* was to give this to Eli, it would be special — more special than if *I* simply bought it and gave it to Eli. Because from Esther, it would be as much about the time and love she put into it as any warmth or coziness it might provide.

"And those candleholders I made?" She made her way back to Ben and the shelf he'd yet to leave. "While I hope they'll make good gifts for many of my customers, I think Aunt Diane would enjoy them even more knowing *I* made them as opposed to just buying them. Make sense?"

"But I do not make such things," Ben protested. "I am a farmer."

"You make things all the time, silly. It's why you have an envelope of cash in my office right now with your name on it. People love the small chests and step stools you make."

"I do not think Rebeccah needs a step stool. She is staying with Emma and the children, and I am sure Emma has such things."

"But she won't *always* be living with Emma, right?"

Claire prodded, grinning. "Someday she'll live somewhere else . . ."

A flash of crimson on his cheeks was quickly coughed away. "What do you think Jakob will give *you* for Christmas?"

Instinctively, her gaze skittered past Ben to the large front window and its partial view of the white clapboard building that housed Heavenly's police department. "I can't answer that. Part of the fun is the surprise."

She took advantage of his answering silence to note a non-sweeping Annie on the front porch, passersby on the sidewalk beyond, and a familiar horse and buggy parked on the opposite side of the street. "Why didn't you hitch your buggy in back? Annie has feed and water back there for her horse, Katie."

"I did."

"That's not your horse?" she asked, pointing toward the window.

"No, that is . . ." Ben stepped around the shelves closest to him and strode over to the window. "Yah . . . That is Samuel's horse and buggy."

"But Samuel has a hitching post behind Yoder's Furniture."

"That is true. Perhaps he is running an errand or making a delivery."

"He has English who do that, doesn't he?" she asked.

"Yah." Ben took one last look at his new brother-in-law's buggy and then turned back to Claire. "Will you give Jakob one of your candleholders for Christmas?"

She forced her thoughts off the buggy's odd placement and back to her Amish friend. "I could, I'm sure. But I'm thinking about more of an experience instead of a gift for him this year. Like he did as a 'just-because' for me one day last year."

"What did he do?"

"Do you remember that big snowfall we had last year? The one that closed all the shops on Lighted Way?" At Ben's nod, she left her lookout spot and wandered over to the counter and the pair of stools it blocked from customers' view. "Jakob showed up at the inn that day with a sled and took me sledding. It was . . . magical."

"It was the first time you went sledding?" he asked, surprised.

She pulled out the stools, slid one out for Ben to take, and perched atop her own. "No, I'd been sledding many times as a kid. But it was my first time sledding as an adult, I'm pretty sure, and it was definitely my first time sledding with Jakob."

Hiking her ankle boots onto the bottom rung of the stool, she tipped back against the counter, smiling at the memory of the perfect winter day. "I can't tell you how good it felt to laugh. We stayed out so long, I'm pretty sure my lips were as blue as your eyes when we finally called it quits and went inside the inn for some hot cocoa and cookies. But that time with him? Laughing and acting like kids? I'll never forget it. Ever."

Ben swept his hand toward the window as he, too, sat.

"There is no snow."

"Yet. But that's what *Jakob* did, Ben. I'm sure you can come up with something equally special. Something Rebeccah will never forget." She pitched forward, hijacked the bowl she kept beside the register, and offered Ben a wrapped candy. When he declined, she helped herself to a butterscotch, the crinkle of the wrapper unusually loud in the otherwise quiet shop. "Maybe a horse-drawn carriage ride, or a winter picnic up by the covered bridge. I'm pretty sure she'll love anything you come up with just so long as it means she can spend a little quiet time with you — talking, laughing, making memories."

He seemed to consider her words as her own attention drifted toward the sound of the back door opening and closing and, soon, Annie's footsteps on the tiled hallway. "Hey, kiddo, I was beginning to think you weren't ever coming back."

Annie hurried over to the counter, her eyes wide, her cheeks flushed from the cold air. "I'm sorry, Claire. I noticed Samuel Yoder's buggy across the street and then Mr. Glick from the hardware store walked by and said he saw Ruth go into the police station just before lunch."

She felt Ben stiffen on the stool beside her and quickly rested a calming hand atop his own. "It is nothing to worry about. I imagine Jakob summoned her to the station to get a feel for how things seemed at the Esch farm yesterday. You know, during their visit."

At Ben's questioning eyes, she continued. "Probably things like whether they may have noticed any strange cars lingering on the road outside Daniel and Mary's farmhouse . . . whether Daniel and Mary seemed upset or worried about anything . . . stuff like that."

"Why does Jakob need to know such things?"

"Because, at the moment, Samuel and Ruth appear to be the last people to have seen the couple alive."

Ben cupped his bare chin with his hand. "They were not there when Daniel and Mary passed."

"I know that. And Jakob knows that. But they might have seen something or heard something — something that didn't seem important at the time but might now in light of what happened."

"Daniel and Mary were in their eighties," Ben said, dropping his hand back to his lap.

"It was their time to be with God."

She felt the weight of Annie's gaze on the side of her face and motioned the teen over. "Annie . . . Why don't you come sit here on my stool for a moment? I have something I need to tell you."

Slipping off the stool, she stepped to the side and waited for Annie to get settled. When the teen was in position, Claire looked from Annie to Ben and back again. "Your friends — Daniel and Mary — they didn't . . ."

She stopped. Took a breath.

"Claire? Are you okay?" Annie asked, her voice revealing the same worry now inching its way into the lines around Ben's eyes.

Swallowing, she took Annie's hand in her own and looked between her friends once again. "Your friends did not pass because of their age or because it was their time."

Ben drew back.

Annie traded worry for confusion. "They did. I saw their feet. And — and Henry said they were gone."

"But it wasn't age," Claire rasped. "They . . . they were murdered."

Annie's gasp, like the distinctive thud of Ben's boots as he returned to his feet, echoed around the shop. "M-murdered?" Annie eked out.

Claire pulled the distraught teen close. "Jakob told me this morning. But when you got here for your shift, I was waiting on a customer. When I finally finished, you were busy with a different customer and I needed to head back into my office to work on the —"

"Is Jakob certain?" Ben asked. "That someone did this to them?"

"He seems to be, yes. I don't know the specifics or what led him to that conclusion other than time of death, I think, but that's what he said." She looked at Ben across Annie's shoulder. "When he heard that Ruth and Samuel had been visiting at the Esch farm earlier in the day, he said he'd need to talk to them."

"But who would want to do such a thing?" Annie asked as a pair of tears slipped down her milky skin. "Mary and Daniel were so good, so kind. They would not hurt anyone. Ever."

Claire stepped back, wiped the wetness from Annie's cheeks with her thumbs, and then wandered back to the window, Annie's words and Ben's growing silence adding to her sudden listlessness. "I don't know who. And I don't know why, either. I can't imagine the answers to questions like that any more than you can. But I know one thing for sure: Jakob will find those answers — one way or the other. And when he does? He'll make sure justice is served — for Daniel, for Mary, and for everyone who loved them."

CHAPTER 5

Even without his third yawn in as many minutes, Claire knew Jakob was exhausted. She could see it in the dullness of his eyes, the dark circles beneath them, and the unusual slump to his broad shoulders as he maneuvered his way around tables and chairs with a lidded cup of hot chocolate in each hand.

"I wish you would have let me get that," she said, liberating their drinks from his grasp and setting them atop their favorite corner table in Heavenly Brews. "*I* slept last night. *You* didn't."

He dropped into his chair with a quiet thud. "Being a gentleman is not sleep dependent," he teased.

"Jakob, I'm serious. You look like you could fall over."

"I'm okay. Really."

"We could have rescheduled, you know. I would have understood."

"I didn't want to reschedule." He accepted the cup she slid in his direction, popped the lid off, and took a long sip. "With the exception of that too brief visit at your shop this morning, I feel like we've been doing the two-ships-passing thing a little more than normal lately. When I'm free, you've been in meetings about your holiday event or up to your eyeballs with customers at the shop. When you're free, I've either been working with our new officer, Derek, or . . ." He waved away the rest of his unspoken words and took another sip of his drink. "Anyway, all I'm trying to really say here is that I wasn't going to let this opportunity to see you disappear — tired or no tired."

She smiled at him over the rim of her own cup. "And I'm glad, I really am. I just need you to promise that you'll find a way to get some sleep tonight. Before you end up getting sick."

"I will."

"Good. And now that that's out of the way, can you tell me what it was that made you first realize Daniel and Mary had been —"

Lifting his finger, he reached into his back pocket, extracted his phone, and, after a quick glance at the screen, silenced the buzzing and flipped the device, upside down, on the table.

"Is that the station?" she asked. "Because I understand if you need to take it, especially with everything that's going on right now."

"It's not the station."

When he didn't elaborate, she rewound back to the point of the interruption. "So what was it that made you realize Daniel's and Mary's —"

"You know what? I actually think it might be best if I return that call." He picked up the phone and pushed back his chair. "You'll be okay in here by yourself for a few minutes, right? I shouldn't be long."

She followed his eyes down to his phone, and when he didn't bring them back to her, she swallowed. "Um . . . sure. I'll be fine. Make your call. There's no rush. I'm not going anywhere."

"Good. Thanks." And then he was gone, his tall form disappearing out the door with nary a glance back.

Not sure what to make of his odd behavior, she fingered the coffee shop's logo on the front of her cup and then busied herself by looking at the various flyers tacked to the bulletin board on her left.

The Heavenly Public Library was hosting a Cookies with Santa event on December sixteenth . . .

Heavenly Brews was having a hot chocolate tasting on the eighteenth, with a variety of winter flavors being unveiled . . .

For the third year in a row, Gussmann's General Store had collection bins behind the store for the purpose of its annual holiday food drive. And for every five food items donated, customers would receive $5 toward their own in-store shopping purchase . . .

The Breeze Point Assisted Living Community, slated to be open by next December, was taking leasing applications for its new state-of-the-art apartments . . .

Marty Linton, a celebrated baker from the popular Tasty Desserts Network, was returning to his childhood hometown of Heavenly, Pennsylvania, to host a Spring Bake-off. The contest, open to anyone sixteen or over, required an original from-scratch recipe. The grand-prize winner and their recipe would be a featured guest on Linton's show, *Dreaming Up Desserts.* Additionally, the recipe would be made and featured in every Linton Bakery location across the country for the entire month of June, with 50 percent of the profits from all sales of the dessert going directly to the winner . . .

"Wow." Scanning down to the end of the

flyer, Claire narrowed in on a quote from Marty Linton himself: *Bring me your best dessert, and you just might end up like me — baking your way to your dreams.* "Oh, Annie," she whispered, "you can win this, I know you can."

"It's Claire, right? You own Heavenly Treasures down the street?"

Startled, Claire looked up to find a vaguely familiar face smiling back at her. It took a moment, but just as she was fearing she'd have to admit she didn't know the woman's name in return, the stocky build, the muted blue-green eyes, and rounded face added together to form a name if not a context in which she belonged. "Yes, and you're . . . *Nancy,* aren't you?"

The woman she guessed to be in her early to mid-fifties nodded, clearly pleased that Claire remembered her name. "That's right. I met you for the first time at Esther and Eli's wedding last fall, and then again at Samuel Yoder's wedding just a few weeks ago."

She pondered the woman's words, her thoughts racing back through both events in search of the limited number of English who'd been invited. Besides herself and Jakob, it had been Harold and Betty Glick, and a solo Aunt Diane, at Eli and Esther's wedding. The same had held true at Ruth and Samuel's wedding, save for the addition of Aunt Diane's new beau, Bill. Everyone else had been Amish, except —

"Yes . . . yes . . . okay, I've got it now." Claire extended her hand to the woman. "I'm sorry. It took me a moment. You drive some of the Amish to the stores and stuff when it's too far for them to go by buggy or scooter."

"An Amish taxi driver, as we're known among the English." Nancy took Claire's hand and shook it warmly before her gaze led Claire's back to the bulletin board. "I noticed you reading about the Spring Bake-off. Are you a Marty Linton fan, too?"

"Marty Lin — no. I mean, I don't really know that much about him, to be honest, so I can't really say one way or the other. But I've heard of him. I think my aunt has tried a few of his recipes out on me."

"Pretty incredible, aren't they?"

"I don't really remember, I'm afraid. But that's because I'm a little biased toward my aunt's tried-and-true recipes, myself. So, too, are all the returning guests we get at the inn."

Nancy drew back. "Do you mean Sleep Heavenly?"

Nodding, Claire reached into her purse

for a pen and paper. "My aunt is Diane Weatherly."

"Ohhhh, Diane, yes. Of course. Our paths have crossed on occasion over the years, most often out at Weaver farm when I'm dropping the Amish off to test-drive a new buggy horse."

"I'm not surprised. Diane is a horse lover. She goes out to Weaver farm a few times a week just to meet any newcomers that might have arrived since her last visit, and to check in on the regulars. It's her way to unwind." Claire set the pad on her thigh, leaned back to get another view of the bake-off details, and then transcribed them onto her paper, pausing every few lines to look back at Nancy lest she appear rude. "*My* way to unwind is sitting on the front porch of the inn trying whatever dessert my aunt has made on any given day."

"She's that good?" Nancy asked.

"She's that good."

Nancy's eyes narrowed behind her glasses as she pointed at Claire's notepad. "Is that why you're taking notes about the bake-off? Because you think she'll enter?"

Was it possible? Would Aunt Diane actually . . .

Shaking the momentary question from her thoughts, Claire continued writing, noting the recipe guidelines, the submission requirements, and finally the Valentine's Day deadline. "No, Aunt Diane wouldn't enter something like this. I've tried to get her to enter the pie category at the county fair each of the last few summers and she always refuses. Says she bakes to feed people, not win ribbons."

"You thinking about entering yourself?" Nancy prodded.

She couldn't help laughing. "Uh . . . no . . . I mean, I can bake, sure. I even like to do it on occasion just to clear my head after a particularly busy week. But no, I'm more of a basic baker. Chocolate chip cookies, and brownies from a box, are my go-to recipes these days."

Nancy shifted her ample weight across her legs. "Recipes for this contest have to be completely original. As in not taken from a cookbook."

"I saw that." She made a second and third underline beneath the word *original* in her notes and then returned the pad and pen to her purse. "I'm quite certain that won't be a problem for my friend. She has a gift for putting fairly simple things together and turning them into something amazing. I've seen her do it in the store with displays time and time again. But what she can do in a

kitchen with flavors and textures? It's —
well, I can't even begin to do it justice."

"There you are!" A male, Claire guessed
to be twenty-five, maybe twenty-six, skid-
ded to a stop not far from Nancy. "I was
beginning to think you'd gotten lost."

"Nope, not lost. Just talking to this nice
young lady here." Stepping to the side,
Nancy drew the young man into the conversation with a single swoop of her arm.
"Claire, this is my son, Tommy. Tommy, this
is Claire Weatherly. She owns that gift shop
right down the road here — you know, the
one next to Shoo Fly Bake Shoppe."

A momentary hesitation gave way to a
single bob of the man's head before he
hiked his thumb in the direction of the coffee shop's front door and pinned his mother
with a not so subtle *we've gotta go.* "Abe
called. Viewing starts tomorrow at eight,
which means we start at seven."

"Where is it being held?"

"Greta's."

"Greta's?" Nancy echoed, pulling a face.
"Why?"

"They're not gonna let *Abe* run things,
you know that."

Turning back to Claire, Nancy's smile
dimmed. "While I normally drive the Amish
for happy reasons, every once in a while it's

72

for something sad, like a funeral. Most of the time I don't know the person they're bidding farewell to. This time, though, I knew them both."

"You're talking about Daniel and Mary Esch, aren't you?" Claire asked.

Nancy's bushy dark eyebrows rose with surprise, only to settle back into place with a slow, even nod. "You knew them, too, I take it?"

"Only by sight, really. Though I did speak with each of them a little at Ruth and Samuel's wedding last month." Claire set her hand atop Nancy's arm. "They seemed like really nice people — very open and welcoming."

"Daniel Esch? Welcoming?"

Startled, Claire followed Nancy's angry eyes back to the woman's son. "Tommy! This is not the time nor the place."

"I think it's the perfect time, actually. But . . . whatever." Again, Tommy hooked his thumb toward the door. "We've still gotta go. Preferably now."

Nancy started to speak, shook her head, and then, falling into step behind her son, glanced back. "It was nice speaking with you, Claire."

"You, too, Nancy."

She watched as they exited the coffee shop

and headed down the front steps, her view of their similarly colored parkas quickly overtaken by that of Jakob bounding up the stairs, two at a time.

"I'm back, I'm back." With two long strides, he was at their table, his cheeks ruddy from the cold. "Sorry that took so long, but it couldn't be helped."

"Do you need to go back to the station?"

"The station? No. Why?"

She pointed at the phone still clutched inside his gloved hand. "I figured that's what that call was about?"

"Not this time." Tucking the phone back inside his pocket, he reclaimed his chair. "So where were we? What were we talking about?"

"You needing sleep, and the case."

"Right . . . right." He pulled off his gloves and rested his bare hands on the table. "I'm sorry if my showing up put a stomp on your visit from Esther this morning."

"You're never a stomp on anything. Besides, it led you to Ruth, right?"

"It did, indeed. Though I imagine she and Samuel would've preferred it hadn't . . . Oops, I'm sorry, one more second." Again, he reached into his pocket, and again, he pulled out his phone. This time, though, he held the phone below the table line while he checked the illuminated screen.

She watched him for a few seconds and then forced a smile into her voice and prayed it sounded more believable to his ears than it did her own. "If you need to take it, I understand. You know that."

"I know, and I appreciate it, but I'll just let it go to voice mail this time." He silenced the continued vibration and shoved it back into his pocket. "Right about now you're probably wishing you hadn't agreed to this meet-up, huh?"

Reaching across the table, he interlaced her fingers with his own. "The ME put a rush on the autopsies so we could get Mary's and Daniel's bodies back to the family. Viewing will start tomorrow."

"I just heard that. So I take it this means you know how they were killed now?"

"I knew last night. The second Henry said he had to move a pillow to see Mary's face."

She felt her mouth gape at his words. "Oh my gosh. I . . . I remember Annie saying something about a pillow now, but . . . So you think they were suffocated to death?"

"I *know* they were. And the medical examiner confirmed it."

She waited for him to elaborate more and was surprised when he didn't. "Jakob? Is everything okay? You're acting a little . . .

different. Distracted, even."

Releasing her hands, he sat back in his chair. "Well, considering I just had a double murder dropped in my lap roughly twenty-four hours ago, I would imagine that makes some sense, no?"

"Yes . . . of course . . . I didn't mean *that.* I mean, I get you have a lot on your plate right now. It's just that lately, even before . . ." Feeling suddenly foolish, she pulled her abandoned hands onto her lap. "I'm sorry, Jakob. I didn't mean to sound so insensitive. If there's anything I can do to help, just say the word, okay?"

"I might need you to help run interference for me with Eli after he gets wind of how things went today."

"Today? Why? Esther wasn't upset by anything you said."

"Ruth was."

"Ruth?"

"I stopped by Bishop Hershberger's place after I spoke with you and Esther and asked him to have Ruth and Samuel come in to speak with me. Samuel was working, but Ruth came in."

"Annie noticed Samuel's buggy outside the station this afternoon. How'd that go?"

Jakob made note of the half dozen or so patrons scattered at tables around the coffeehouse and then leaned in close. "Let's just say the questions got a little intense."

"Intense? From Ruth? I . . . I can't really picture that, but if she got a little upset, I'm sure she didn't mean it. You know Ruth, she's about as easygoing as it gets." She reached for his hand again, but when he didn't take hers, she wrapped it around her lukewarm cup instead. "I'm sure she's just grasping for an explanation as to how two people she'd just spent time visiting could be dead later that same day."

He stared, unseeing, into his own cup, his voice becoming almost wooden. "By the time I cut her loose for the evening, Ruth was pretty much in tears. Which, as I'm sure you can imagine, means Eli is going to be gunning for me once he gets wind of it all."

Sighing, he shoved the cup into the center of the table and palmed his face. "So, one step forward, ten steps back, where my family is concerned . . ."

"One step forward, ten steps back? I don't understand." She tugged his hand off his face and back onto the table with her own. "Hey . . . asking Ruth questions regarding her and Samuel's time at the Esch farm makes sense. It's your job."

"I know that and you know that. And yeah, I want to believe Eli and Esther will understand that, too. But you and I both know that's not going to be the case. I kissed that kind of understanding good-bye the moment I decided to leave the church to pursue police work in the first place."

"Wait. Slow down." She squeezed his hand until his troubled gaze was on her once again. "Daniel and Mary Esch were *Amish.* Daniel was a respected elder in the church. Surely Eli and Esther and everyone else will want the person responsible for their deaths to be apprehended, yes?"

"You'd think so, wouldn't you . . ."

"No, I *know* so. And so do you. They know you need to ask questions to get to the truth. You've done it before, and sadly, you're having to do it again."

"Yeah, but this is *Ruth.* She's Eli's twin . . . She's Ben's little sister . . . She's Esther's sister-in-law . . . She's —"

"Hey . . . hey . . ." She scooted her chair closer to his. "They'll get that you had to ask her a few mundane questions. And if they're upset about the timing in relation to Daniel's and Mary's deaths, I'll explain how important that is in a case like this. They'll get it, I promise."

"They weren't *mundane* questions, Claire."

"Okay, I'm sorry. I don't mean to make it

sound as if I'm trivializing —"

This time, when he took his hand back, he used it to push away from the table. "Ruth is a suspect, Claire."

She heard herself gasp, even felt the curious glances it drew from neighboring tables, but in that moment all she could do was stare at the man now gathering their napkins into a ball.

"They *both* are," Jakob added, shoving the balled-up napkins into what was left of his drink.

"You — you can't be serious."

He stared at her across the mounded napkins. "What kind of questions did you *think* I was asking Ruth?"

"Stuff that would give you a starting place like you said this morning," Claire argued. "Something she or Samuel might have seen or heard outside the window when they were visiting . . . or something Mary or Daniel might have said to them that could have indicated they were worried about something. You know, stuff that could help lead you to someone with real means and motive."

"Someone with real *means and motive*?" he repeated.

"Yes!"

Setting the cup and its mound of napkins

on the table, Jakob slowly lowered himself back onto the edge of his seat. "You mean like being the last known people to see the victims alive? Like Daniel's cabinetry business securing the bid for that new senior housing development project going up in Breeze Point — the one that Samuel Yoder was positive he was going to get right up until Esch Cabinetry did?"

"*Someone* had to have been the last ones to see them," she argued.

"You're right. The killer, or killers."

Her mouth grew dry as his words hit her. "But we're talking about Ruth and Samuel Yoder here, Jakob . . . not *killers.*"

"You don't think I'm aware of that?" He stopped, pulled in a breath, and then slowly released it along with a growing anger he didn't even try to hold back. "Two people are dead, Claire. *Murdered.* It is my job, as an officer of the law, to conduct this investigation the same way I would any other. That means the last known people to see the victims alive are top on my suspect list until I can replace them with someone else. And while they're *on* that list, I have to explore all possible motives they may have had to commit that crime."

"But —"

"Claire, please." He turned his chair

80

toward her so fast, his knees slammed into hers. "I need you to understand this. I can't, in good conscience, turn a blind eye to the facts just because they happen to cast Samuel and Ruth Yoder in a bad light. I just can't."

Oh, how she would love to give him what he wanted, to tell him she understood. But every time she tried to speak, to offer him the assurance he clearly needed, she just couldn't get the words out.

"Please, Claire, I need you to stand by me on this, to support me as I do my job," he whispered. "Can you do that for me?"

She dropped her gaze to her cup as his question, his plea, looped its way through her thoughts.

Could she do that? Could she stand by him even knowing he was making a horrible mistake? Could —

"C'mon, let's go." With one quick swipe, he picked up both their cups and stood, his expression a mask of hurt and anger. "I'll drop you off at the inn."

CHAPTER 6

Tucking her chin inside the collar of her winter jacket, Claire waited until his taillights disappeared back onto Lighted Way before she finally let herself breathe and process. Jakob was angry. At her.

She knew this. She even understood it. But even so, she'd hoped the time in the car from Heavenly Brews to the inn would be the calming force they needed. Instead, neither had spoken. And now, with her silent count to ten rounding the corner to twenty-five, any lingering hope she had for a sudden U-turn on Jakob's part was over.

"Nice going, Claire," she whispered as she took one last glance toward the now darkened road and then stepped inside Sleep Heavenly's front hallway.

"Claire, dear? Is that you?"

Squaring her shoulders with a fortifying breath, Claire closed and locked the door. "Yup, it's me."

"Splendid! We're here, in the parlor."

She recognized the explanation as the invitation that it was, but really, the last thing she wanted to do was put herself in a position of having to make small talk with the inn's latest round of guests. It wasn't that she didn't enjoy meeting new people; she just didn't have the heart to partake in the necessary back and forth at that moment. No, what she really wanted was to go up to her room and be alone. Maybe if she did, she could come up with a way to fix this thing with Jakob before it did irreparable harm to their relationship.

"Claire?"

Forcing her thoughts away from the daunting stalemate that had stymied their evening together, she wriggled out of her coat, hung it inside the hall closet, and headed for the steps. "I'm a little tired tonight, Aunt Diane. If it's okay, I thought I'd just head upstairs and be back down here in time to help with breakfast in —"

"You're not really going to make me wait until morning to say hello, are you?"

Freezing mid-step, Claire turned toward the parlor entrance and the distinguished yet quietly playful face beaming back at her. *"Bill?"*

"In the flesh." Saying nothing else, the

83

sixty-something met her in the middle of the hallway with exactly the hug Claire needed at that moment.

She buried her head in his warm, sturdy shoulder and breathed in the faintest hint of cologne that clung to his cable-knit sweater and salt-and-pepper hair. "I didn't know you were coming today! I thought it was Saturday."

"It was. But the second I finished wrapping your aunt's presents, I knew I couldn't wait five more days. So I hopped in the car and crossed my fingers all the way here that there'd be a room for me when I arrived."

"I'm so glad you did!" Stepping back, she peeked around the travel agent's broad shoulder to her aunt's room-lighting smile. "You didn't know, either, Aunt Diane?"

"I was just getting ready to sit down with a bowl of stew and the latest copy of *A Stable Life* when I heard a knock at the back door." Diane motioned them both into the parlor. "There were no guests on the schedule for the night, so I figured it was some sort of late delivery."

Bill drew Diane to him in a side arm hug that served only to deepen both their smiles. "I could see her from the door and I figured that's what she was thinking as she headed in my direction. But then, as she got closer and saw it was me? Yeah, well, I won't be forgetting *that* look of pure joy anytime soon, I can tell you that."

"I'm glad." And she was. Seeing Diane so happy, and knowing that someone else saw her the way Claire saw her, was everything she could have ever hoped for the woman. The fact that this person happened to be pretty amazing in his own right was simply the icing on the cake.

"Come. Sit." Diane guided Claire toward the couch and its matching lounge chair. "Bill has a toasty warm fire blazing away in the hearth, and the cookies I put in the oven should be done in about six minutes."

"I'm not terribly hungry, but I'll sit for a few minutes."

Diane and Bill exchanged a glance, with Diane breaking it in favor of placing a kiss on Claire's forehead. "No fever, although you just came in from outdoors, so I should probably check you again in a little while."

"I'm not sick, Aunt Diane."

"Tired?" Bill asked.

Claire sank onto the lounge chair and watched as one of the logs split in two, scattering glowing embers every which way. "Some, yeah. But I have a feeling sleep isn't going to come all that easy tonight."

"Oops, that's the oven timer letting me

know the cookies are ready." Turning toward the hallway, Diane squeezed Bill's shoulder. "See if you can find out what's troubling her before I get back, will you?"

Bill patted Diane's hand and then held it to his lips for the briefest of kisses. "I'm on the case."

Together, Claire and Bill watched Diane disappear, her soft but purposeful footsteps fading into a silence broken only by the fire's crackles and snaps. Seconds turned to minutes as neither rushed to fill the room with chatter, both content to soak up the coziness that was Claire's favorite room in the old Victorian.

"How's your young man?" Bill finally asked as he settled onto the couch across from Claire.

"You mean Jakob?"

"Do you have another young man I don't know about?"

Shrugging, she glanced back at the fire. "Actually, after the mess I made of things tonight, I'm not sure I *have* a young man anymore."

"Do you want to talk about it?"

She stared at the bluest part of the flames for a few beats and then, reaching behind her back, pulled out a throw pillow and hugged it to her chest. "An elderly Amish couple was found murdered in their home last night."

"Oh. Wow. I didn't know. Your aunt told me about the lights you two saw last night and the couple that died, but she didn't mention a murder."

A quiet gasp stole their attention from each other and sent it racing toward the doorway and the woman standing just inside it with a plate of cookies in one hand and a stack of napkins in the other. "There's been another murder?" Diane rasped. "When? Where? Here in *Heavenly*?"

"Yes," Claire said. "Last night."

"Last night? I don't understand this." Diane carried the plate around to the coffee table and set it down. "But I didn't see or hear any more sirens after —"

Claire met Diane's widened eyes with a nod.

Clutching her hand to her chest, Diane shook her head as if trying to prevent the truth from taking route. "Please tell me you're not talking about Mary and Daniel Esch . . ."

"I wish I could."

Diane dropped onto the couch. "I . . . I don't understand. They were such a lovely couple, so unassuming, so . . ."

"I know. And I've had all day to process it."

"Heavenly didn't use to be like this," Diane murmured. "Two years ago, before Walter Scott, the most we saw in this town was an occasional crime of opportunity — a wallet stolen after it was left on a park bench, a bike stolen out of an open garage, that sort of thing. And even those were rare. But once Walter was killed, it was like some sort of floodgate opened."

Bill found Diane's hand and squeezed it. "This Walter Scott fellow — was he a friend of yours?"

"No. He was the previous tenant where Claire's shop is now." Diane brushed a piece of graying hair off her forehead and leaned back against the couch. "Walter was a most unlikable soul, but he certainly didn't deserve to die."

"You say someone killed him?" Bill asked.

Nodding, Diane stretched her feet onto the oval hook rug. "That's right. First murder in Heavenly in more than fifteen years at that point."

"So there had been another?" Bill looked from Diane to Claire and back again. "Before Walter?"

Claire pushed the pillow off her lap and scooted forward on her chair. "That very first murder? The one Diane just referenced? That's the case that propelled Jakob to leave his Amish upbringing and his baptismal vow to become a cop."

"Why *that* case?" Bill asked.

"Because the victim was an Amish farmer."

"Ahhhh. And Jakob wanted to help catch the person who'd murdered one of his own?" At Claire's slow nod, Bill hiked his ankle onto his knee and draped his arm across the back of the couch. "But you just can't become a cop out of the chute like that. There's a test to take first. And then, if you pass, you have to get called up for a particular police academy. Surely the person who killed that Amish farmer was caught before Jakob even got into the academy, yes?"

"He was, but Jakob had already walked away from his Amish life by then, not that that mattered." Claire crossed to the hearth, retrieved a log from the holder, and added it to the fire. "He wanted to be a cop. That particular case just gave him the courage to make his desire known."

"I still can't believe this . . ." Diane took a deep breath. "About Daniel and Mary . . . I mean, Annie didn't say anything about them being murdered when she called last night."

Claire returned the poker to its spot beside the other fireplace tools and wandered over to the picture window and its view of the Amish countryside. Parting the drapes with her left hand, she stared out at the darkness. "That's because she didn't understand what she was seeing and she never actually went inside."

"But she said Henry did . . ."

"You're right, he did. But he didn't recognize the scene for what it was, either. He, like Annie and their friends, assumed Daniel and Mary died of old age."

"I take it they were a married couple?" Bill asked.

"Yes. A married Amish couple. In their mid-eighties!" A quick shift in the volume of Diane's voice let Claire know the woman was headed in her direction. "Who on earth would want to do them harm?"

Bill, too, stood and made his way over to the window. "I imagine that's what Jakob is trying to figure out as we speak."

"Does he have any leads?" Diane asked, stepping in beside Claire. "Anything to go on?"

Pressing her forehead against the glass, Claire used the limited moonlight peeking out from behind a cloud to locate a few barns and silos in the distance. "He does.

Or at least he thinks he does. But he's wrong."

"I'm sure that has to be defeating — thinking you've got something and then realizing you don't." Diane tsked softly beneath her breath. "I can't even imagine how truly frustrating that must be for him."

Slowly Claire let the curtain fall back into place as she turned toward Bill and her aunt. "It might be if he actually realized he was wrong, but he doesn't. And now, on top of that, he's upset with me for not standing by him."

"Not standing by him?" Diane echoed. "Oh, don't be silly, dear. You have been by his side, supporting him, through every case he's had since Walter Scott."

Claire tried to smile, to lighten the atmosphere back to what it was when she'd first seen Bill standing in the parlor doorway, but now that she'd let the proverbial genie out of the bottle, she couldn't really see a way to stuff it back inside all that easily. "I don't think Jakob sees my disagreeing with his choice in suspects as being terribly supportive . . . And I suppose, if I'm being honest, he's right. But that's just because he's barking up the wrong tree."

Diane trailed her back to the seating area and its cozy proximity to the fire. "Do you want to talk about it, dear?"

"He thinks Ruth and Samuel are viable suspects."

"Ruth and Samuel?" Bill echoed as he stopped en route back to the couch to poke a smoldering log into a better burn position. "Isn't that the couple whose wedding we went to last month? The bakery owner and the furniture store owner?"

Diane's delayed gasp let Claire know her aunt had caught up to the ridiculousness of Jakob's suspicions. "Oh, Claire . . . Surely you misunderstood something! Jakob Fisher is too smart a man, and much too good of a detective, to suspect either of them in something so . . . so . . . horrible."

"But he does! And that's the problem!" Claire dropped onto the edge of the lounge chair and buried her head in her hands. "How can I possibly support that when I can't even wrap my head around how he *got* there, let alone the fact he's giving the theory any credence whatsoever?"

"Thinking Ruth Miller could harm anyone, let alone an elderly couple, is like thinking" — Diane threw up her hands — "I don't know . . . I can't even come up with an analogy for how preposterous that is."

Claire slid her hands down her cheeks

until she could see Diane across the tips of her fingers. "I know, right? That's how I feel. But instead of agreeing or telling me he was kidding, he got upset that I didn't see it from his perspective."

Diane wandered her way over to the floor-to-ceiling bookshelves that lined the northern wall of the room, only to turn back before she'd actually reached them. "You know how highly I think of Jakob . . . He's smart, he's funny, he's kind, he's everything I could want for you, dear. But this? I don't understand."

"Why is he looking at Ruth and her husband?" Bill asked, placing the poker back in its holder. "Do you know?"

"That's my fault, I'm afraid."

Diane stared at Claire. "*Your* fault?"

"Esther stopped by to see me with the baby earlier today, and we got to talking about what we assumed was Daniel's and Mary's passing from natural causes. She mentioned how Ruth and Samuel would have seen them right before it happened, as they'd gone to the Esch farm to visit and collect their wedding gift."

Halting the rest of Claire's explanation with her hand, Diane swept her attention toward the fireplace and Bill. "In Lancaster, an Amish bride and groom don't usually receive wedding presents on their special day. Rather, over the next several weeks, they'll go off visiting the various people who attended their wedding. It is during these visits they are given their gifts."

"Why is that?" Bill asked, crossing back to his previous spot on the couch.

"It helps establish the newlyweds as an adult couple in their district and gets them in the habit of visiting — something the Amish believe in as a way to keep one another close." Diane turned her attention back to Claire. "Go on, dear . . ."

"Jakob stopped by while Esther and I were talking, and he heard that Ruth and Samuel had been at the Esch farm shortly before the murders. At first, he seemed to just see that little tidbit of information as a starting point for his investigation — even used those very words. But somehow, over the next few hours that followed, he went from seeing Ruth and Samuel's presence at the Esch farm as *helpful* to them now being on the top of his list of suspects."

"Were they the last known people to see this couple alive?"

Claire shifted her gaze to Bill's. "You mean other than the real killer? Quite possibly. I really can't say for sure, though."

"If they were, it makes sense they'd be

suspects."

She didn't need to look at Diane to know her surprise was wholly shared. But before she could dispute his claim, Bill continued, the calm rumble-like quality of his voice luring Diane back to the couch. "When a child goes missing, the parents are questioned. When one half of a married couple goes missing, the other half is questioned. It's just the way things are done, a way to rule out possibilities — no matter how remote they may be — so the investigators can get to the truth sooner."

Diane perched on the arm of the sofa. "Come to think of it, that makes sense. That's the way they do it on all the police procedural shows on TV. So maybe that's all this is, Claire. Maybe Jakob is just following a standard checklist. Ruth and Samuel saw Mary and Daniel before they died. Therefore, they need to be questioned, regardless."

"That's what I thought initially, too." Claire pushed off the chair, only to lower herself back down seconds later. "But he's got a motive for them and everything."

"Good heavens!" Diane gasped. "A motive?"

She looked down at her hands and then back up at first Bill and then Diane. "Apparently Daniel Esch made kitchen cabinets or something like that?"

"He did. Some years ago." Diane slid off the armrest and onto the actual couch cushion. "Esch Cabinetry. In fact, he did the cabinets in my kitchen."

Claire settled back into her spot with the throw pillow on her lap. "I didn't know that."

"There was no reason to really mention it, I guess. He, along with Abe and the boy's friend, installed them for me about six years ago."

"Why didn't I know he had a cabinet business?"

"Because my kitchen was one of the last he did before shuttering his business. Three of his daughters moved out of state with their husbands, and one stayed here in Heavenly with a husband who's pretty much all thumbs in everything he does. Daniel's oldest son, Amos, moved to upstate New York a good decade or so earlier. He's a farmer, I believe. Anyway, I imagine he and Mary, like everyone else, had always assumed Abraham, his youngest son, would take it over when Daniel was ready to retire, but that didn't happen." Diane helped herself to a cookie, handed it to Bill with a sweet smile, and then turned back to Claire.

"One day, the Esch Cabinetry shingle that used to hang outside Daniel's farmhouse just came down. After that, there were no more Esch cabinets made."

"Well, *something* must have changed. Because, according to Jakob, Daniel's cabinetry business just won some bid out at that new senior housing project you first told me about last month."

Diane's eyes widened. "You mean the one out in Breeze Point?"

"That's right. In fact, I just saw a pre-leasing flyer for the place on the bulletin board inside Heavenly Brews this evening."

"That's a huge project, with something like two hundred and fifty units being built in just the first phase alone," Diane mused. "And the second phase is set to be every bit as big, according to that original article in the Lancaster paper."

"That's a lot of cabinets," Bill said around his cookie. "Especially for a mom-and-pop-size company, like I imagine this man's operation was."

"It was small, for sure. But Daniel's work was so good that builders from around the area loved using him."

"Did you know he was getting back in the business?"

Diane's head began shaking before Claire

was even done with her question. "I had no idea. The man was in his mid-eighties, after all."

"So what does this bid have to do with Jakob and your friends?" Bill asked.

"From what Jakob told me tonight, Samuel had bid on the same project and was virtually certain his reputation in the area would give him the edge over the competition." Squeezing the throw pillow to her chest, Claire rested her chin on the soft material. "Only he didn't get it. *Daniel* did."

Bill's long, low whistle had both women looking to the man now making his way back to the fireplace. "I can see why Jakob is looking at Samuel for this now. It makes sense."

"It makes *sense*?" Diane held the cookie plate out to Claire and, when she declined, set it back on the table and folded her arms across her chest. "How do you figure that?"

"Samuel's business is small in the grand scheme of things. He's not a national chain, he doesn't have franchises, he's just a mom-and-pop-style furniture store in a tourist-friendly town in southeastern Pennsylvania. A job like the one you just described? Supplying kitchen cabinetry for five hundred apartment units? That would've been a big coup for him. And I mean, *big.* Surely people have murdered over far less."

"And I'm sure you're right." Claire tilted her head against the back of the couch and stared up at the ceiling, the stress of the day beginning to take its toll on her patience and her energy level. "But they weren't Samuel and Ruth Yoder."

"I agree with Claire."

Bypassing the last few remaining pieces of wood in the copper holder, Bill grabbed the poker and maneuvered the burning pieces into a centralized pile. When he had them the way he wanted, he braced his hands against the mantle and watched the shoots and sparks that rose up toward the chimney. "Please know I'm not saying I think your friends did it, because I don't. I found them to be lovely people when I met them at their wedding. But if I was Jakob, I'd have to give them a closer look for this crime, too. They had means and they had motive. You can't wipe your hands of that just because you know them. Not if you believe in the integrity of your job the way Jakob does."

"Wait." Claire focused all her attention on Bill now. "Say that again?"

"Which part?"

"The last part. About the integrity?"

"Oh. Sure." Bill turned his back to the fire. "I was just saying that if you believe in the integrity of your job the way Jakob does, you have to follow protocol. So you can know, beyond a shadow of a doubt, that you dotted all your *i*'s and crossed all your *t*'s."

"For any other case, maybe," Diane protested. "But looking at Ruth and Samuel for the Esch murders is really just taking time away from finding the *real* killer — time he or she could be using to get as far from Heavenly as possible."

"He'll find the real killer, I'm sure. He just —"

"He has to do his job." Claire palmed her mouth as the reality behind Bill's words churned in her stomach. "I . . . I can't believe I couldn't step off my high horse long enough to see it . . . to know Jakob is only doing what he has to do, and that instead of judging him, I should've tried hard to be what he needed — a listening and supportive ear."

Bill wandered back to the couch but refrained from actually sitting. "So be that now."

She knew he was right, she really did. But —

"I still know, with everything I am, that Ruth and Samuel had nothing to do with Daniel's and Mary's murders."

"Then help prove that to Jakob."

Tossing the pillow to the side, Claire wiggled her way off the lounge chair and onto her feet. "I think it's time for me to head upstairs. I have a call to make, and an apology to give."

She crossed the hooked rug, kissed the top of her aunt's head, and then covered Bill's warm hands with her own. "Thank you, Bill. For listening and for helping me to see. You really are a very special person."

"As are you, Claire." Bill pulled her in for a quick hug. "Now go. Make things right. For Jakob *and* for Ruth."

CHAPTER 7

One by one they appeared to her left and disappeared to her right, each front bench inhabited by a bearded man in a black-rimmed hat and a woman in her black winter coat and kapp. Some buggies were filled to capacity with children of non-driving age crammed into the back; others carried less. All were pulled by horses tasked with getting their occupants from point A to point B.

Sighing, Claire made herself step away from the front window and its somber view, the day's tasks oblivious to the heaviness in the air. The morning had been busy all on its own thanks to the tour bus of senior citizens that had arrived just as shop signs were turned to OPEN up and down Lighted Way. In fact, she'd barely finished filling the register with the day's starting money when the bell over the front door began to jingle . . . and jingle . . . and jingle still more.

The first half dozen or so were those who wanted to know why Shoo Fly Bake Shoppe was closed. When she'd explained it was Amish owned and there was a funeral going on, a few had grumbled and walked out while others had stayed to wander the shop. Those who left still grumbling went in search of Heavenly Brews. Those who opted to stay asked questions, ooh'd and aah'd over the many Amish-made items on her shelves, and, in most cases, made a purchase.

Annie, like every other Amish employee or shopkeeper along Lighted Way, did not come in to work. Instead, the teenager was likely at the first of three viewings for Mary and Daniel Esch — a viewing Claire, too, hoped to attend with Jakob once the workday was done.

Jakob . . .

Glancing at the clock over the register, Claire headed toward her office and the brown bag lunch waiting in her desk's bottom drawer. More than anything, she wished she could take her sandwich and cookie across the street to the police station in the hope that she and Jakob could eat together, but with Annie gone and Jakob knee deep in yet another murder investigation, a solo lunch at the counter would have to do.

Still, the handsome detective was up-permost in her thoughts as she retrieved her lunch and carried it back inside the main room. For several stressful moments the previous night, she'd feared he wouldn't answer the phone when she'd called to apologize. But after the fourth ring, he'd finally picked up, his usual pre-bedtime greeting void of its usual warmth and enthusiasm . . .

"I have your glove. You left it in the front seat."

"I didn't know I dropped one."

"Oh."

Before he could say anything else or possibly end the call entirely, she'd stammered on, Bill's words serving as a road map of sorts. "I . . . I'm calling to apologize. For the way I reacted to you questioning Ruth. I was wrong and I'm sorry. Truly."

She set the paper sack beside the register, pulled out her sandwich and napkin, and settled onto one of the two stools tucked behind the counter, the memory of Jakob's answering sigh of relief stirring up the same emotion she'd experienced during their call.

"I get it, Claire. I really do. And it's not really fair of me to only appreciate your steadfast loyalty when it works in my favor."

There were so many things about Jakob

she loved — his kindness, his work ethic, his ability to listen . . . the list went on and on, actually. But perhaps the thing she loved most was his willingness to see things from the perspective of others, a trait that had allowed him to really hear what she'd had to say and to understand that while she knew in her heart Ruth and Samuel were innocent, she knew, too, that Jakob was doing what he needed to do. By the time she'd finished explaining and apologizing for her lack of sensitivity, the warmth he so easily exuded when it came to her was back, enabling her to get at least some sleep when they'd finally ended their call.

Reaching for the pad of paper she kept on a shelf beneath the register, she flipped to a clean page and took a bite of her sandwich. One of the best ways she could help Jakob was to expedite the removal of Ruth and Samuel from his list of suspects. Yes, he was working on that, but maybe, if she could help do it faster by pointing him in more believable directions, it would help minimize any fallout with Jakob's former Amish brethren. To do that, though, she had to know more about Daniel and Mary — their business, their family, their neighbors, that sort of thing. How, exactly, she'd go about learning those things, though, was the question.

She took a second bite of her ham and cheese sandwich and then rested it atop her napkin in exchange for a pen from the holder beside the register. For as far back as she could remember, she'd always been a list maker. In elementary school, her lists had been typical of her age: friends' names, things to play outside, and who she wanted to come to her birthday parties. In high school, the lists had changed to the more organizational to-do variety: homework assignments, after-school tasks, and job responsibilities. Now that she was an adult and a store owner, her to-do list had morphed into something more road map–like, guiding her through each day in manageable chunks.

That's what she needed now — a road map with point A being Daniel's and Mary's deaths, and point B being the removal of Ruth and Samuel from any and all cloud of suspicion. To do that, though, meant either proving they had nothing to do with the murders or proving who did.

Tapping the end of the pen against her lips, she let her gaze wander across the shop, through the front window, across the street, and then left toward the police station she could see in her thoughts if not with her eyes at that very moment. Jakob, too, was a list maker of sorts, with his lists being composed of motives and means and suspects, and being written across the white board in his office rather than in a simple notepad like the one in front of her now. When she'd asked him about it early in their relationship, his reason for liking lists had resonated with her, too. Because really, there *was* something about seeing things written on paper that made them feel more real, more approachable.

Her mind made up, Claire dropped her focus back down to the paper and began to write, the words scattered at first and then linking with others to form the beginning of her road map through Ruth's dilemma.

Ruth.
Samuel.
Mary and Daniel Esch, murdered.
Ruth and Samuel last to see them alive?
Ruth: Too sweet, too shy, too gentle.
Samuel: Never seems to get ruffled by anything. Has a solid customer base both locally and via tourists. Senior community nice push, but okay without, right?

Claire stopped, doubled back, and reread her last entry. Granted, she wasn't privy to the financial specifics of her friends' lives any more than they were of her own, but Samuel's shop was doing well to the best of her knowledge, and Shoo Fly Bake Shoppe couldn't be any more successful than it was . . .

Slipping off her stool, she wandered over to the side window and its view of the alleyway between her own Heavenly Treasures and the bake shop in which Ruth had worked until her wedding to Samuel. Today, the line that so often wound across the front porch and down onto the sidewalk for one of Ruth's fresh-from-the-oven pies was absent, the bakery's CLOSED sign and darkened windows slumping more than a few shoulders of passersby. Then again, since Ruth's wedding and subsequent departure from the day-to-day running of the popular shop, the lines, while still par for the course, weren't as long anymore. People wanted the tasty treats sold inside, but maybe with a little less intensity as they had when Ruth herself was making them on the premises.

"I've been looking out my window that same way all morning."

Startled, Claire turned away from the

window to find the man that matched the voice grinning at her from the front of her shop. "Harold! I . . . I'm sorry, I didn't hear you come in."

"Not sure why." The balding man shrugged his thick shoulders and stepped farther into the shop. "Bells rang just like they always do. But I'm not surprised, I guess. You sure seemed mighty distracted looking out at Shoo Fly just now."

She glanced back at the bake shop across the alleyway and then headed across the carpeted floor, the smile the hardware store owner always managed to elicit twitching at the corners of her lips. "I don't know, maybe I was dreaming about one of Ruth's cookies. Or imagining what it would be like to have folks lined up outside my front door the way they do over at Shoo Fly."

"You mean the way they used to," Harold said, tucking his thumbs inside the upper straps of his Glick's Tools 'n More smock. "Now don't get me wrong, that little sister of Esther's is doing a fine job of tempting me up those stairs with her own assortment of treats. But she isn't Ruth, and Shoo Fly's most loyal fans know this."

"There are still lines," she protested. "I mean, just this Saturday, the line stretched across the mouth of the alley."

Harold poked a finger through the bin of holiday-colored linen napkins to his left and then returned his hand to its normal resting spot atop his stomach. "That's because it was a Saturday, and the official start of the holiday shopping season. But the week before? The line didn't even reach the steps."

"Ruth had days like that, too," she said, her words hollow even to her own ears.

Chuckling, Harold ventured over to the front window and its view of Lighted Way. "You're right. Ruth did. When she was getting ready to close and there wasn't much more than a few cookies left in the case . . ."

Claire swept her own gaze toward the side window and the part of Shoo Fly Bake Shoppe's white clapboard exterior she could see from where she stood. "Do you think they're seeing a difference in the bottom line, then? You know, since Ruth left to marry Samuel?"

"I'm not sure how they couldn't. A drop in business is a drop in business, even if the drop in question simply went from crazy-good to everybody-else-good," Harold mused. Abandoning his belly in favor of the five o'clock shadow that was two hours too early, he rocked back on his heels with an audible *hmmph.* "And then there's the little matter of having to pay someone to do what Ruth was doing . . . Makes me wonder why the Miller clan didn't just give the job to the younger girl."

"Because Ruth's younger sister is still in school for another month or so. And even when she finishes, she'll only be what? Thirteen? Maybe fourteen? That's probably a bit young to be running a shop all by herself with only occasional check-ins from Ben or Eli, don't you think?"

Harold nodded. "I do. But the Amish do things younger than the rest of us, as you know. In fact, I'm not so sure Ruth wasn't much older than that when the family opened Shoo Fly to begin with. Granted, Eli spent a good part of the day helping his twin back then, but that didn't stay the case for long. By the time the two of them were fifteen or so, Ruth was running that shop on her own. Course Ben and/or Eli stopped by a half-dozen or so times a day, but that was just to lend a little muscle with shipments. The baking and the running of the store were all on Ruth. Alone."

She forced a nod even as her thoughts jumped ahead to a fresh new set of questions and thoughts for her notepad — the kinds of questions and thoughts she hadn't really entertained until that moment.

"You planning on going to that double funeral today?"

Now that Ruth was married, did she have any financial ties to Shoo Fly? If so, how?

"Claire?"

She snapped her attention back to the window and the man now studying her with a mixture of curiosity and amusement. "I'm sorry, Harold, I guess I zoned out a little there for a minute. Can you repeat your question?"

"I can." He folded his arms and leaned heavily against the room's lone upright. "I asked if you plan on going to that double funeral I imagine your Annie is at today?"

"Oh . . . yes . . . she is. And yes, I . . . I'd like to. I'm actually hoping to go with Jakob when I've closed up here for the day." At Harold's slow nod, Claire closed the gap between them with her latest question in tow. "Hey, I've got an odd question for you . . . Do you happen to know if Ruth is still tied to Shoo Fly in any way?"

"I know Benjamin delivers some of Ruth's famous pies to the shop shortly before lunch sometimes. I've seen him unloading them from his buggy when I've happened past the alley at just the right time. Seeing them makes my mouth water just like always, but the smell? It's just not the same as it was

when the actual pie baking happened" —
he nudged his chin to their left — "next
door there."

It was a daily delivery she well knew,
although it wasn't always Benjamin who
made it. In fact, at least several times a week
it was Ruth herself who pulled into the alley with at least a half-dozen or so pies to
be carried into the shop. Which, now that
Claire thought about it, probably meant
Ruth was compensated for her contribution
in the same way Claire compensated Ben or
Esther or Eli when something they made
sold at Heavenly Treasures. Still, even with
that, the money Ruth made from a handful
of pies each week had to be considerably
less than what she'd made working at Shoo
Fly six days a week, unless . . .

"Do you, by any chance, happen to know
whose name is on the lease for that space?"
she asked.

Harold paused his fingers against his
stubbled chin. "Shoo Fly? I imagine the
parents — Ruth, Eli, and Benjamin's, that
is. But Al could tell you for sure one way or
the other."

Al — Al Gussmann. Owner of Gussmann's General Store and the landlord for
most if not all of the businesses on Lighted
Way . . .

"You could ask him next time you see him," Harold suggested. "It'll give him a reason to yammer on the way he does."

She knew he was talking. Even knew she was missing an opportunity to tease him back. But honestly, the minute he'd mentioned Al, her conscious thought scampered back to her notepad and the pen her fingers were itching to pick up.

CHAPTER 8

The crunch of the sparsely graveled road gave way to silence as Jakob pulled the department-issued sedan onto the shoulder and cut the engine. Glancing across the seat, Claire's eyes mingled with his before traveling, together, toward the dirt driveway on the opposite side of the street. The season's early nightfall made it difficult to discern specifics, but the glow of lantern lights made the outlines of certain things easy to pick out.

To the left of the driveway, and about twenty yards in, were rows of matching rectangular objects lining the vacant field — rectangles Claire knew were all gunmetal gray, the chosen buggy color for the Lancaster sect of the Old Order Amish. To the right, under a temporary tent lit by lantern light, were all of the horses, each one sporting a blanket to keep the animal warm in the chilly December air.

Down the driveway, beyond the buggies and the tent, were flashes of movement; people Claire knew from experience to be clad in simple black coats waiting in line to enter the farmhouse for the viewing part of the funeral. The part of the line that had made it inside the home was surely filing, one by one, past the deceased. Only this time, instead of there being one simple pine casket with a single body lying in rest, there would be two caskets, likely side by side, with the bodies of Mary and Daniel Esch, clothed completely in white.

The bodies themselves would be embalmed as per state regulations, but there would be no makeup, no attempt to doctor them up for the benefit of the living. Because in death, as they'd been in life, the Amish were modest people . . .

"Are you ready for this?" Jakob asked, his voice pulling her attention back inside the car and onto him.

Claire ran her fingers through her auburn-colored hair and then let them drift down to her lap and his waiting hand. "I know I only spoke with them for a few moments at Ruth and Samuel's wedding, but they both seemed so nice, so unassuming. It just doesn't make any sense that someone would kill them."

"Murder rarely makes sense to anyone but the killer." He squeezed her hand and then nudged his chin toward the road. "Well? Shall we?"

Nodding, she opened her car door and stepped out, the quick pop of the gravel beneath her shoes echoing in the still night air. Glancing left and then right, she crossed around the front of the car and joined Jakob on the other side. "Do you think there will be any issues with you being here? From Bishop Hershberger or anyone else?"

"The bishop knows this is an active murder case; we talked about it the night it happened. He knows, too, that my job is to figure out who did this. He just wishes, I'm sure, I'd do it somewhere else, far from his district and its people."

She matched his stride as they crossed the road and made their way up the driveway, his comments pulling at a distant memory. "I remember, back when I lived in the city, there was a case in the suburbs involving a woman and her children who were killed in a home invasion. The killer didn't know anyone was home when he first broke in. Is it possible this could be something like that?"

"It is, of course. But the things we'd expect to see in such a case weren't present here." He set his hand on the small of her back and gently guided her around a series of rain-induced ruts. "There was no sign of forced entry — although there is a possibility the killer came in through a window that was partially open — no indication the victims were in fear for their lives, nothing of significant value missing from the home."

"So that's out, then?"

"It's never completely off the list until the crime is solved, but yeah, I'm not seeing this as a home invasion gone wrong."

She considered his words as the farmhouse drew closer, her eyes scanning the slowly moving line snaking around the eastern corner of the house. "You believe they knew their killer?"

"I do."

It was on the tip of her tongue to again plead Ruth and Samuel's case, but she let it go. Now was not the time or the place to revisit that subject. And even if it was, the best way to truly revisit it was through solid suggestions based on information gleaned rather than simply returning, again and again, to her own personal convictions.

"Which means," he continued, his hand tightening on hers while dropping his voice to a volume only she could hear, "the killer could be here tonight, sitting out on the road somewhere, watching, or even standing on the viewing line just like everyone else."

It was a boldness she found difficult to imagine, yet she knew it existed. People capable of doing harm to another human being were cut from a different cloth. She just wished they were easier to identify from a safe distance. If they were, maybe they couldn't wreak such havoc in the world.

"Eli is here."

She followed Jakob's gaze to the left, her own quickly cataloging her way from the back of the line forward.

There was the farmer she recognized from her summer walks . . .

The woman she'd passed in the candy aisle of Gussmann's General Store the previous week . . .

The teenage girl she knew to be a friend of Esther's sister, Hannah . . .

An Amish man and woman she'd never seen before . . .

And finally Eli Miller, in his black winter coat and brimmed hat, his blue eyes void of their usual spark. Like his dat and all married men of the Old Order Amish, Eli now sported a beard, the year's worth of growth blocking his neck from view. Drifting her focus beyond Eli for just a moment, she

119

noted Esther and Sarah's absence, chalked it up to the hour and the baby's age in relation to the plummeting temperature, and then returned her thoughts and her smile to Esther's husband. For a second, maybe two, his lack of an answering smile led her to believe he didn't see her, but when the addition of a wave garnered a single nod in return, she knew otherwise.

"Well, that didn't take long," Jakob murmured, his pace slowing in tandem with an audible breath in and a whoosh of frustration out.

"What?"

"The shutdown."

"What shutdown?" She dragged her lingering gaze off Eli and, instead, followed the rest of the line as it stretched across the front lawn and up the porch steps, the movement forward offering no sign of stopping. "I thought these viewings go far into the night. Has that changed?"

Palming his jawline, Jakob shook his head, the simple movement pained. "No, it'll go straight through until tomorrow night if people keep showing up." He dropped his hand to his side and jerked his chin and her attention back toward the line. "I'm talking about Eli just now. You saw it. He's already different."

"Different?" she echoed. "Different how?"

"I could feel his anger before I even saw him. And when I caught him staring, he kept right on doing it, almost daring me to look away."

"I didn't see that."

"Because his anger isn't directed at you — yet. Though even with you just now, he wasn't the same."

His words pushed her back a step. "Eli isn't angry, Jakob. He's just at a wake, or — or a viewing or whatever the proper word is in the Amish community. People aren't usually peppy at things like this."

"His reaction to seeing me just now? That wasn't about being at a viewing or mourning the deaths of Mary and Daniel Esch. No, that was all about what went down yesterday. With his twin, Ruth."

"With his . . ." The rest of her sentence fell away as her focus skittered back to the line and the twenty-something male now actively pinning Jakob with a death stare.

Oh, how she wanted to believe anger was not the reason for Eli's demeanor, that, in fact, the aura he wasn't even trying to disguise was simply his way of dealing with grief. But she knew better. So, too, did her stomach if the sudden clenching in its pit was any indication.

"Oh, Jakob," she whispered.

"It's okay. I knew this was going to happen, knew Eli and Benjamin would be furious when they found out about my talk with their sister. You know, you've seen it. Those two have always been very protective of Ruth. So my going at her the way I did yesterday pretty much guaranteed that look I'm getting right now — a look that would likely be followed with strong words if there wasn't a funeral going on. But somehow, last night, after you called and told me you understood why I have to consider Ruth and Samuel for these murders, I let myself believe, even a little, that maybe those two would understand, as well. That maybe, just maybe" — his voice broke only to return in a hushed rasp — "there was still a chance I wouldn't lose ground with Esther because of all of this, but that was wishful, deluded thinking. I knew, the second I put on my cop hat and went at Ruth the way I did, I was done. Whatever relationship I've managed to build with my niece and her husband, thanks to you, is over. I am, once again, the turncoat — the guy who turned away from his baptismal vows and his family to pursue an English path."

Gently she guided him off the driveway and over to the empty paddock, her hand finding his as they reached the fence. "If you're right and Eli is upset, he'll get over it when he sees that you're just checking the boxes you need to check in your investigation."

"And if it turns into more than that?" He hiked his foot onto the bottom edge of the fence and leaned heavily against the top. "You and I both know Eli and Esther have been walking a mighty fine line engaging with me the way they do. Something tells me, by the time I'm done, they won't risk being shunned at a church service for me."

"But you're almost done, right?"

"With?"

"Checking the Ruth and Samuel box . . ."

Pushing off the fence, he tilted his chin upward until the cold night sky was his only view. "If another lead, another name, comes up, I can start looking in that direction, too. But right now? They're all I've got. And that bid-losing thing with Samuel? I wouldn't ignore a thread like that in any other case, so how can I ignore it in this one?"

It was on the tip of her tongue to point out the Samuel Yoder they both knew, but she held it back at the last minute. Even in the limited moonlight, it was clear Jakob was wrestling with a lot. The bags under his eyes told that story just fine all on their own.

"It'll be okay," she said instead.

His answering laugh lacked anything resembling humor. "I wish I had your confidence."

"You didn't think you'd ever have a relationship with your niece, did you?"

"That was before you." He draped his arm across her shoulder, pulled her against his side, and pressed his lips against her hair. "Before you became a link back to my past — to my sister, Martha; to my niece and Eli; and now, to my precious great-niece, Sarah."

"I'm still here, aren't I?" she asked, looking up at him.

"You are. But this" — he swept his free hand forward — "*this* changes things. I've crossed a line."

"We'll see about that."

His eyebrow arched in a welcome hint of playfulness. "Oh, we will, will we?"

The headlight beams of an approaching car bounced across the fence and onto the frozen earth beyond before extinguishing as fast as they appeared. Together, Claire and Jakob turned toward the driveway and the small two-door car that rolled to a stop just outside the barn.

Ever the observer, Claire made a mental note of the color (black, maybe dark blue), the model (a two-door Corolla), and the familiar note or two of the Casting Crowns song she detected before it faded to silence along with the engine. "Even though I've seen it before, it still surprises me to see a car on an Amish farm."

"You and me both," Jakob said, shrugging. "But between the Amish taxi drivers and the delivery guys who worked for Esch in the past, it makes sense in this situation."

"It might make sense, but visually, it still doesn't fit. Not for me, anyway." She returned her attention to the man beside her, and wiggling free of his arm, she rose up on the toes of her ankle boots and met his waiting lips. "So . . . What do you say we get on that line, pay our respects, and then head back to the inn? I happen to know where Aunt Diane keeps the evening's leftover cookies."

Smiling, he kissed her again. "You mean there's a secret stash?"

"Of course."

"And you've been holding out on me all this time?"

"Maybe . . ."

"Any other secrets I should know — ?"

Rapid-fire shouts stole the rest of his words and sent their collective attention racing back toward the barn. Just beyond the car, a handful of Amish men stood shoulder to shoulder across the open doorway, seemingly unmoved by the anguished voice slipping past them into the night. "Jakob?" she rasped. "What's happening?"

"I don't know, but someone in that barn isn't happy, that's for sure." Glancing back at the line waiting to get inside the farmhouse, he gestured in that direction. "Get yourself in line and I'll go check out whatever is going on."

"Jakob, I —"

"I'm fine. Go on. Besides, maybe Eli will be his normal self if I'm not standing next to you."

"He's over there," she said, pointing back toward the growing crowd of males by the barn. "See?"

Another shout, followed by the distinctive sound of metal thumping against wood, had Jakob on the move, his destination clear. For a moment, she considered following, her curiosity over the noises and the crowd of men only growing. But when she started in that direction, a brief peek back at the line of mourners yielded a familiar yet troubled face standing inside the shadow of the farm's lone tree, watching.

Reversing course, Claire hurried across

the mouth of the driveway. "Ruth? Are you okay?"

"Is he coming back?"

"Who?"

"Your Jakob — the detective."

"When he's done at the barn, yes. Why?"

Again, Ruth peered at the barn, her anxiety palpable. "Your Jakob, he had many questions for me. Some I could answer, others I could not."

"That's okay. Jakob doesn't expect you to give answers you can't —"

"Your Jakob said he is to find out who sent Mary and Daniel Esch to be with the Lord, that the person who did it will go to an English jail for a very long time."

"As he should. No one has a right to do to someone what was done to Mary and Daniel. No one."

"He said someone who does not tell what they know can get in trouble, too," Ruth said, fidgeting with the sides of her coat.

"That's true, I'm sure, but that's not really anything you need to be worrying about." Claire inched closer to her shy friend, her voice calm and steady. "On a lighter note, did you speak with Samuel about the cookies I'd like you to make for One Heavenly Night? Is he okay with you doing that?"

For a moment, she wasn't sure Ruth had

heard her, but after a beat or two of silence, she was rewarded with a single fierce nod. "It is just one day of baking, yah?"

"One day."

"And Mr. Glick and the others will pay for them?" Ruth asked.

"The Lighted Way Business Association will, yes."

"I know cookies are not furniture or kitchen cabinets, but cookies are how *I* can help Samuel."

Something in Ruth's tone caught her up short. "Is everything okay with you and Samuel?"

Even with the winter shadows created by the moonlit tree limbs, Claire didn't miss the flinch or the awkward shift that followed in rapid succession. Before she could question them, though, Ruth cleared her throat. "Samuel did not like to hear of your Jakob's questions, and I did not like to see Samuel upset by them. He has a very full plate without such things."

Again, she followed Ruth's eyes down the driveway and over to the barn, where they remained. "Ruth? You need to know that those questions Jakob asked you yesterday were standard fare for a murder case. You and Samuel being the last known people to see Mary and Daniel Esch alive simply means you might have information he needs to find the person responsible for their deaths. Once he's satisfied you don't, he'll move on."

"But what if he doesn't," Ruth whispered.

Claire pulled a face. "Of course he'll move on. You're one of the gentlest people I've ever known. Thinking you could hurt someone is absurd."

"He says he will talk to Samuel next."

"Again, Ruth, this is Jakob just doing his job. Checking the boxes that must be checked. That's all."

"I . . . I hope you are right." Ruth's body convulsed in a shiver.

"Of course I'm right."

Ruth's long lashes closed over her eyes like a thick curtain. "When will the questions stop?"

"When he's satisfied he has the answers he needs from you and from Samuel, or when another, more viable suspect emerges," Claire said.

"I wish that would happen soon. I do not like Samuel having more worries. He does not smile as he did at our wedding. Or before."

Claire studied her friend — the nervous hands, the darting glances, the downward tilt of her full lips, and the pervasive sadness that loomed large — then sucked in a fortifying breath. "Maybe, if we work together, we can get Jakob on to that more viable suspect sooner rather than later. What do you say?"

Clamping her hand atop Claire's arm, Ruth leaned forward. "Can we really do that?"

"Absolutely. I just need to pick your brain a little. About your visit to the Esch farm, things they may have said, that sort of thing."

Like a balloon pricked by a pin, Ruth's whole body deflated. "Your Jakob asked those same things."

"And I'm sure I'll ask even more things that are the same. But maybe" — she closed her hand over Ruth's — "we'll hit on something he hasn't even thought to ask, something that will make it so he won't need to talk to you or Samuel about this case anymore."

"Yah. That is good." Ruth stood tall, her chin lifting little by little. "Tomorrow morning, before you go into work, perhaps it would be a good time for you to come to the house. I will tell Samuel you are there to talk about the cookies for your festival. When he goes out to the barn, I can answer your questions."

CHAPTER 9

She wasn't sure how long she'd stood there, staring after Ruth as the young woman slipped into the darkness that lapped at the edges of the property, her simple black boots and coat swallowed up by the night. All Claire knew for certain was the inexplicable unease snaking its way up her back and spreading outward toward her neck, her arms, her legs — a chill that had nothing to do with the date on the calendar.

Ruth was nervous — terrified, even; that much was obvious. What wasn't so obvious was why. Sure, Ruth was shy. One only had to be in her vicinity for a few minutes to come to that truth. Yet there was something more to the newlywed's angst, something off. It wasn't anything Claire could put a finger on well enough to articulate to herself, let alone Jakob, but it was there. And the longer Claire stood there, playing their conversation over and over in her head, the less certain her next step became.

Yes, she could tell Jakob, but what was there to say? Ruth was upset? He'd likely think that was normal in light of Ruth's personality. But if he didn't, if his radar began to ping like Claire's, would it be fair for Ruth to open the door the next morning to Jakob instead of Claire?

Probably not.

Besides, would waiting to tell him until tomorrow, when she'd had a chance to see Ruth on her home turf, really make much of a difference in the grand scheme of things? After all, it would only be what? Maybe fourteen, fifteen hours from now?

Her mind made up, Claire headed toward the barn and the occasional rise and fall of a voice from somewhere inside. The group of Amish men that had assembled en masse during the shouting had largely dissipated, with only a few holdouts scattered about. At the open door she peeked inside, scanned the horse stalls, the owner's parked buggy, the water troughs and feed buckets, and finally, near the back wall, spotted Jakob sitting on a bale of hay next to a dark-haired man dressed in an ill-fitting suit, staring down at his knees with a somber expression. A few feet away, pacing between stalls, was another Englisher — one she vaguely recognized but couldn't yet place in the proper context.

She couldn't hear what was being said, but she could tell, from Jakob's demeanor, that he was sharing something important with the man in the suit. Drawing in a breath, she took a step backward, only to stop when Jakob looked up, spotting her immediately.

"C'mon in, Claire. There's someone" — he paused, slanted a glance toward the man still restlessly pacing — "some *people* I'd like you to meet."

She stepped inside the barn, slid the door closed at Jakob's request, and made her way across the uneven and straw-littered aisleway that ran the length of the building from front to back.

"Abe, I'd like you to meet my girlfriend, Claire Weatherly. She owns the Heavenly Treasures gift shop on Lighted Way."

The dark-haired man lifted his chin to reveal equally dark eyes rimmed red by tears that had long dried. Pushing off the hay bale, he stood, cleared his throat, and extended his hand. "Claire Weatherly," he repeated. "Might you be kin with Ms. Weatherly from the inn?"

She shook his hand, his grip gentle yet firm. "I am, actually. Diane Weatherly is my aunt. I live with her at Sleep Heavenly."

"My father and I did some work for her about six years ago."

"*I* was there, too, Abe."

Recognition dawned swiftly as Claire turned toward the second Englisher who'd stopped, mid-step, to join the conversation. "Wait. I know you. I met you last night . . . at Heavenly Brews. You were there with your mom, Nancy." She held out her hand, letting it drop to her side when the gesture was not returned. "You're Tommy, right?"

"Yep."

"Ms. Weatherly was so happy with the work we did, she sat us down at this big table when we were done and fed us the best pot roast I ever had in my life." The faintest hint of a smile played at the corner of Abe's mouth at the memory. "After the meal, when we were heading back home, I told my father that, asked him not to tell my mother in case her feelings got hurt. He pulled us over to the side of the road, reached down beside his feet to a container I hadn't noticed him leaving with, and showed me the helping of pot roast Ms. Weatherly had sent home for my mother. He looked at me, square in the eyes, and told me there was no need to keep it from her because she'd know for herself soon

134

enough."

Claire's soft laugh mingled with Abe's. "I'll be sure to tell my aunt that story when I get home tonight. I'm sure she'll get quite a chuckle out of it, as well."

"Send her my regards, will you?"

"Of course. Will she know you by Abe?"

"She'll likely know me as Abraham — Abraham Esch."

The last name, spoken with anguish, smacked her back. "Oh . . . Abe . . . I . . . I didn't realize." She dropped her gaze to his suit, his tie, his wrinkled shirt. "I was so intent on your story just now, I didn't realize" — she stopped, glanced at Jakob, and tried again. "I didn't realize you were Amish."

"That's because he's not," Tommy sneered.

Abe bristled but kept his focus on Claire. "There'd be no reason for you to know that, seeing as how you weren't living out at the inn when Dat and I put those cabinets in." He ran his faintly scarred and trembling hands down his rumpled front. "And I am wearing English clothes."

"Abe left after baptism like I did," Jakob said by way of explanation. "Mary and Daniel were his parents."

And just like that, she didn't need a

rewind button to know what Jakob and Abe had been discussing when she'd first looked inside the barn. Jakob's calming hand on the man's back and the man's broken demeanor came together to form a picture she knew well — a picture that had Abe floating in the world alone, void of the grounding tether that was a person's childhood family.

Without thinking, Claire stepped forward, wrapped her arms around the man, and pulled him close, the quick yet stifled sob that followed nearly breaking her heart in two. "I'm sorry for your loss."

"Thank you," he murmured, stepping back.

"As you can imagine from what you've lived through with me so far, Abe's arrival here — to his sister's farm just a little while ago — wasn't exactly welcomed."

The shouts . . .

The angry words . . .

She looked between Abe and Jakob as the reality she didn't want to believe loomed large. "But Mary and Daniel . . . They're still his parents . . . They raised him . . . He loved them . . . Surely they can understand he would want to say good-bye to them, too!"

"The Ordnung trumps all, don't you

know that?"

Jerking her head to the left, she stared at Tommy. But it was Jakob's voice and the calming and familiar touch of his hand on her arm that eased her heart enough to listen. "It's the rules, Claire. I knew it when I chose to leave and so, too, did Abe. No, knowing doesn't always make it easier, but it is what it is. All we can do is make peace with our choice and hold our head high."

A glance back at Abe showed him nodding, albeit sadly, along with Jakob.

"So that means he can't go inside and see them one last time?" she rasped.

"It might. But I have faith Bishop Hershberger will do the right thing if I ask." Jakob turned to Abe. "You ready to see if we can make this happen?"

Abe nodded but remained in place, his voice, his very gaze, suggesting he was no longer standing there in the barn but rather somewhere else — a different time and place. "I always knew this day would come, knew it was coming closer with each passing day. But I just didn't think anything I could ever say would make a difference for him."

"Him?" Jakob prodded.

"Dat."

"You can tell him now, in your prayers."

137

Jakob's own voice grew strangled as he clamped his hand down on Abe's shoulder. "Perhaps, with the Lord by his side, he will listen with his heart instead of the Ordnung."

It took every ounce of restraint she could muster to keep from crying — for the distraught Abe who'd lost his parents and for Jakob, who was getting a bird's-eye view of what lay ahead in his own life. Still, as Jakob passed by with his arm on Abe's shoulder, she leaned forward and whispered a kiss against his cheek. "I'll wait for you out here," she said softly.

"You want me to come, too, Abe?" Tommy asked, trailing behind his friend.

Abe shook his head. "No. I'm good. Thanks."

She watched as Abe and Jakob walked, side by side, down the barn's center aisle, each lost in thoughts she could only imagine. When they'd disappeared out into the darkness, Claire turned back to Tommy. "How long ago did Abe leave the church?"

"Six years."

"Six years," she repeated as she wandered over to the closest stall. Its occupant — a sturdy chocolate brown mare — studied her with avid interest. "Six years of being completely cut off from his family. I have such a hard time wrapping my head around that. I mean, how many kids did Mary and Daniel have?"

"Six. Four of them live elsewhere — upstate New York, Indiana, Ohio, and someplace in Wisconsin. Unfortunately Greta and ol' Lloyd stayed here, in Heavenly. If they hadn't, maybe things would have been different."

She stilled her hand atop the mare's head. "Greta is Abe's sister?"

"Yep. And Lloyd is the wackadoodle she married," he said, spreading his arms wide. "And *this*? This is *their* barn . . . *their* farm . . . *their* house . . . *their* district . . . *their everything.* Make no mistake about it, those two won't bend the rules for anyone, under any circumstance."

"How long have you and Abe been friends?"

"Since we were six. My maw became an Amish taxi driver when my twin sister, Trishy, and I started first grade. Said it gave her something to do when we were at school. Most of the time, she just trekked the Amish around when we were gone, but sometimes she'd get a call to drive one of them somewhere when we were home. When that happened, she'd take us along, too. That's how we met Abe."

"There wasn't any issue with the two of you being English and Abe being Amish?"

"Not that I ever saw. Maw, neither."

Liberating a brush from the hook beside the stall door, Claire began to brush the mare's back, the soft, rhythmic strokes proving to be every bit as relaxing for her as for the horse. "You said something about helping Abe and his father with the cabinets out at my aunt's place?"

"My dad walked out on my maw when I was thirteen. Went out for some milk one day and never came back. So Maw started picking up even more runs just to make ends meet, and Abe's mamm let Trishy and me hang out with them. By then, Abe was helping his dat out with the cabinet business — sanding them, painting them, and sometimes installing them. In the beginning I just watched, maybe handed them some tools when they needed them, but that was it. After a while, Abe started showing me how to do certain things. Next thing I knew, I was going along on jobs with them. They'd install everything, but I was there to help with little things that came up — like putting on whatever knobs the customer wanted or swapping them out when they decided they wanted something else. My part was never anything too big, but I liked it. And Abe? He was really good at all parts of the business. Even came up with a few new designs that ended up catching the eye of Harper Construction out in Blue Ball."

Intrigued, she finished grooming the part of the horse she could reach from outside the stall and returned the brush to its hook. "I've heard of Harper! They build some really pretty homes out in that area. But isn't that kind of far to take the buggy?"

"It is. So that's when Abe suggested hiring a few Englishers to get the cabinets from his dat's workshop to the farther-away job sites. I had a truck of my own by then, but it wasn't big enough to hall everything we needed."

She wandered over to a barrel, checked its sturdiness, and then pulled herself onto its closed lid, her feet dangling off the edge. "Did that work out for Daniel and Abe — hiring English?"

"Business took off fast. A few months in, Abe's dat hurt his back so bad he couldn't build anymore. Abe tried to keep up with everything on his own by working late into the night and starting long before dawn every morning, but it cost him big-time. The Amish girl he'd started courting a few months earlier moved on to someone else — someone who wasn't too busy to linger at hymn sings or drive her around in his buggy." Tommy's throat tightened with a hard swallow. "Abe took it real hard. Between losing her, worrying about his dat's health, and taking everything on his own shoulders, he had a lot to deal with. But he always wanted to do right by his dat, no matter what.

"Then he dropped a big ball. He missed a critical deadline for Harper, and they severed ties with Esch."

The barrel wobbled beneath her as she drew back. "Ouch."

"A few months before all this went down, Abe's sister Greta had married Lloyd Chupp, this guy from some place I can't even remember. When Abe lost Harper, Lloyd suggested *he* take over the company, since Daniel was wanting to get out — he, the guy who couldn't hammer a nail straight even if his life depended on it . . . But Daniel was adamant it was going to Abe — said Abe knew the business, knew how to build the cabinets, had grown it to what it was."

"Okay . . ."

"Then one Sunday, Abe is shunned at church. For drinking."

"Had he been baptized yet?"

"Yeah."

She winced. "Oh. Yeah. Not good."

"It wouldn't have been if it were true. But it wasn't."

She stared at him. "Then why was he shunned?"

"Near as we can figure, Lloyd told the then bishop he'd caught Abe drinking. Told him he'd talked to him multiple times and he just kept doing it. So he was shunned."

"That's horrible!"

"Trust me, it gets worse. Without Harper, Abe had to let both delivery drivers go. I tried to tell him they'd be okay, they'd find other work, but he felt like he was disappointing everyone — his dat, Harper, the girl he'd wanted to marry, and now the drivers."

"What happened?" she prodded.

"He started actually drinking. I was cool with it because he was my bud and we were having fun. But one night, Lloyd — who was always nosing around and is as old-school Old Order as they come — and Greta saw Abe cutting through the field, and they followed. Caught him drinking and horsing around with Trishy. Lloyd went straight to the bishop at the time, and once again, Abe was shunned. Which, in the event you're unaware, means no one speaks to you until you repent — they turn their backs on you and refuse to do business with you. Abe repented, said he wouldn't drink anymore, and he didn't. But Lloyd? He said otherwise. Which meant, Abe was shunned a third time, and his dat's company suffered again. The shame of that alone started him drinking again for real. After the fourth or fifth shunning, he left the church in an effort to spare his father's business."

"Why would Lloyd say that stuff if it wasn't true?" Claire asked. "Didn't he risk being shunned himself if he'd been caught lying?"

"Lloyd was older. He was married. That alone made him more trustworthy, more believable in the eyes of the bishop."

"Oh. Wow . . ."

"And as for your first question? About why Lloyd would say that stuff? He thought it would play out differently than it did, I guess."

Claire shifted her weight across the barrel, the heels of her ankle boots making a soft thump against the aged wood. "Meaning?"

"When Abe left, Daniel closed the company down. Said it was time. Lloyd, of course, got angry, tried to make a go of his *own* company, but it never took off. Of course, Lloyd blamed his lack of success on Abe, and considering the way the Amish have a stranglehold on just about every business in this town, it's an accusation he's allowed himself to wallow in for years. But the reality is Lloyd Chupp isn't someone most people would want to work with. On anything."

"Wait." She rewound the conversation back a sentence. "The Amish don't have a stranglehold on every business in this town."

He pinned her with a stare. "You're kidding, right? You ever try to make a go of something around here that the Amish are already doing? It doesn't work. Period."

"I own a gift shop and it's thriving."

"That's just because it's the only one in town," he countered. "Had they had one first, you wouldn't. Not for long, anyway."

She considered challenging him but let it go as her thoughts drifted back to the man with the rumpled suit and red-rimmed eyes — a man who was likely standing beside his parents' bodies at that very moment. "Is Abe still drinking?"

"Hasn't touched a drop in nearly a year, and it was something he was excited to tell her when they spoke."

"Her?"

Tommy rubbed at his cheek, his chin, his throat. "His mamm."

"But Abe left the church . . ."

"He was still her son," Tommy said, his

voice tight.

She waved away his rebuttal. "No, I get it. I'm glad they spoke. I . . . I just know, from my relationship with Jakob, that's not the way things usually go."

"My maw said Mary was never the same after Abe left. Thinks she might've been one of the Old Order who'd have broken the rules to keep him close, but Greta and Lloyd weren't having that. There's no gray with those two. Ever."

"So what changed? What made her risk talking to him now — or whenever it was they talked?"

Pulling in a breath, Tommy raked his fingers through his hair. "Abe was at our house this time last year, and he was drinking. My maw told him it was time to stop, that he was letting his life slip by. He said something about it not mattering, and Maw went off on him. Told him how it was up to him what kind of man he wanted to be in life.

"That's when he got himself cleaned up, even started building things again. Then, one day about three or four weeks ago, he asked Maw's help in finding a way for him to talk to his mamm. She did, and they did."

"Good for Abe." Again, she glanced toward the barn door, the hands of her internal clock making it likely Abe and Jakob would be returning sooner rather than later. "I imagine that'll be a comfort for him in the days and weeks ahead — knowing he got to reconnect with his mamm?"

His answering laugh held no humor. "You sound like my maw; ever the peacemaker. Trishy and me? We're not like that, not like Maw is, anyway. Trishy can fake it better than I can, but I don't see much use in that. If I don't like you, I'm not gonna pretend I do. The day Abe left that farm for good was the last time I stepped foot on that farm or his sister's. Maw says I should forgive, that a job is a job. But I'd sooner riffle through a garbage can for food than make so much as a penny driving the likes of any of them around."

Claire brushed a piece of straw off the half wall to her left and wandered over to a different stall, a different pair of soulful eyes watching her every move. "I remember the first time I witnessed the back-turning thing in regard to Jakob. I knew he'd left after baptism, and I knew it meant he couldn't go back, but to watch his own family act as if he didn't exist? That was hard to see. Still gets me worked up sometimes, even though Jakob is the first one to tell me he knew the consequences of his decision."

"Did you know him when he was Amish?" Tommy asked.

Grinning, she shook her head. "No. But I wish I could've, even if only for a few minutes."

"You getting worked up when his family treats him like dirt? It'd be even worse if you'd witnessed the before and after the way Trishy and I did. Growing up friends with Abe, we watched him pick wildflowers for his mamm, we stopped our playing because he wanted to help his dat with a cow or a lame horse or whatever . . . Abe was always thinking about his family, even when he left. But when he *did* leave, he might as well have been dead. Because to them, he was" — Tommy splayed his hands toward the barn door — "*is.*"

She looked beyond him, to the images filing past her mind's eye in rapid succession: Jakob's own father turning his back to Jakob at Esther and Eli's wedding, the way Jakob's sister, Martha, acted as if Jakob didn't exist if other Amish were near, the —

"You know what I'm talking about, don't you? I can see it on your face."

"I do," she admitted. "But it's not always like that." Though, even as she said the words, her thoughts lit on Eli's face as she and Jakob had approached the mourners' line. Had his blatant dismissal of the detective really been about the questioning of his sister, Ruth, or was it because he was surrounded by other Amish and Jakob was the black sheep. The thought, the question, was unsettling at best.

Tommy's eyes narrowed on hers. "You know, if you two were to get married and have kids, they'd speak to you, right? Even have a relationship with you and your kids. But not him . . . In theory, he could be there, wherever you all are, but they'd keep their backs turned to him while engaging with you and your kids."

"I know. But that's just the way it is. The way it's always been."

"Said Jakob. Said Abe." Tommy threw his head back in disgust. "And they'd be okay with that happening because they actually think that kind of treatment is what they deserve. But they don't. No one does. Except Lloyd and Greta."

Slipping his hands into the pockets of his coat, he nudged his chin toward the door. "At least now Trishy won't be having to grin and bear that kind of thing with Abe's mamm."

"Your sister?" Claire asked, wandering back to Tommy. "Why?"

"She and Abe got hitched a few months

after Maw set him straight that time. They're expecting their first next summer."

"I see. So you're going to be an uncle . . ."

Something resembling a genuine smile flashed across his face, only to disappear as a long, steady creaking sound pulled their full attention toward the barn door. Less than a second later, Abe stepped through the opening, followed by Jakob, the former's eyes cast down at the floor.

Tommy closed the gap between them with a half-dozen long strides, his focus flitting between Abe and Jakob. "Did they give you any trouble?"

"Abe's sister and her husband weren't pleased to see either of us inside their home, but Bishop Hershberger saw to it that Abe and I got some time alone in the room." Jakob clapped a hand on Abe's back en route to Claire. "He's a good man, Annie's father; a fair man."

Abe's nod was slow and labored but genuine, too. "It wouldn't have been that way with the last bishop, so I'm grateful — to him and to you, Jakob. I . . . I needed that chance — to say good-bye."

"And I'm glad you had it, Abe."

"Hey, you okay, man?" Tommy asked, moving in beside his friend.

"I don't know. Verdict's still out."

"Feel what you need to feel for however long you need to feel it and then get back to the business of living." Jakob slid his arm across Claire's shoulder and pulled her close to his side. "You have good memories from your Amish upbringing. I know this because I do, too. Focus on those. They're every bit as real as the stuff that came later, but a whole lot nicer to think about."

Again, Abe nodded. "I just wish my son or daughter could have met them."

"They still can, through your memories. Tell them about your life — the stuff you did, the fun you had. No one can take those memories away from us unless we let them." Jakob looked down at Claire and motioned toward the still-open door. "Well, shall we? It's getting pretty late, and I want to stop at the station on my way back from bringing you home."

"Jakob, you need some sleep," she protested. "The station will still be there tomorrow."

"It won't be a long stop. I just want to make a few notes about the case and see if anything came in while I was here."

"You'll let me know as soon as you know anything, right?" Abe asked, stepping forward to shake Jakob's hand. "Because I'm pretty sure Lloyd and Greta won't tell me anything."

"You were Mary and Daniel's son, yes?"

Abe's Adam's apple moved with his swallow. "I was — I mean, *am.*"

"Well, in the eyes of the law, that makes you their next of kin every bit as much as your sister Greta." Jakob met and held Abe's sad eyes. "Which, translated, means we'll be in touch."

CHAPTER 10

They weren't more than a few car lengths away from the Chupp farm when she abandoned her passenger side view of the moonlit countryside in favor of the man behind the steering wheel. Jakob Fisher was, in a word, handsome. Even in the dark cabin of his station-issued sedan, she could make out so many of the features she could lose herself in if given the chance.

The sandy blond hair that looked like spun gold when the sun hit it just right . . .

The amber flecks in his hazel eyes that seemed to dance when he smiled at her . . .

The dimples that had a way of weakening her knees every single time she saw them . . .

The broad frame capable of shouldering whatever life threw his way . . .

Aware of the growing mist in her own blue-green eyes, Claire reached across the center console for his hand. Sure enough, he lowered his hand to hers, threaded their fingers together, and then gently kissed her skin. "Hey, I'm sorry that went longer than either of us planned."

"Are you kidding me? You were incredible back there with Abe. Everything about the way you handled that was perfect."

His laugh, low and short, filled in the space between them. "You really need to stop making me sound like Superman all the time. It's going to go to my head one of these days, and you'll be wishing you'd held your tongue."

"Not a chance. If I make you sound like that, it's because, in my eyes, you are. In all the best ways, anyway."

"Wait. Does that mean there are things about Superman you *don't* like?"

She followed his gaze to the road in front of them, the gas-powered lanterns of Lighted Way growing closer. "The way he went off into those phone booths all the time? I don't know . . . that could get a little weird."

"Note to self: Stay out of phone booths when with Claire." He let up on the gas as they transitioned from the graveled country-side road to the cobblestones of the quaint shopping district. "Anything else I should avoid?"

Grinning, she tapped her chin in thought.

"Hmmm . . . the web thing could get cumbersome."

"Superman was the one with the cape; Spiderman was the one with the web. But since you brought Spiderman into this, I have to say I think the web thing would be pretty cool."

"I'm listening . . ."

"Think about it," he said, swinging his attention from Heavenly Brews on their left to Gussmann's General Store on their right. "If I wanted one of your aunt's cookies and they were on a table on the other side of the room, I could use my web to get one. And when I'm at work and I'm craving a little time with you because the chief is driving me nuts, I could open the window and snag you with my web."

"The chief's window faces the back of the station," she reminded.

"I know. But Spiderman is gifted enough, his web isn't limited to just one direction."

"Ahhh . . ." She squeezed his hand once, twice, and then rested her left cheek against the headrest as they inched their way past the first few storefronts. "But seriously, so you know, I really did think you were amazing with Abe. The way you talked to him, the things you shared, I think you reached him in a way no one else could have tonight.

You should be proud of yourself."

"Maybe because I get it, I get *him*. I just wish things could be different, you know? I wish he didn't have to beat himself up over a life choice . . . I wish he could mourn the way he needs to without the added pain of being told he's unwelcome . . . And I wish the head and the heart didn't have to be at such odds all the time . . . because if they weren't, then I'd be better able to navigate the waters between rebukes and kindness, kindness and rebukes."

It was subtle, the shift in subject, but she caught it and it made her heart ache. "Hey, it *is* possible Eli didn't even see you. He does have a three-month-old at home. Which means he's probably short on sleep most days."

"He saw me, and he saw you, too. His re-action had nothing to do with lack of sleep."

"Okay, so maybe you're right. Maybe he is angry about you questioning Ruth. Eli has always been ultra-protective of his twin, you know that. But he's married now. To *your niece.* I think that will swing this back into your favor in the end."

"We don't know how Esther feels yet . . ."

She motioned for him to pull over. When he shifted into park in front of Glorious Books, she released her seat belt and turned so her back was parallel to the passenger side door. "Esther loves you, Jakob. There is no doubt to be had on that one."

"Maybe. But Eli is her husband. The second he becomes anything but okay with me stopping out at the farm, or the desserts on his front porch with everyone facing out at the driveway, or the subtle nods and smiles in my direction when they see me in town . . . it'll all stop. Because the truth of the matter is, they've been defying the Ordnung where I'm concerned this past year or so. If it's seen by someone like Abe's sister, Greta, or Greta's husband, Lloyd? Eli and Esther will be shunned at church. Eli might've been willing to risk that before, but he's not going to be willing to risk it for someone who upset his sister the way I did, and it will get even worse when I start questioning Samuel, too."

"Jakob, I really think this will all go away when you start looking at people who —"

He released her hand to hold up his own, stopping her mid-sentence. "Can we talk about something else for a little while? I really don't want to go back to where we were yesterday when this subject came up."

She wanted to protest, but really, when the top thing she wanted to say involved pleading Ruth and Samuel's case again, it was best to do as he asked. After all, if everything went according to plan with Ruth in the morning, Jakob would be on to a real suspect soon enough. Action always trumped words. Always.

"What would you like to talk about?" she asked.

"You . . . sleep . . ." He peeked out at the shops and the decorations. "How people are going to flock to Lighted Way even more than normal because of how magical this place looks right now . . ."

She laughed. "From your mouth to God's ears."

"Really, it looks amazing. You guys outdid yourselves this year."

He was right. They had. Every shop, every front porch, every nook and cranny of Lighted Way, was dressed to the nines in its holiday finery. Festive . . . inviting . . . warm . . . They were all words that came to mind as she looked ahead toward Heavenly Treasures, the lighted garland each storefront sported glistening like a thousand twinkling stars.

"Tommy Warren thinks the Amish have a stranglehold on business in this town," she said, widening her field of vision to include Taste of Heaven(ly) and the other shops beyond Glorious Books.

"A stranglehold?" Jakob echoed. "How does he figure that? You're English, Harold is English, Drew is English. That's three shops right there. And Sandra with Heavenly Brews . . ."

"He seems to think the only reason I have a gift shop is because the Amish don't. Same with Harold's tool shop and Drew's bookshop. But it's not about Amish versus English, not on Lighted Way, anyway. That's more about Al not wanting to lease to doubles of anything. He thinks we'll all succeed if we complement, instead of compete."

"Did you tell Tommy that?"

"I didn't, but I wish I had. By not doing so, I let his misperceptions continue."

"I wouldn't sweat it. If you get another opportunity to do so in the future, you take it then. After all, your festival is right around the corner. Maybe he'll be there."

"I wish everyone would stop calling it *my* festival. One Heavenly Night belongs to everyone — the shopkeepers on Lighted Way, the folks who live here year round, the tourists who are drawn to the very town we" — she flicked her finger back and forth between them — "already love. I want everyone to embrace it as a chance to show this place off a little *and* come together as neighbors and friends."

"I'm kind of hoping Abe shows up. I think that guy needs to feel like he's connected somewhere, you know? I mean, it's made a world of difference in my life. Maybe it will do the same in his."

"Maybe, once you get his contact info, you can bring him by a flyer," she said. "I have extras."

He returned her smile with a dimple-laden one of his own. "Sooo, we're a little over a week away until One Heavenly Night? Are you excited?"

She let her gaze drift beyond the confines of the car once again, her thoughts ricocheting between the decorations and the things on her checklist that still needed to be done. "More like *terrified.*"

"Terrified?" Hooking his finger beneath her chin, he guided her eyes back to his. "Why? It seems to me that Harold and the rest of the shopkeepers are all on board with this event."

"That's because they are . . . because I made it out to sound like this idyllic way to showcase our town and forge connections as neighbors."

"And you think it won't be?"

She looked past him to the opposite side of the street and the simple yet tasteful wreath adorning the front door of Yoder's Furniture. "I *want* it to be."

"Claire, I've seen your plans for this thing, I've seen the effort you've been putting into it since the board gave you the okay — an okay you got on first mention, I might add. There's no way this thing isn't going to be incredible. I mean, just look at this place" — he gestured past the windshield — "it's stunning."

"Al, Harold, Drew, and everyone else have done a wonderful job with their decorations, there's no debating that," she said. "But we drew up a plan, and everyone followed it to a tee. The event itself? That's where the unforeseen variables will pop up — the mistakes, the issues, that sort of thing."

He took one last look outside the car and then grabbed hold of her hand. "So if those happen, you roll with it. You're resourceful and clever. You'll find a way to make it all work."

"If only I had your confidence," she murmured.

"I can spare some. I've got plenty when it comes to you and what you're capable of doing in this town."

Nibbling against the sudden quiver in her lips, she took a moment to breathe, to revel in the man seated just inches away. Yes,

Jakob was handsome for all the obvious reasons. But it was everything else — the sincerity, the kindness, the empathy, the loving nature — that made him someone truly special.

Their hands glowed blue as Jakob's phone came to life inside the cup holder. A glance at the part of the screen she could see yielded little more than the first letter of the caller's name before it disappeared completely with the quick push of his finger. "So, anything new about the festival? Any new surprises you've come up with?"

Even with the limited light streaming in through the windshield from the closest lamppost, she could tell Jakob was flustered. The rubbing of his jaw, the evasive eye contact, and the sudden shifting in his seat made that obvious. Equally as obvious was the why.

Twice in as many days, Jakob had gotten calls he didn't want Claire to see or hear. The previous night, while at Heavenly Brews, an incoming call he'd first silenced and then returned had him leaving her alone on their evening date for close to ten minutes. Within seconds of his return to the table, he'd gotten another call — one he'd let go to voice mail rather than answer in front of her. Now, just twenty-four hours

162

later, there was a third call and yet another rush to keep her from seeing the screen.

With anyone else, she wouldn't give either incident a second thought. In an age when people were reachable twenty-four/seven, people dismissed incoming calls all the time. She did, Jakob did, and everyone did at some point. But never had those deliberately dismissed calls left him so . . . *odd,* so uncomfortable, so clearly anxious to be somewhere where he could take the call.

Without me being here . . .

She tried to shake off the troubling thought, to relegate it to the *impossibility* compartment in her brain, but try as she did to stuff it inside, it refused to go. "Jakob? Is — is something going on I should know about?"

"Going on? What do you mean?"

"I don't know . . . It's like you check out on me sometimes. And" — she drew in a fortifying breath — "that call just now. Why did you silence it?"

"Because I'm with you and it can wait."

"But I've never had an issue with you taking work calls when we're together, Jakob. You know that."

He cupped his hand over his mouth, only to let it slip back to the steering wheel. "I know."

163

"Then why won't you take it?" she persisted.

"Shouldn't you be glad I'm not? That I want to spend this time with you instead?"

Claire drew back at his words. "Of course I'm glad, Jakob. I'm just . . ."

Wondering who keeps calling you when we're together?

Worried that you're keeping something from me?

Suddenly afraid you're going to break my heart?

Repositioning herself against the seat back, Claire pulled the belt across her torso and clicked it into place. "It's been an incredibly long day for both of us, and I certainly don't want to keep you out any later than necessary, especially if you still want to stop at the station before calling it a night."

Oh, how she wanted to read the sudden sag of his shoulders as disappointment. But the quiet, almost imperceptible sigh of relief he emitted made that impossible.

CHAPTER 11

She knew the second she bypassed her bed in favor of the window seat that Aunt Diane's knock would come. It was as much a given as the answering gladness she felt clear down to her toes.

Pulling her forehead from its resting place against the cold glass, Claire turned toward the slowly opening door and the face that had a way of inducing hope even when all else seemed bleak. "I'm sorry if I woke you when I came in; I tried to be quiet."

"You didn't wake me, dear. I was on the last chapter of a really good book when I heard you coming up the stairs." Diane closed the door with a quiet touch and crossed the room to Claire. "We really need to get a new bed frame in here. One that's less squeaky."

"I haven't even gotten in bed yet."

"That's why I'm here."

It was a dance they danced often, the two

of them, and it was one Claire treasured for the deep bond it represented. "I know," she whispered, swinging her gaze back to the night sky. "Do you remember how Grandma always used to say that thing about when it rains, it pours? It's really true, isn't it?"

"It can be. But it just makes the sun all the more beautiful when it comes back out."

"Well, it needs to hurry up before the rain makes a complete mess of things."

Diane crossed to Claire's dresser, retrieved her brush from the top drawer, and carried it back to the window seat for the ritual Claire had loved since she was a little girl. Sure enough, as she traded her view of the stars for her aunt's reflection against the glass, she saw the brush moving toward her head mere seconds before she felt its soothing touch. "I'm listening, dear."

"It's just that it's almost Christmas and things are supposed to be calm and peaceful and good. But it's not any of that right now — not even close."

With careful, loving strokes, Diane started at the top of Claire's head, her warm brown eyes seeking and holding Claire's reflected gaze with each pass of the brush. "Is this about what you shared with Bill and me last night? About Jakob looking at Ruth as a suspect in Mary's and Daniel's murders? I thought, based on your lightness at breakfast this morning, you two must have worked through it on the phone."

"We did. Sort of. I told him I understood he was just doing his job and that seemed to help clear the air a little. But there's something else going on, something I don't think has anything to do with Ruth or this case."

"Maybe it's the time of year? It can be hard for some people, especially if they've lost loved ones. Remember, it was only a few months ago that Jakob lost Russ. That man became like a father to him when his childhood family shunned him."

Was that it? Was that the reason for Jakob's odd behavior? It made sense right up until . . .

She shook her head. "He's been getting phone calls. Three in the past twenty-four hours that he doesn't want me to see, doesn't want me to hear him taking. And when I ask about them, he changes the subject."

"If they've all come in the past twenty-four hours, maybe they're just about the case."

"He's gotten all sorts of calls from the station in my presence since we've been dating — calls about robberies, and calls from the chief about this, that, or the other. I was even with him when he got the call about Russ. He's never been one to worry about me overhearing work calls." She looked past her aunt to a blinking orange light in the distance — the nighttime light a mandated safety addition for all buggies in the state of Pennsylvania. "That's why I don't think they were calls from the station."

Diane finished brushing the final section of Claire's hair and then lowered herself onto the edge of the bed. "You're not worried they're from another woman, are you?"

Oh, how she wanted to say no. To be able to laugh off the question as the preposterous notion she wanted it to be. But something inside her kept her from doing either.

"Claire?"

"I don't want to be," she whispered past the rising lump inside her throat. "But I don't know what else to think. He's being so . . . *strange.*"

At Diane's answering silence, she squeezed her eyes closed and did her best to breathe through the tears she didn't want to feel, let alone shed. Seconds turned to minutes before, at the feel of Diane's hand on her cheek, she looked up and into the face she cherished for the grounding force it had been all her life.

"Claire, I've seen the way Jakob looks at you. I've heard the way he speaks about you. I can't believe he'd risk that. He, of all people, knows how rare you are and how foolish it would be to lose that."

"I want to believe that, Aunt Diane. I really do. And there's times, like in the car on the way home from Mary and Daniel's wake, when things feel normal. But then his phone rings, he turns it so I can't see the screen, and then he gets cagey."

Reaching forward, Diane gathered Claire's hair in her hands in a pseudo-ponytail and then let it fall back down into place. "I'd be happy to talk to him if you'd like? See if he'll open up to me?"

She was shaking her head before her aunt had even stopped speaking. "I don't think he's going to feel real comfortable telling you he's found someone else . . ."

"He couldn't have. There is no one else for that young man." Diane squared her shoulders, scooped the brush off the bed, and carried it back to the dresser, her steps one of purpose and determination. "That said, perhaps he needs a man to talk to. What with Russ gone, he really doesn't have another father figure to confide in. Maybe Bill would be the better choice. Those two are quite comfortable with one another, don't you think?"

"They are, but I don't think it's fair to put that on Bill. He's dating you, Aunt Diane, not you and me."

"If he's dating me, he gets you, too," Diane said. "And he adores you, dear. Says, routinely, that you feel like the daughter he never had."

The lump was back. "That's sweet."

"He means it. And he thinks very highly of Jakob, as well. I don't see any harm that can come from them talking."

"I suppose. But only if Bill sees Jakob, and only if he can do it in a roundabout way. I don't want Jakob to feel as if he's being put on the spot." Claire followed the blinking orange light for another minute or two and then turned so her back was flush to the window. "Then, on top of all that, there's this stuff with Ruth. I saw her tonight, and she's just so distraught at the notion anyone could think she'd do something so heinous."

"No one does."

"In Ruth's eyes, *Jakob* does," she said, grabbing the window seat's lone throw pillow and holding it to her chest. "And that's one person too many for Ruth."

"Just keep reassuring her until she's gotten the all-clear."

Claire rested her chin on the top edge of the pillow and gave in to a yawn. "I want to do more than just reassure her. I want to get the all-clear *for* her."

Diane made her way back to the bed and the corner closest to Claire's spot on the window seat. "Meaning?"

"I want to pick her brain about what happened on Sunday. You know, while she and Samuel were visiting Mary and Daniel."

"Isn't that what Jakob is doing? As the detective on the case?"

She felt her aunt's probing eyes but kept her own gaze fixed just above the woman's head. "He is. I just thought maybe I could help move things along a little faster seeing as how Ruth and I are friends."

"Or make Jakob doubt your faith in him," Diane mused.

Pushing the pillow off her lap and onto the seat beside her, Claire rose to her feet. "I have faith in Jakob," she protested. "I just know he's busy and —"

"Your festival is next week, isn't it, dear?"

She dropped her gaze to her aunt's. "It is . . ."

"Then you're no less busy."

It was the same argument she'd had with herself the previous night as she'd waited for sleep to descend. She was busy. Very much so. But —

"The longer Ruth and Samuel remain on his list, the more damage is going to be done to his relationship with Eli and Esther." Claire splayed her hands. "I mean, I know it will never be normal the way it should be with family, but at least he had something with them and they regarded him with genuine, albeit restrained, affection. And his relationship with Ben? That's come such a long way since what it was when Jakob first moved back here. You know that.

"I don't want those things to go backward. And maybe, if I can move this whole Ruth and Samuel issue along faster, any damage will still be recoverable."

Diane gathered Claire's hands in her own and squeezed. "You take too much on your shoulders, dear. Far too much."

"Said the pot to the kettle," she joked. "Seriously, if I tend to get wrapped up in a lot of things at one time, it's only because I've watched you do it for years."

"You've seen less of that from me these past few months." Diane released her hold on Claire and reclaimed her seat on the edge of the bed. "I've turned down several committees at church and with our business owners' group. And I've extended my annual no-reservations policy for Christmas

Eve and Christmas Day to include the day/ night on either side this year, as well."

Claire, too, sat again, her back to the darkness outside. "I thought you turned down the January-Thaw Committee because you didn't want Harold and Al chairing the Sweet-Valentine Committee in February. Is that not the case?"

"Not really, no. In the past, I'd have taken January and then helped Harold and Al with February, too. But all that's done is turn everything into a blur. I want to slow that down, *slow me* down."

She stared at her aunt as something that felt a lot like fear niggled in the pit of her stomach. "Is there something you're not telling me, Aunt Diane? Are you sick or something?"

"I'm fine, dear. Actually" — the woman scooted back on the bed until her slipper-clad feet dangled above the floor — "I'm better than fine. I'm great."

Leaning against the window, Claire allowed herself a moment to take in her aunt's larger-than-normal smile, the way the sparkle in the woman's eyes seemed to flash and pop, and the almost childlike giddiness that bubbled just below the surface. "You're positively glowing."

"I love this time of year," Diane said, patting at the sudden redness in her cheeks. "You know that."

"I do, but this is different, Aunt Diane. It's . . . deeper." Then, before there was any chance her words could be swatted away, she grinned. "You've really taken to him, haven't you?"

Diane started to speak, stopped, and then flopped back onto Claire's pillow with a hushed yet no less real laugh. "I have. Bill Brockman is everything I never expected to find in life. He's thoughtful, he's funny, he's fun, he's interesting, he's creative, he gets why I love Heavenly so much, and he fits so perfectly with me. With you. With us. It's like he's this missing piece I never knew was missing until it was. And now that it's here — that *he's* here — I want to hold on tight so it doesn't slip away."

Swapping her spot on the window seat for one on the bed, Claire smiled down at her aunt. "Have you seen the way that man looks at you? He's not going anywhere. Ever."

"Neither is Jakob. For all the same reasons and then some."

She felt her smile falter but did her best to recover it. "I hope you're right."

"I know I am, dear. Just have faith."

"I'll try," Claire whispered.

"Good." Diane sat up, swung her legs over the edge of the bed, and stood. "Well, I should probably let you get some sleep. Tomorrow morning will be here before we know it, and I have two rooms to turn over before check-in at three."

"Who's leaving?"

"The Dickinsons in room three, and the Loombas in the downstairs suite."

"Where are the new folks coming in from?"

Diane tapped her chin, her gaze traveling to the ceiling in thought. "The Steeles are from Tennessee, and . . . the Kelleys are from Delaware."

"Very nice," Claire said, stretching her arms above her head and yawning. "Oh. Wow. I guess I am getting a little tired."

"Good. You need your sleep." Diane crossed to the door. "You're at the shop all day tomorrow, right, dear?"

"I am."

"Then the eggs, bacon, and cinnamon rolls I have planned for breakfast should send you off with some good sustenance."

"Actually, Aunt Diane, would you mind terribly if I skip out on breakfast altogether tomorrow? I wanted to stop out at Ruth and Samuel's place before work. I know she could use a friend right now, and maybe

175

something she tells me will help Jakob."

Stilling her hand atop the doorknob, Diane glanced back at Claire, her expression void of its earlier lightness. "Of course, dear. But be careful. There's a fine line between helping Ruth and second-guessing Jakob. I'd hate to see you cross it even if you did so with the best of intentions."

CHAPTER 12

It was half past seven when she pulled into the dirt driveway, the plume of smoke billowing up from the home's chimney easy to pick out against the morning's charcoal-colored sky. Decreasing her speed to little more than a crawl, Claire steered her aunt's car past the old German-style bank barn that housed Samuel's workshop, some chickens, two cows, and Gussy the goat, and parked in front of the house Samuel had purchased in preparation for his marriage to Ruth. The home, itself, wasn't particularly large — maybe three bedrooms. It didn't sit on acres upon acres of lush farmland the way their neighbors' homes to the left and right did. But for a man who made his living making and selling furniture rather than farming, it was perfect.

The front porch, which ran the full width of the house, featured two rockers. Turned so as to face west, they were the perfect place for Ruth and Samuel to sit at the end of a busy day. On the door, suspended from what was likely a single nail hammered into place by Samuel, was the heart shaped WELCOME, FRIENDS sign Claire had given the couple as a wedding gift. Beneath the frontfacing windows on the first floor were freshly painted and newly hung window boxes. Empty now, Claire knew that come spring, they'd be bursting with pink and purple flowers — Ruth's favorite colors.

She slid her gaze to the left and to the young woman she could just barely make out through the window. Even sitting there, some distance away, she could tell Ruth was flitting around, going about her morning chores with the same efficiency she'd shown at Shoo Fly Bake Shoppe. Only now, instead of starting her day sweeping the shop's front or side stoop and popping croissants and muffins and other breakfast treats in and out of the oven, Ruth was cooking for just two — herself and her husband.

Glancing down at the dashboard clock, Claire muttered to herself about wasted time and then pushed open her car door to the distant whir of whatever machinery Samuel was using in his workshop. For a moment, she considered stepping inside the barn to say hello to her fellow Lighted Way shopkeeper but, in the interest of time, headed toward the house instead.

She was barely up the porch steps when the front door swung open and Ruth peeked out. "Good morning, Claire," Ruth said. "Come, come. It is quite cold this morning, yah?"

"That it is . . . And if the weatherman on the local news station was correct last night, we'll be seeing snow soon, too!" She heeded her friend's invitation to come inside and then, when the door was closed, gave her a quick hug. "Ohhhh, you're so warm."

"That is because of the fire Samuel had going in the wood stove before I even came downstairs. It makes the whole house seem as if it is summer."

Lifting her nose into the air, she closed her eyes and inhaled. "Mmmmm . . . And that smell? That makes me feel as if I'm standing in the alley outside the shop, smelling all those amazing smells that were always floating on the air around Shoo Fly." She took a second sniff and opened her eyes. "You're making banana bread, aren't you?"

"It is already made and waiting for you to have a piece," Ruth said, pointing the way down the hallway and into the neat-as-a-pin kitchen. "I know it was your favorite of my breakfast breads."

"It still is."

"Then come, sit at the table." Ruth led the way over to the table and its two waiting place settings. "Would you like something to drink? I have fresh milk from Nettie."

"That sounds wonderful, but I don't want to take Samuel's spot."

"Samuel has already eaten. He is in his workshop now, finishing a rocking chair for the store. It is a beautiful chair and I think it will sell quickly."

Taking the seat closest to the window, Claire waited as Ruth crossed to the counter and the cloth-draped mound that was the young woman's famous banana bread. "Do you know how much I've missed that bread this past month? The smell, the sight, the *taste*?"

"Perhaps Annie will bring you some one morning."

"I didn't know Annie makes banana bread."

Ruth opened a cabinet to the left of the stove, extracted two plain white plates from inside, and set them on the counter beside the bread. "It is Annie's recipe that I use."

Claire looked from Ruth, to the bread her friend was actively cutting, and back again.

"*My* Annie?"

"Yah. She made it for me a few years ago when I was not feeling well. The second I took my first bite, I knew it was something my customers at Shoo Fly would like, too."

"A few years ago?" Claire echoed.

"Yah. Four, maybe five."

"But that would have had Annie being what? Twelve? Thirteen?"

Nodding, Ruth carried the bread-topped plates to the table, setting one down in front of Claire, the other in front of the opposing bench. "Yah. Perhaps twelve."

"Wow." Claire bit into the still-warm bread. "Wow . . . I still can't believe Annie wasn't snatched away from me when you left Shoo Fly. She would have been a natural replacement."

"Annie would not come," Ruth said, her tone matter of fact.

Claire grinned. "Does that mean you tried?"

"I spoke with her about it one day. It is no secret Annie likes to bake or that she likes to take recipes many have tried before and turn them into something better. But it has always been a quiet thing. Someone will say, *'Who made the chicken soup,'* or *'Who made this bread, it is quite good,'* and Annie will say thank you so quietly many do not hear her."

"I know what you mean. There were times, those first few months she worked with me, she would share something with me from her lunch pail. I would go on and on, gushing about how wonderful it was, but she would not tell me she made it until I asked who did."

Ruth's slice of bread remained untouched atop her plate, her fidgeting fingers moving between the edge of the plate, her glass of milk, and the table. "Yah, that is Annie."

"She clearly loves it, though. Her face just lights up whenever I try something she's made." Claire took a second bite, the banana flavor popping in her mouth. "That's why, as wonderful as I'm sure Hannah is, I can't help but wonder if maybe Annie would have been a better fit to replace you when you and Samuel got married."

"Perhaps. But as much as Annie likes to bake and to cook, it is working with you that has her smiling again after her mamm's passing. Even her father, Bishop Hershberger, says that is true."

Claire paused, mid-chew, and stared at Ruth. *"Me?"*

"Yah. Your kindness and your friendship have put smiles where there were none — for many in my district."

Claire set the remaining bite of bread back on her plate while Ruth continued. "For Annie, for my brother Benjamin, for" — Ruth's voice quivered — "your Jakob."

"They did the same for me, too," Claire rushed to say. "As did you . . . and Eli . . . and so many others."

If Ruth had processed Claire's words, it didn't show. Instead, the newlywed's high cheekbones and ocean blue eyes dropped behind the curtain that was Ruth's trembling hands.

"Ruth?"

When there was no response, Claire pushed the remaining piece of Annie's bread to the side, left her spot on the bench, and made her way around the table to sit beside her troubled friend. "Ruth, please talk to me. I can be a good listener if you let me."

Dropping her hands to the table with a soft thud, Ruth looked past Claire to the kitchen's lone window and its sweeping view of the next-door neighbor's land, the muted green of the cover crop a welcome contrast to the stark brown of winter's earth. "I do not want to be a burden on Samuel, but I am."

"A burden?" Claire echoed, guiding Ruth's eyes back to hers. "What are you

183

talking about? Samuel loves you, Ruth."

"But it is because of me — our marriage — that he must buy this house."

"That's what you do when you get married, Ruth. It's normal."

"I see the way he worries, the way he paces when he thinks I am not looking. And pie does not help when he sits at the table with pencil and paper, adding and subtracting numbers."

She weighed her friend's words, turning them over in her thoughts. "Wait a minute. Are you saying Samuel is worried about money?" At Ruth's nod, she felt her stomach begin to churn. "But how? When? The tourists talk incessantly about his furniture."

"They may talk about it, but a bed or a desk is not like a pie from Shoo Fly, or a tool belt from Glick's. People cannot put such things in their car or take them on a bus the way they do place mats or dolls from your store."

It made sense, it really did. But —

"Yoder's Furniture has been on Lighted Way for longer than I've had Heavenly Treasures," Claire protested. "If it wasn't successful, how has Samuel kept the store open this long?"

"It is the orders that allow Samuel to keep the shop."

"Orders? You mean *custom* orders?"

"Yah."

"Oh. Wow. I guess I didn't realize he did that. I mean, I know he can build anything, I just didn't know people could hire him to make something a certain way." She reached across the table, pilfered another smidge of bread from her abandoned plate, and popped it into her mouth. "So, okay, what's different now?"

Ruth swung her long legs over the bench seat and wandered over to the window. "The orders do not come like they once did. At first, he was not worried. He said there was enough work for many. But soon there was not enough work. And now, instead of four hand-carved headboards as there were before we married, there has not been one. There have not been any cribs or kitchen tables, either. Just one rocking chair and one small dresser."

"Maybe it's just the time of year and it'll get better after the holidays, when people aren't thinking about the kinds of presents they can put under a tree."

"It is not the holidays," Ruth said, leaning her forehead against the glass pane.

"You can't know that." Claire stood and joined Ruth at the window. "I've had slow periods at the gift shop, too. Everyone on

Lighted Way has at some point or another, you know that. Early November is a particularly tough time for Harold because raking season is over, but there's no snow to be shoveled yet. It gets better for him as the holidays approach because wives tend to flock to hardware stores when trying to figure out what to get their husbands for Christmas. And Drew, at the bookstore, has his light seasons, too. But then summer draws closer and folks start going on vacations and suddenly they think about reading again. I think it's cyclical for all of us, even if our cycles don't necessarily match up with one another's."

Ruth ran her finger across the window's sash, her breath rising and falling against the glass. "But when people that visit Heavenly want to buy books — they go to Glorious Books. When people want to shop for tools — they go to Glick's. It is no longer that way for Samuel. Now they go to others."

"Others? What others? Yoder's is the only furniture store in Heavenly."

"It is the only shop, but it is not the only maker." Ruth rocked back on the heels of her simple lace-up boots and released a sigh so protracted, it seemed to sag her entire being.

"Okay, so then maybe Samuel needs to run a sale — something to put himself back in people's minds."

"That is what I said last week, when Samuel could not sleep. But he did not seem to hear me." Ruth lifted her hands to her cheeks, only to let them drop down to her dress in short order. "I even told him I could go back to the bake shop, but he did not like to hear that."

"Because you're married now," Claire said. "That is when Esther stopped working for me, too."

"But the baby will not be here for many months."

"Whoa, whoa, whoa, hold on a minute." Setting her hand on Ruth's forearm, she gave her friend a gentle shake. "Are you pregnant?"

Ruth's milky white skin flamed red just before her gaze dove toward the floor. "Yah. But there is much time to go — eight months, Mamm says."

"Oh, Ruth — this is wonderful news!" She pulled her friend in for a hug and held her tight. "You and Samuel are going to be wonderful parents!" Then, stepping back, she let loose a quiet squeal. "And Sarah? She's going to have a little cousin close to her age to play with!"

The answering smile she expected to see stopped short of Ruth's eyes. "Yah."

"Ruth, this is *exciting*! For you *and* for Samuel."

"It is also more worry for him. Like these questions from your Jakob."

"A baby is not a worry, it's a joy," she said, pulling Ruth close once again. "And these questions from Jakob? We're going to make them stop."

Ruth drew back. "How?"

"We're going to put our heads together and find the thing that will point Jakob in the right direction."

"We will?"

"You bet we will."

"When will we do such a thing?"

Claire peeked at her wristwatch and shrugged. "I still have a little time before I have to be at the shop. So how about we start now?"

"Yah," Ruth cocked her ear toward the front of the house and, when she was satisfied with whatever she was seeking, led the way back to the table. "What can I do?"

"You can tell me about your visit with Mary and Daniel. What you spoke about, who else might have been on the farm at the same time, who you may have passed in your buggy when you were leaving . . . Basi-

188

cally anything and everything you can remember."

Ruth swung her leg over the bench and sat, her forehead creased in thought. "It was a Sunday, so there were no cars at the Esch farm that day."

"And there had been no church service that day?"

"No. Bishop Hershberger was in his other district. That is why it was a perfect day for Samuel and I to finish up the last of our visiting. We saved the Esch farm for last because we knew it would be a longer visit." Swallowing quickly, Ruth cast her eyes down at the table. "Visits always made Mary happy."

Claire leaned forward against the table. "I need to ask you something . . . Did Samuel *know* Daniel was going after that Breeze Point job when he threw his hat in the bidding ring?"

"At first, he did not. But soon, he did."

"I would imagine that upset him?"

"It surprised him," Ruth corrected softly. "Like many in our district, we did not know Daniel was working again. It had been many years since he stopped making his cabinets, and he did not put his sign by the mailbox as it once was."

"I imagine a job like that would've more

than offset the drop in custom orders Samuel has been encountering the past —" Claire sat up so tall and fast, the legs of the bench scraped against the wood planked floor. "Wait. Daniel just made cabinets, right?"

Ruth's cheeks flamed pink, but she said nothing.

"Ruth?"

"When we were at their house on Sunday, I . . . I saw cards," Ruth whispered.

"Cards? What kind of cards?"

"Business cards. Like Samuel has for Yoder's Furniture, but more fancy."

"Okay . . ."

Ruth brought her hands to her cheeks and held them there for several beats. "They were nice cards — black with gold letters and trim. They said *Esch Custom Woodworking.*"

"Oh. Wow. Okay." Claire let Ruth's words sit in her thoughts for a few moments. "Did . . . did they say anything else that you can remember? Or was it just —"

"They said *Furniture done the right way.*"

Claire drew in a harsh breath as she stared at the woman on the other side of the table. "What did Samuel say?"

"I put Mary's dish towel over them so Samuel would not see them."

"Why? Isn't the fact that he had new competition something he'd want to know?"

"Perhaps. But I knew, if he saw them, my news would be met with more worry than joy."

"Your news? You mean about the baby?" At Ruth's answering nod, Claire leaned forward again, her gaze seeking and holding her friend's. "You hadn't told him yet?"

"I wanted to tell him that afternoon, on the way home from visiting. I thought maybe we could take the road across from my dat's farm — the one that goes over the stream." Ruth let loose a long, tired sigh. "But that did not happen."

"Why not?"

"Mary moved the dish towel." Rising up and onto her feet, Ruth gathered their plates with quick, jerky motions, her sudden need to be busy not lost on Claire. "At first, I did not think Samuel saw the cards, but when he no longer heard the things Daniel and Mary said, and offered only a polite nod at their gift, I knew that he had. I tried to talk to him about it on the way home, to tell him it did not matter how many furniture makers there were, but it was as if I said nothing."

"Surely he was still excited about the baby, though, right?"

The clatter of the plates against the inside of the sink did little to disguise Ruth's answering silence.

"Ruth?" Claire repeated. "He *was* still excited about the baby when you told him, though, right?"

"I did not tell him," Ruth whispered, her back to Claire. "I couldn't. Such news should bring joy, not more worry."

"Oh, Ruth, you have to tell him!" She touched the woman's shoulder, the tension she felt there both surprising and heart-breaking all at the same time. "He's going to be so excited!"

Ruth reached for the soap and a sponge. "I want to believe that is so. But news of another mouth to feed will bring even more worry."

"Whoa, whoa . . . wait." Claire took the soap and the sponge out of Ruth's hands and then gently turned the woman until they were facing each other. "You can't keep something like this to yourself for long. In another few months, you'll be showing."

Ruth's blue eyes sank to the floor, only to return, ever so slowly, to mingle with Claire's. "When your Jakob is done with his questions of me and of Samuel, I will tell him then."

"Okay, good. Because joy trumps worry.

Always."

"When the questions are done, there will be no more worry for Samuel," Ruth said, her voice unusually hoarse.

"I don't understand . . ."

"With Mary's and Daniel's passing, there will be many orders for Samuel's custom furniture again. When there is, his worry will be gone."

Claire didn't need a mirror to know she'd flinched. She'd felt it just as surely as she did the chill working its way up her spine and outward toward her fingers and toes. Closing her eyes, she willed herself to breathe . . . to think . . . to see her friend's words as the innocent statement of fact they surely had to be . . .

"Would you like to see their gift?" Ruth asked, her words like ice water on Claire's burning-hot cheeks. "It is on the desk in the other room. Come, I will show you."

Ruth led the way out of the kitchen and into a den-like area nestled off the back of the house. The room itself was quite small, with the simple wooden desk and chair easily taking up half the square footage, while Ruth's sewing machine, a small end table, and a pair of rocking chairs took up the rest. "See?" Ruth said, pointing toward the desk. "Daniel made the box, and Mary painted

193

the pretty heart and the words."

Claire mentally inventoried the pencil cup and the pad of scratch paper beside it before aligning her attention with the narrow yet deep box now in Ruth's hands. Sure enough, painted in pink and white across the top of the wooden lid was a whimsical heart. Beneath it, in careful black lettering: ALWAYS CLOSE AT HEART.

"It is for sending and receiving letters from faraway kin." Slowly, almost reverently, Ruth traced the outer edges of the heart with her long, delicate fingers, her trademark shy smile tugging at the corners of her cupid bow lips. "I always looked forward to the letters Mamm would get in the mailbox from her sister in Ohio. She would gather Ben and Eli and the rest of us around the table after dinner to hear stories of our kin — the weather they were having, the crops they'd planted, the new baby animals in the barn, and silly things that made us laugh. And Mamm always looked so happy when she read them aloud. When I asked her about that one day, she told me those letters made it so she and her sister were not so far apart. That is why, many times before the next letter would come, I would see Mamm reading the letter again and again.

"Soon, I will read the letters *I* get to my own children just the way Mamm did. And when I am done reading them, I can keep them here, in this special box." Ruth turned the box to reveal three knobbed drawers. "That way, I can still feel close to my faraway kin in between letters, too."

Claire knew Ruth was waiting for some sort of reaction to the letter holder, but it was hard to concentrate on much of anything beyond the pounding in her head. Everything she knew about Ruth was standing right there in front of her — the sweet smile, the shy enthusiasm, the love of family. Yet suddenly it was like they were standing in front of a fun house mirror and everything was distorted. Only instead of her eyes doing the distorting, it was Ruth's words, playing in a continuous loop in her head, that were messing everything up.

"Claire? Are you okay?"

Shaking off the troubling thoughts, she made herself focus — really focus — on the woman looking at her with a mixture of confusion and uncertainty. Ruth Yoder was a good person, a kind person.

She knew this . . .

"Yes, yes, I'm fine, Ruth," she said finally. "I'm sorry, I think I just zoned out there for a moment. Your letter box is lovely. Truly.

And the place to keep your special letters? Such a neat idea."

Ruth beamed. "There is more." Again, Ruth moved her fingertips down to the second of two small knobs and gently pulled. "This is where I will keep the envelopes and stamps I will need to send letters back to Mamm's sister in Ohio and my cousin in Wisconsin. And see? Mary even put some inside to get me started."

Leaning closer, Claire peered inside the shallow drawer, her eyes following Ruth's finger as it moved down the outer edge of the waiting envelopes. "I just hope I remember to write Yoder, instead of Miller. That is hard to do when I have been Ruth Miller for so long."

"I'm sure it will become second nature soon enough." Claire's gaze skipped to the bottom of the drawer and the book of stamps peeking out from beneath the edge of a pale yellow envelope. "What's that one, there?"

Ruth peeked around the back side of the holder. "That is just an envelope. That is what goes in this drawer — envelopes and stamps. The paper to write the letters is in the last drawer. See . . ."

"No, wait." Claire stilled Ruth's hand with her own, then pointed inside the open drawer. "That last one, just above the stamps — it's not like the other envelopes."

"Oh . . . that does not matter," Ruth said, shoving the drawer closed. "I . . . I am sure Mary just ran out of white ones. It happens. Do you know, when I worked at Shoo Fly each day, I had to use different napkins — plain ones — when I ran out of the special ones? I did not like to do it, but sometimes it could not be helped. Soon, it did not bother me so much. Perhaps that is why I did not notice that envelope until now."

"Ruth? Are you in the house?"

"That is Samuel! He must have finished in his workshop." Gently, Ruth lowered the wooden holder onto the desk and hooked her thumb in the direction of the door. "He told me this morning that he wanted to show me the chair he's been working on when he finished. So I will go see that now and then come back."

Claire was pretty sure she nodded, maybe even eked out a yes as Ruth headed toward the hallway, but the pull to inspect the one lone yellow envelope in a pile of pristine white counterparts was too strong and too all-consuming to be one hundred percent certain. Glancing back at the letter holder, she opened the second drawer, reached inside, and pulled out the last envelope, the sight of Ruth's name scrawled across the top pushing her back a step.

Confused, she studied the uneven, almost stop-and-go writing style her late grandmother had adopted during the final years of her life, her thoughts darting from birthday cards and just-because notes to Christmas cards and the occasional full-fledged letter. The memory, while good, left her blinking back tears and rushing to clear her throat.

Like her grandmother, Mary Esch had been in her mid to upper eighties. Clearly writing had become an effort for her, as well. But just as Claire had hung on to each and every tangible link to her grandmother, she suspected Ruth, too, would forever treasure whatever sweet sentiment Mary had painstakingly written for —

Snapping her full attention back to the envelope, she took in the solitary name scrawled across the front, its expected mate nowhere to be seen. Odd, considering it was a wedding gift, but maybe it was simply a part of the Amish culture she'd yet to learn, some tradition or way of doing things she could ask Jakob about over lunch or after work.

Work . . .

Uh-oh.

She glanced down at her watch, noted her rapidly closing pre-work window, and then froze as her shifting fingers caught something on the underside of the envelope. Glancing toward the door and then back at the envelope, she flipped it over, her ensuing gasp echoing against the walls of the sparsely furnished room.

For a moment, she just stared at the unsealed opening, her thoughts, her feelings, too scattered to nail down over the roar in her head. But soon, they bowed to one — one voice, one sentence: *Perhaps that is why I did not notice that envelope until now.*

Ruth had lied.

The only question now was why.

CHAPTER 13

Claire leaned against the door frame and stared out at the faces making their way up and down Lighted Way on what had to be her busiest day of the season to date. From the moment she'd let herself in through the back door and mad-dashed her way across the shop to unlock the front door, she'd been going nonstop.

She'd helped a few men decide on gifts for their wives . . .

She'd held up more than a few Amish quilts for potential buyers wanting to find just the right shade of blue or yellow or green . . .

She'd answered the near-daily question as to why the handmade dolls didn't have faces . . .

She'd offered her opinion on the lunch options at Taste of Heaven(ly) . . .

She'd engaged in a lively discussion about the book a particular customer had sticking out of her tote . . .

She'd bagged postcards and napkin rings and place mats and a little bit of just about everything else she had in the store . . .

She'd gift-wrapped a few items . . .

She'd counted back change and tucked receipts into shopping bags . . .

She'd encouraged people to come to next week's One Heavenly Night if they were in the area . . .

And more than a few times, while standing behind the register, she'd glanced longingly at the empty shelf where Annie's lunch pail would have been if the Amish teen had been able to keep her shift.

It was a good problem to have — a busy shop. Especially when the holidays would soon give way to Lighted Way's biggest nemesis: January. But try as she had to be in the moment all morning long, the persistent churning in her stomach had made it difficult to forget her visit with Ruth. In fact, more than a few customers had asked if she was okay when, according to one woman from Chicago, she'd looked as if she was going to cry. She'd covered, of course, by claiming she'd gotten something in her eye, but the second the lie was uttered, her thoughts had gone racing right back to the mysterious letter and her own decision not to confront Ruth about it when she'd returned from the barn.

"Busy day?"

Startled into a full stand, Claire turned toward the back of the shop and the somber-faced teenager looking around the room, wide-eyed. "Annie! I didn't hear you come in!" Then, leaving her view of Lighted Way completely, she met her part-time employee in the middle of the room. "Aren't you supposed to be at the viewing for Mary and . . ." She paused, sniffed the air, and then peeked around Annie into the back hallway. "Um, sweetie? Did you leave the back door open by any chance?"

"It is closed."

Again, she sniffed the air, the answering aroma kicking off a very different churning inside her stomach. "Then why am I smelling cinnamon as if it's under my nose?"

"Because it is." Annie pulled her hand from behind her back and held up a covered plate. "When Dat and I returned from the viewing a little while ago, I asked if I could bring you a slice of my cinnamon bread. I made a loaf for Dat with his breakfast this morning, and there are many pieces left."

"You drove here just to bring me a piece of cinnamon bread?"

"Yah. It is one I think you will like." Annie made a second visual pass of the room before pushing the plate closer. "Especially since I do not think you have had time to eat."

"I haven't. It's been nonstop since I opened." Reaching out, she peeled back a portion of the cover and squealed. "Oh. My. If I didn't know any better, I'd think I was imagining this right now."

Annie giggled. "No. It's real."

"So this is really for me?" she asked, taking the plate and lifting the opening in line with her nose.

"Yah."

"You, my dear, are far too good to me."

"It is just a piece of cinnamon bread," Annie protested.

"Nothing you bake is ever *just.*" Claire motioned toward the counter with her chin. "Can you stay for a few minutes, or do you have to get back to the viewing?"

"I have a few minutes." Annie trailed Claire to the counter and the pair of stools housed on the other side. One tug pulled Claire's out, the other, Annie's.

"You do realize I'm going to become a food snob thanks to you, right?"

Annie paused, mid-sit. "A food snob?"

"That's what you call someone who is so used to five-star dining, they refuse to eat anything less." Claire peeled back the rest of the covering and helped herself to the generous slice. "And if this tastes even half as good as it looks and smells, I'll be a goner. Especially after that banana bread this morning."

"Banana bread?" Annie echoed, scrunching her nose. "I didn't make you banana bread today."

"I know, but Ruth did — from your recipe." Then, anxious to correct the slump born on her own mention of the morning, Claire bit into the cinnamon bread. "Oh . . . wow . . . Annie . . . This — this is . . . amazing, incredible" — she stole another bite — "*insanely* good. How on earth do you do this with every single thing you make?"

"Do what?"

Claire looked down at the bread and then back up at Annie. "Make everything taste like the best thing I've ever had in my life. Every. Single. Time. And that's *me* saying this — the niece of an absolutely amazing cook in her own right."

Annie's cheeks glowed red with the praise before disappearing from view altogether with the help of two well-placed hands. "I just make food."

"Trust me, kiddo, it's way more than that." She took another bite of the bread, only to pause mid-chew. "Wait, wait, wait! I have something for you!"

Slipping down off her stool, Claire reached into the first of two cubbies beneath the register, unzipped her purse, and rummaged around among the receipts and old shopping lists lining the interior until she found the paper she sought. "Here. I think you need to try this. Read it."

Annie took the scrap of paper, scanned Claire's hurried handwriting, and then looked back at Claire, confusion mingling with curiosity. "I do not understand."

"It's a contest — a baking contest! This man" — she pointed to Marty Linton's name at the top of the paper — "has a baking show on TV. It's really popular. He grew up here, in Heavenly, apparently, and he wants to do something to honor his roots. That's why he'll be doing a big bake-off here in the spring. For residents of Heavenly, aged sixteen and over! You enter with an original from-scratch recipe. If he likes your recipe more than anyone else's, he'll put you on his TV show and . . . wait. I'm such a dunce. You couldn't do that part of the prize, but *this* part" — she pointed farther down the page — "you could. If you won, he'd feature your recipe in every Linton Bakery location in the country, and you'd get fifty percent of all the profits from the sale of your dessert!"

"Claire, I could not do this. My desserts are not special."

She stared at the teen. "Annie, yes, they are. They're incredible. You could win this thing, I know you could. You just need to enter. The deadline to put your hat in the ring for this is mid-February, but it doesn't hurt to enter sooner. I could go online and enter you if you want." Closing her hand over the top of Annie's, she squeezed. "What do you say, kiddo? Can I?"

The flush was back in Annie's cheeks. "I . . . I would have to ask Dat."

"Will he let you?" she asked.

"I don't know."

"But you will ask him, right?" Claire squeezed the hand again until Annie's eyes were back on hers. "You have to do this, Annie. You're way too talented not to give this a go."

"I do not want to be on TV. It is not the Amish way."

"I know that. Though when I first wrote this stuff down for you, I'd forgotten about that part." She glanced at the rules and details she'd written down in Heavenly Brews and narrowed in on the part in the middle. "But the money . . . You could win

that. It would be no different than you getting a paycheck from me, right? Only with
this, if you won, you'd be getting paid for
the work you did in the kitchen."

Annie scratched the tip of her nose, her
eyes glazing over in thought. "I do like to
help Dat as much as I can . . ."

"So you'll give it a try?" Claire prodded,
grinning.

"It is just like a job, yah?"

"If you win, it would be kind of like having one of your quilts here" — she motioned
around the shop — "for sale. Only your dessert would be in lots of stores or, rather,
kind-of-famous bakeries. But before that, in
terms of the bake-off itself, you simply bake
one of those amazing desserts you've come
up with on your own. That's it. Then, on
the day of the bake-off, you drop it off at"
— she dropped her eyes back to the paper
— "town hall, like you might drop off a dessert at one of those mud sales the Amish
do."

Annie looked from the paper, to Claire,
and back again, her initial hesitation quickly
fading into excitement. "Do you really think
I should?"

"I really do."

"Perhaps" — Annie stopped, swallowed,
and tried again — "perhaps I could keep it

a surprise from Dat."

"But if you win, he'd have to know."

"That is a big if."

Claire guided Annie's eyes back to hers. "I don't think it's a big *if* at all. In fact, I think you *not* winning is the more appropriate *if* here."

"Then I will try. If you are right, and I win, I will surprise Dat with such news." Annie wiggled the paper between them. "May I keep this?"

"Of course. Just let me take a picture of it first. That way I have the website I need to go to in order to sign you up." She reached into her purse, made a second pass through the papers and loose change, and then pulled out her phone.

"I could write it down for you," Annie offered.

"Nah, this is just as easy, and there will be less chance of me misplacing it — a win-win right now with everything I'm trying to keep track of." She took temporary custody of the paper again, set it on the counter, took a quick picture, and then went into her phone's album to make sure the bake-off website was, in fact, visible. "Perfect. I'll take care of that once I'm done here for the night."

She closed out of the picture, its

thumbnail-size version taking its place beside yet another piece of paper she'd felt the need to capture — a piece of paper she wished she'd never taken out of its envelope . . . never unfolded . . . never read.

"Claire? Are you okay? You look sad all of a sudden."

It was an observation she couldn't argue. Not unless it was to demand *confused* and *scared* be added as well. Instead, she stepped off the stool, pulled off another bite of cinnamon bread, and mustered up the closest thing to a smile she had. "It's been a crazy day, kiddo. People were waiting outside when I opened this morning, and they've been coming and going nonstop ever since. That's why, when you walked in, I didn't hear you. The last customer had just left, and I think I was in shock over the sudden quiet."

"I'm sorry I could not work yesterday or today, and I am sorry I am taking time away from what might be your only break all day. But soon, Mary and Daniel's funeral will be over and I will be back to work. When I am, I can handle things in here so you can spend all of your time finishing plans for your festival. But if there are no customers for me to take care of and I have done all of the tasks on the clipboard, perhaps I can help you with some of those things."

"Sounds good, kiddo." She pulled Annie in for a quick hug and then motioned toward the clock on the back wall. "You better get going before your dat wonders what happened to you."

"Yah." Annie pushed in her own stool but remained standing where she was. "I know you are worried you will not get everything done, but I know you will and I know your festival will be very special. It is how you do everything."

It was Claire's turn to blush, and blush she did. "Thanks, kiddo. Your faith in me means a lot. Now . . . off with you. Go . . ."

Annie opened her mouth as if to say something else, but in the end, she made her way around the counter and over to the back hallway. At the doorway, she glanced back, her eyes pinning Claire's. "When I started Rumspringa, I wanted to have a phone like you have. I wanted to send texts, and make calls, and take pictures the way I'd seen English girls do for so long. And the first few times I used one, I thought it was . . . *cool.* But I do not think so anymore."

Intrigued, Claire leaned against the side of the counter and silently compared the confident girl in front of her now with the angry, boundary-pushing one who'd first walked into her shop ten months earlier.

The old Annie couldn't get far enough away from her Amish ways. The new Annie embraced them . . .

The old Annie couldn't wear enough makeup. The new, fresh-faced Annie glowed from the inside out . . .

The old Annie had worn anger as a cover for intense sadness. The new Annie sought to find lightness everywhere . . .

The old Annie had talked a good game about her abilities but hadn't believed her own words. The new Annie was humbler, wiser . . .

"Why? What changed?" she finally asked.

"I see the distraction Dat speaks of. I see conversations that stop because a phone dings. I see smiles and waves that are not returned because someone is looking down at their phone instead of up at God's people. I see animals and babies that are not seen because people are moving their fingers instead of their eyes. And today, I watched your smile disappear because of a picture you keep on your phone."

Claire drew back, ready to protest, but the reality behind Annie's words made it so she couldn't. Instead, she dropped her gaze to the floor.

"I know you are busy with many things to do. But I also know there is more."

Lifting her chin, Claire released the breath she hadn't realized she was holding. "And you're right. There is. Or at least, I think there is. But I'll figure it out, Annie, and everything will be —" She stopped and looked away.

Everything would be what? Okay? Fine? Hunky-dory? She didn't know that. How could she? Mary's letter to Ruth changed everything.

For her, if not for Jakob.

"When I first came into this store many months ago, I didn't think anything would ever be better. Mamm was gone, Dat was busy all the time, and I was always alone. I was angry at Dat because he did not have time for me, I was angry at Mamm for dying, I was angry at" — Annie's voice faltered — "God for his will, and I was angry at you for smiling at me. I didn't want you, or anyone else, to smile at me. I just wanted to make enough money to run away.

"I know you should not have hired me that day. But you did. And you made me work. You taught me things about this place, and you, and even me. And you taught me to share the things that upset me with the people I love. That is why Dat and I have dinner together every night now. It is why we talk about my day here with you, and his day in the fields or with someone in the district, and why we talk about Mamm sometimes, too. Dat could not help when he did not know what was wrong. You taught me that, Claire. But it seems you do not know these same things for yourself."

"Annie, I —"

"I know I just turned seventeen and that there are many things I still do not know about the English world. But ears do not need to be old or English to listen."

Claire felt the familiar prick of tears gathering just behind her eyes and did her best to blink them away. "Trust me, kiddo, I know you're a good listener. You've proven that many times since that first day. And seventeen or not, I value your input every single time. But this thing, on my phone? There's a chance I'm reading more into it than there really is. That's why I need to sit with it by myself for a little while, okay?"

"Yah." Annie started down the hallway, only to return seconds later. "Claire?"

"Yes, kiddo?"

"I saw someone last night. At the viewing. It is someone I remember from that night."

Pushing off the counter, she joined Annie by the doorway. "From what night?"

"The night my youth group went caroling. To Daniel and Mary's."

She stared at the girl. "You mean the night
you and Henry found them?"

"Yah." Annie stepped over to the disheveled display of place mats and quickly
neatened them into Claire's preferred piles.
"It was because of the pebbles that I saw
him, but then Henry said something about
the moon and I looked away."

"Pebbles?"

"On the dirt outside Mary and Daniel's
home."

"Do you mean the driveway?"

"Yah," Annie said, moving on to the bin
of napkin rings. "They made a funny sound
when he ran. I saw his face, but it was so
quick and it has been many years I did not
remember. But last night, when I heard Dat
say his name, I knew he was the one that
made Mary sad."

She swallowed. Hard. "Who did you see,
Annie?"

"Abe Esch."

CHAPTER 14

She was exhausted. Plain and simple. Yet something about flipping the sign from OPEN to CLOSED filled her with such dread, she actually entertained the idea of keeping the door unlocked and the lights blazing. But she couldn't. Not in good conscience, anyway.

Her whole upbringing had been centered around three simple principles: Be kind, work hard, and be truthful to yourself and others. And while she'd always found them reasonably easy to honor thus far, it was the last one she'd been doing her best to ignore all day.

Every customer that had come in, every question she'd fielded, every phone call she'd answered, every purchase she'd rung up, every item she'd bagged, had kept her from this exact moment — a moment with no distractions and no excuses.

Wrapping her fingers around the same

rectangular placard that hung in every shop up and down Lighted Way, she pulled in a breath, let it out through pursed lips, and flipped it over, her gaze finding and then quickly discarding the police station. Inside its four walls, Jakob was likely interrogating or getting ready to interrogate the victim's son — a young man who hadn't been on anyone's radar until Annie's visit.

She knew she should be relieved Annie had spoken up, that Ruth and Samuel had likely been pushed to the bottom of the suspect list because of the teen's admission, but she wasn't. At least not in the way she would have been before she'd stopped out at Ruth's — before Ruth had looked her in the eye and lied.

When she'd woken that morning, Claire had still been certain Ruth and Samuel were no more viable suspects in the double murder than she was. Ruth's lie had stolen that certainty, leaving in its place the stomach-churning fear she could no longer ignore under the guise of a busy day.

No, the customers were gone, the phone silent, the register closed and locked. There were no more excuses to be had.

Drawing in another deep breath, she took in the garland-wrapped streetlamps lining the sidewalks, the wreath on Glorious

Books' door she knew matched her own and every other shopkeeper's on the street, and the last of the day's shoppers heading into Taste of Heaven(ly) for a home-cooked meal, and then turned her back on it all in favor of the one thing she didn't want to look at.

With heavy footsteps, she made her way past the doll display that needed resupplying, the candle section that needed reorganizing, the quilt section that needed refolding, and the baby section that needed straightening. Had she not been running so late that morning, her purse would be in her office, tucked away in her desk's deepest drawer with the bag of pretzels she kept on hand for days like this, when a real lunch hadn't been an option.

Instead, her purse and her phone were below the register in a cubby normally taken up by Annie's lunch pail and, in the winter, the teen's scarf and gloves. Here, thanks to the day's busyness, the bowl of wrapped candies she kept out for customers stood empty, thus negating any chance of a quick food-break diversion.

She wandered behind the counter, pushed the stool out of the way, and reached for her purse, the churn in her stomach growing more intense. Maybe, if she was lucky, she'd have a text from her aunt asking her to pick up something at Gussmann's General Store on the way home — a text she'd feel obligated to answer lest Diane doubt she'd gotten it and head to the store herself. Or . . . or maybe there would be a voice mail from Harold Glick's wife regarding the Santa suit she was making for One Heavenly Night. If there was an issue with the suit, Claire would have to address it right away. Time was ticking, after all . . .

Yet when she unzipped her purse and pulled out her phone, a tap of the button tasked with waking the device yielded no little red indicator next to the text or voice mail icon.

Great . . .

Slumping back against the edge of the stool, Claire glanced up at the ceiling, murmured her way from one to ten, and then, dropping all focus back to her phone, pressed the flower petal. Instantly, a checkerboard of thumbnail-size pictures filled her screen.

Pictures of the countryside from Sleep Heavenly's front porch . . .

Shots of Aunt Diane with various horses at Weaver's farm . . .

Farm animals that had caught her eye while walking the less-traveled roads on the

Amish side of town . . .

The cover of a book she'd seen at Glorious Books she'd been certain (and right!) her aunt would enjoy . . .

Her feet beside Jakob's during their last walk of the autumn season, the reds and golds and oranges around their shoes so breathtakingly pretty she'd had to take a picture . . .

The drawings Annie had made of the various scenes Claire had described when imagining what One Heavenly Night could actually be if everything went off without a hitch . . .

Left to right, row after row, she took in each and every tiny picture until she came to the one she wished she could accidentally delete. But accidental would mean without thought, and it was all she could think about.

For a moment, she let her gaze skip ahead to the one she'd taken during Annie's lunchtime visit, the wrinkled paper with its bake-off information promising the distraction she'd been silently praying for since the door-mounted bell jingled good-bye to the day's last customer. On one hand, it would make perfect sense for her to hop on the Internet and sign Annie up for the competition. After all, Annie, who was technically still on Rumspringa while waiting to be baptized, didn't have any Internet-capable devices at her disposal, and Claire had said she'd sign the teenager up. But considering it was only five fifteen and entries were being accepted for another eight weeks, it was a distraction that could wait.

This thing with Ruth? It couldn't wait. Not if Claire was being true to her upbringing and the whole *be truthful to yourself and others* thing.

She hovered her finger above the second to last picture, mustered every ounce of courage she could, and then pressed. Instantly, the letter that had stolen her breath in just the first two sentences she'd managed to read before Ruth's returning footsteps had sent her scrambling for her phone took center stage. Looking back, she'd felt the heat of shame as she'd unfolded the letter that hadn't bore her name. But in the moment, she'd been so thrown by the ripped seal and Ruth's lie, she wasn't exactly thinking clearly. All she knew was the way her thoughts were focused on the lie and stirring up all sorts of *what if's* — *what if's* that had her starting to doubt her belief in Ruth.

Opening the letter, though? And actually starting to read it? That split-second, poorly thought-out decision had taken all those silly little doubts and turned them into something not quite so little or so silly. Now, where there had been idle curiosity and irritation over a lie, there was fear and dread.

Fear that Jakob's questioning of Ruth was no longer about checking a box.

And dread over everything that meant — for Jakob, for Eli, for Ben, for Samuel, and for Ruth's unborn baby . . .

Setting her thumb and forefinger on the screen, Claire spread them apart, bringing the letter she both wanted and hated to finish reading into full view.

Dear Ruth,

I know you will not think too kindly of me by the time you finish reading this letter, but the Bible says, "These are the things that ye shall do; speak ye every man the truth to his neighbor." That is why I must tell the truth.

By the time you read this, you will know that Samuel's bid for the Breeze Point job did not win. You will also learn that the one Daniel put in for Esch did. Many, including Samuel, will think it is because his was better, and that is truth. But it is also truth that it was a better bid because we made sure it was so. For many years Esch was good and strong because of him — his work, his name.

Claire felt the hitch of her breath as she stopped, skimmed the paragraph again, and then resituated her fingers so she could keep reading, Mary's words holding her captive.

I know it was wrong. I know there will be confusion and disappointment and pain, but that is what forgiveness is for. That is what I must remind myself, too. You cannot change what you have done. You can only change what you do. That is what Daniel and I are doing.

You and Samuel are young. You have each other. There will be many years to fix the mistakes I pray you do not make with your loved ones.

From,
Mary Esch

Moving her shaky fingers from the screen, Claire used them instead to help steady her phone-holding hand. The letter she'd been so afraid to read for the answers she wasn't sure she really wanted had merely doubled — even tripled — the feeling of dread that seemed to claw at every square inch of her being.

Now, instead of *Why did Ruth lie about never having seen the yellow envelope* and *What, if any, tie could that have to the murders of Mary and Daniel Esch,* Claire was holding in her hand a picture of what could very well be the case's proverbial smoking gun. The fact that said gun looked to have a treasured friend's fingerprints all over it took everything to a whole new level.

Mary and Daniel Esch had fixed a bid for a cabinetry job that Samuel Yoder wanted, bid for, and desperately needed according to his young wife. It was the kind of sickening and underhanded act that made an honest person's blood boil. It certainly did hers, and she wasn't the one who stood to lose financially because of it . . .

The trembling under control, she rubbed at her cheek as she tried to recall a moment when the furniture shop owner had ever displayed even a hint of anger. But no matter how many business owners' meetings she cycled through in her thoughts, or how many buggy sightings she'd had of the quietly confident man, she couldn't think of a single one.

Ditto for Ruth.

Unless she counted the time she'd been conversing with the former bake shop owner across their respective front porches when a passing Englisher had groused about the prices in Ruth's then-fiancé's shop. Ruth had gotten so flustered and so upset, Claire had felt the need to leave her shop unmanned for a few moments while she worked to calm her friend.

At the time, she'd been surprised such a reaction had come from someone she'd always equated as being shy, even timid. But when she'd shared the encounter with her aunt later that same day, Diane had offered the same chilling reminder now looping its way through Claire's head.

Ruth was, in fact, Eli's twin. And up until Eli had set his sights on marrying Esther, he'd been shunned by his district a time or two for his temper — a temper that had been witnessed by many prior to Claire's arrival in Heavenly.

No.

No.

No.

Determined, she willed the troubling thought from her head and instead looked back at the screen, her eyes and thoughts narrowing in on the second part of the letter . . .

I know it was wrong. I know there will be confusion and disappointment and pain, but that is what forgiveness is for. That is what I must remind myself, too. You cannot change what you have done. You can only change what you do. That is what Daniel and I are doing.

You and Samuel are young. You have each other. There will be many years to fix the mistakes I pray you do not make with your loved ones.

What did Mary mean, the part about not making mistakes with loved ones? Wouldn't it have been so much easier to say *I'm sorry* than messing with someone else's livelihood?

She didn't understand people sometimes. The decisions they made, the actions they took, the justifications they used. Then again, she was holding the image of someone else's letter in her hand — a letter she hadn't been given permission to read, let alone copy.

Aware of the slump sagging her shoulders, she wandered her gaze across the section of her shop devoted to home and hearth and then out the window to the white clapboard exterior of her next-door neighbor, Shoo Fly Bake Shoppe, her thoughts traveling back to the first day she'd met Ruth Miller.

It had been a nice day, the bright morning

sun reflecting off the Heavenly Treasures shingle she'd ordered from her landlord. Something about walking down Lighted Way that morning, toward the start of a new dream, and a new life, had been more than a little scary. Yet as she'd unlocked the back door of her new shop, Ruth had stepped out into the alley with a freshly made cookie and a smile of encouragement.

Somehow, those two simple gestures had calmed Claire's nerves and made her feel as if everything would be alright from that point forward. And it had. Ruth's quiet ways, yet willingness to help and encourage, had led Claire to hire Esther. Esther, in turn, had become Claire's best friend. *That* friendship had led to even more inside the Amish community — from both a personal and a professional standpoint.

How different would her life be now if Ruth hadn't reached out to her? If Ruth hadn't introduced her to Esther?

She looked back down at the phone, the words on the screen blurring in her tears. "What a way to thank her, dummy," she whispered.

CHAPTER 15

It was close to six thirty by the time she finally stepped into the alley, her thoughts as jumbled now as they'd been when she'd finished reading the letter. Did she head across the street to the police station? Did she get in Aunt Diane's car and head back out to Ruth's? Or did she turn right, walk straight to Heavenly Brews, and lose herself in the biggest mug of hot chocolate she could buy, thus prolonging a decision she was no closer to making than she'd been an hour earlier?

She pulled the door closed, locked it, and took a moment to look around. The small turnaround spot at the back of her building where Annie hitched her horse, Katie, was empty, the horse's feed bucket dangling from the post by its handle. Across the alley, next to Shoo Fly's side door, was the milk box that, come morning, would hold a few bottles of fresh cow's milk, delivered to the shop in the wee hours by either Ben or Eli. Up ahead and across the street, the display of holiday titles in Glorious Books' front window was slightly visible thanks to one of Lighted Way's many lampposts, which stood sentry along the cobblestone thoroughfare.

Dropping the key into her purse, she made her way down the short alleyway to the sidewalk and the full view of Lighted Way it afforded. At night, during the holiday season, the cobblestones sparkled with the addition of countless twinkling lights, transforming the already picturesque street into something straight out of a Dickens novel. It was, in a word, magical, and at that moment, she was in dire need of a little magic.

To her left, just beyond Shoo Fly, was Glick's Tools 'n More. Like the lamppost across the street had done for the bookstore, the one positioned outside the hardware store shone brightly across Harold's holiday window display — shovels for those snowy days, tools and other assorted gadgets that were just the right size for stocking stuffers, and gift cards scattered about that recipients could use toward one of the many how-to classes the store offered throughout the year. It had taken some coaching to become the visual stunner it was, but the memory of Harold's nearly face-splitting smile when it was finally done helped quiet her troubled heart for a few moments.

To her right, just beyond the *Heavenly Times'* office and Heavenly Hairdo, she spotted a couple, not much older than she and Jakob, stop to look at the Christmas tree in all its glory, the weather-resistant garland and twinkling white lights casting a glow of contentment around them. It was hard not to rewind back to the day the detective had joined her and a few of the shopkeepers to decorate the shared outdoor tree. They'd had such fun winding the light strands around the tree, reminiscing about past Christmases they'd each had, and brainstorming real and even outrageous ideas for One Heavenly Night. Everything had seemed so light and happy and . . . promising.

And for some, like the couple now smiling at each other more than the tree, it was still light and happy and promising.

She wanted that feeling back. She *needed* that feeling back.

The *how to make that happen* part was the issue.

Mary and Daniel Esch were still dead, still murder victims. Jakob was still the detective tasked with solving the case. She still had something in her possession she knew he needed to see. And as busy as she'd been all day, and as troubled as she'd been since finally getting to read the letter Ruth had pretended not to know about, the fact that an entire workday had come and gone without so much as a call or text from him had not escaped her. Even when she'd tried to reach him to tell him about Annie, he hadn't picked up. Instead, she'd called the station's main desk and asked if he was in, and when she was told he couldn't be disturbed, she told the dispatcher that she was sending Annie over and that Jakob would want to talk to her right away.

Yet when Annie left the station an hour later, he hadn't called, hadn't thanked her for insisting Annie speak to him . . .

Something was wrong; she could feel it in her bones. And while she knew the smartest, most effective thing to do was march across the street and ask him outright, the fact that she was in possession of something that more than earned Ruth and Samuel a legitimate spot on Jakob's suspect list kept her feet planted right where they were.

A chime, indicating the arrival of a text, sent her scrambling through her purse for the source. Any hope she had that it was

Jakob, though, was quickly drowned out by the relief that it wasn't.

Can you stop by Gussmann's on your way home and pick up a gallon of milk? I've got some chocolate chip cookies in the oven that would go mighty well with a glass.

She scrolled up, read the text again, and, dropping her phone back into her purse, turned right toward the welcomed distraction.

Tugging her scarf higher onto her cheeks, Claire crossed the street just beyond Yoder's Furniture, her ankle boots making a staccato beat against the cobblestones as she hurried to beat Al Gussmann's seven o'clock close. A glance inside the window yielded the empty aisles she expected to see at this time of day, as well as the stocking cart near the back counter that would be used to return the occasional item ruled out by a customer at the last minute.

With a gloved hand, she pinched the door handle and pushed her way inside the warm interior, her gaze lifting instantly to the mirror that provided Al with a view of the front door and her a view of the now-empty register area.

"Welcome to Gussmann's."

She craned her head around until she spotted the scrap of thinning black hair rising up above the top shelf in the soup aisle. "It's just me, Al. Aunt Diane is baking cookies and she needs a gallon of milk."

"You know where it is." The top of Al's head disappeared temporarily, only to appear along with the rest of him in the milk aisle, his wide forehead glistening in the overhead light. "Saw Harold a little while ago. He said he was hopping all day long. Same for you?"

"It was nuts," she said, reaching inside the refrigerator. "But a really, really *good* nuts."

"And you were on your own, right? On account of the funeral for that Amish couple?"

She pulled out a gallon and let the door swing closed behind her. "I was. But yesterday and today was just the viewing part. Tomorrow is the actual service and burial."

"Is that why you're still here, almost two hours after closing?" Al wiped his hands down the sides of his logo'd apron and then pulled it up and over his head. "Trying to do all the restocking and bookkeeping stuff you couldn't get done with customers underfoot?"

"Pretty much."

"Everything ready to go for the festival next week?"

"I think so." She stepped aside to let him pass and then followed him over to the register. "All that's really left now is reconfirming everyone one more time, checking in with someone about one very important detail for the Living Nativity, and trying not to revert back to biting my nails the way I did when I was a kid and worried about some test or the other."

He rang up the milk, took her money, and counted the change back into her palm. "I know you, and I know you'll worry about every detail until the last minute, but I also know — because I know you — that this event is going to be a success. I don't think a single local customer I've had the past few weeks has left this store without telling me how excited they are for this thing. It's like the adults are the kids this season, eagerly looking forward to the big night. Only instead of wanting to know what Santa brings, they're wanting to celebrate the real reason for the season with their neighbors."

"But no pressure, right?" she said, laughing.

"I didn't intend it to be that." The creases beside Al's eyes burrowed in deep. "I really said it just so you know how electric your idea has been throughout this whole town."

She hiked her purse back onto her shoulder and took her aunt's milk from the man's outstretched hand. "I know you were. This is just me being me, worried I'll let everyone down if it doesn't live up to whatever image they have in their heads."

"Don't be. Just do the things you showed us at the last business owners' meeting and it'll be a smashing success. And know that Harold, Sandra, Drew, and all the rest of us are ready to do whatever you need that night."

"Thanks, Al. You guys really are like a second family for me."

"We're a tight-knit bunch, that's for sure. And I don't see that changing so long as business keeps doing well across the board." He moved out from behind the register and walked with her to the front door. "I'm always wary someone will give up or move on to another venture, leaving me with the task of finding just the right fit. Like I did with you."

At the door, she turned back to her landlord, her curiosity aroused. "Was there interest from someone else in taking over that space?"

"There was, but nothing too serious.

Fortunately for me, though, you being Diane Weatherly's kin made it a little easier to slide you in. But even with that, had it been the Millers' place that had opened up back then, I'd have had more than a few pairs of eyes on me, just waiting for me to hand them something they could try to sue me over."

"Sue you over? I don't understand."

Al checked his watch, compared it to the clock on the wall, and then, looking up and down Lighted Way, flipped his OPEN sign to CLOSED. "I pick and choose my tenants more than I should by law. But that's because I like the mix we have, not only with the kinds of shops but also with the shopkeepers who are running them. The people who keep this street alive with their spending dollars are here because they're fascinated with the Amish. So I don't just lease to anyone willing to pay the rent I'm asking. I want tenants who appreciate the pull of this place for more than just a way to turn a fast buck. Because if that's all it is, the folks who vacation here will spot that a mile away. Beyond that, I want tenants who will see the success of this street as a team effort, and I want each shop or restaurant to be a unique experience. Someone wants an Amish-made rag doll, they go to your place. They want a book about Amish culture, they go to Drew's bookshop. They want to try out a tool the Amish use, they go to Glick's. They want some brown buttered noodles like the Amish eat, they go to Taste of Heaven(ly). They want to order an Amish-made bedroom set, they go to Yoder's. They want to indulge in a little shoo fly or apple pie straight from an Amish kitchen, thankfully Ruth's place is still open. Watering that down with seconds and thirds of the same businesses we already have would come to hurt all of us in the end."

Shifting the gallon of milk to her other hand, she considered Al's words against a very different conversation. "I wish you'd been standing beside me last night when this guy told me the Amish have a stranglehold on business opportunities along this street. His statement caught me by surprise so much that I just sort of stood there, dumbfounded. When I recovered enough to point out the fact that a good half of the shops here are owned by English, the conversation had already moved in a completely different direction."

"Eh, just ignore them like I do," Al said, scrunching his nose as if he'd come in contact with a bad smell. "Some folks like to grasp at straws. That's just the way they're made. And folks like that? They don't want to hear reason, don't want to hear facts and truth. They just believe what they want to believe because it gives them whatever justification they need for whatever shortcoming they have or whatever wrong they've committed."

"So you've heard this before, then, I take it?"

"Only once, and it about knocked me over. So I *did* say the things you wish you'd said last night. But it didn't matter. You ever heard that expression, *Never let the facts get in the way of a good lie?* Well, that way of thinking was in full force that day, and it didn't take me all that long to realize there was no reasoning to be done with that one." Al shook his head slowly, methodically. "I know there's no stranglehold on this street, you know it, Harold knows it, Drew knows it, Sandra knows it, and the Amish know it, too. Heck, anyone with working eyes can walk in and out of every shop on this street and know it for themselves. That's a good enough answer for me."

"Me, too." Glancing outside, she shivered in anticipation of the vast temperature change awaiting her out on the sidewalk. "Well, I guess I better get this milk out to my aunt. Have a nice evening, and I'll see

— wait! I just thought of something I wanted to ask you if you have a minute?"

He paused his hand on the door and grinned. "Seeing as how you're still standing inside my store, I'd say I have a minute," he teased.

"I'll make it quick, I promise. Can you tell me whose name is on the Shoo Fly lease? Is it Ben's dad or the family as a whole?"

"Shoo Fly?" Al echoed, pulling a face. "Why? Is there some sort of issue that I don't know about?"

She waved away his question so fast she nearly dropped her purchase on the ground. "No, no, not at all! I love being alley-mates with Shoo Fly. Not only do they make my place smell amazing in open-door season, I also reap the rewards of being the next shop on the street for some seriously satiated and happy customers."

"Oh. Okay, good. Getting a complaint against Ruth in any form would've been a first."

"Against Ruth?"

"Yep. Shoo Fly is hers and Samuel's now — lease and all. They took it over the first of the month." Leaning against the door, Al scratched at the crown of his head. "Most people don't know, but I let her stay through

November without a lease. But I wasn't ready to give up on her yet. I knew — or rather hoped — that she and Samuel would come to the exact decision they did."

"Who had the lease originally?" she asked.

"The father — Jeb. He owned the lease, Ruth did the baking, of course, and Benjamin and Eli pitched in wherever they were needed. But Jeb is getting up in years, and since Ruth was set to get married a week or so after his lease was up for renewal, he decided to let it go." Al dropped his hand to his mouth, his chin. "I'm not sure who was more heartsick over that — me or Ruth. Shoo Fly Bake Shoppe, as you know, is a big pull for this entire street. The thought of losing that for the rest of us was" — he whistled long and low — "daunting, to say the least. I put out a few quiet feelers to see who might want to come into that same space and do the same thing, but even the most talented of those lacked the complete package that was Ruth and Shoo Fly.

"So that's when I let her stay through November — with Ruth at the helm until the wedding, and then that younger one they've had in there ever since."

"Hannah. She's Eli's sister-in-law."

"Ahhhh, okay, that makes sense now. I thought she looked a little like your Esther around the eyes . . ." Al tried for a smile but cleared his throat instead. "She's good, but she's not Ruth."

Claire half nodded, half shrugged. "*Yet.* She's still young, still feeling her way. But she's got some pretty amazing specialties of her own. Like her candies and her toffees and even her chocolate caramel pie. The returning tourists just need to give her a try the way the new ones do."

"That's good to hear, and something you might want to mention to Ruth or even Samuel at the next business owners' meeting, seeing as how they signed a twelve-month lease with me on December first." Al motioned down the street toward Heavenly Treasures' end. "Maybe encouraging folks toward Hannah's specialties before they even walk in the door will help get business back up in the vicinity of where they need it to be in order to keep from drowning under two separate leases."

Two leases . . .

Double the business expenses . . .

A drop in traffic at Shoo Fly, a decrease in custom orders at Yoder's . . .

No wonder Samuel was feeling stressed.

This time, the shiver that moved through her had nothing to do with the dropping temperatures waiting for her on the other side of Al's door. No, this chill was the kind that was completely immune to heavy coats, thick scarves, and wooly mittens.

"Yeah . . . okay . . . I . . . I'll mention it to them when I see them," she murmured. "Maybe they can put up some new signs or talk up Hannah's candy in an ad or something."

Al's feet shifted forward, prompting her to look up as his hand came down on her shoulder. "Is everything okay, Claire? You're not looking so good all of a sudden."

No, everything isn't okay. I'm afraid Ruth may have acted out of desperation or anger or fear . . .

But she couldn't say that aloud. Not to Al, anyway. Instead, she hugged the gallon of milk to her chest and nudged her chin toward the door. "Just dreading the walk back to Diane's car."

"There's cookies at the other end, though, right?"

She laughed in spite of the fear pressing against her heart. "My own little personal pot of gold."

"We all need one of those at times, don't we?" he mused, opening the door.

"Indeed." She stepped out onto the front stoop and then turned around. "What's yours?"

"My pot of gold?" At her nod, he grinned. "I've got two. The first has my slippers, my remote, and my recliner. The second is a sandy beach — somewhere tropical and cut off from the rest of the world."

"That sounds mighty nice . . ."

"Maybe next week, after the festival is over, you should try one of those for yourself. You've more than earned the recharge."

She was pretty sure she nodded, maybe even offered some lighthearted retort as she finally made her way onto the cobblestones, but it wasn't real. Real was the fear ushered in by Mary's letter to Ruth and invited to stay by the barely dry ink on the bottom of Shoo Fly Bake Shoppe's lease.

CHAPTER 16

Claire was less than twenty feet away from Diane's car when the front door of the police department swung open and Jakob stepped out and onto the mirror image of every front porch up and down Lighted Way. The mere sight of his broad shoulders in the disappearing lobby light at his back stole a quiet sigh from her lips.

Sometimes, when she caught him at just the right angle, she was instantly transported back to the moment she first laid eyes on him in the front-page picture of the *Heavenly Times* — the sandy blond hair cut short along the sides, the quiet confidence he'd seemed to wear every bit as well as the light blue dress shirt he'd sported, the hint of those dimples playing at the edges of his smile . . .

Switching the gallon of milk to her other hand, she had to smile at the memory of the way she'd stared at that picture, momentarily distracted by the handsome face. Little had she known how important that new detective from the big city would become in her life, how he'd quietly, yet oh so definitively, change her world in so many ways.

She stood there, in the shadows cast by the lamppost just beyond Glorious Books, and quietly drank in the man he was now compared to the one she'd met inside the police station not long after she'd seen his photo. That day, armed with Aunt Diane's certainty that Jakob's return to Heavenly would be unwelcome by his childhood family, Claire had set aside her own bent toward shyness and stopped by the department with a welcome gift. That fairly innocuous blue and green striped gift bag — with homemade candles and a framed photograph of winter's Lighted Way — had taken him by surprise and helped kick off the sweet friendship that had quickly ensued. Together, they'd helped each other heal from past hurts: hers from the confidence-crushing pain of a failed marriage, and his from a severing of relationships mandated by a culture he gave up everything to protect. Even early on, she'd have done anything to have gone back in time and somehow spared herself and Jakob the pain they'd endured. But as they grew and learned and helped each other turn lemons into lemonade, their friendship had become so much more — something bigger and better and more beautiful than she could've ever imagined.

And just like that, the urge to step into his arms and breathe in his scent and his nearness propelled her forward one step, two steps, three —

Jakob reached into the pocket of his winter coat, pulled out his phone, and tapped a few buttons, prompting her to fish her own hand inside her purse in anticipation of his call. But when he finished tapping and held the device to his ear, her phone didn't vibrate, didn't light up.

"Hey, it's Jakob. I got your picture, and all I can say is, *wow*! Gorgeous."

Aware of the sudden thudding inside her ears, she reclaimed her spot inside the darkness, his unmistakable excitement, as much as the words flowing from his mouth, making it difficult to breathe.

"Yes, yes . . . definitely. This is everything we both want, you know? It's a million times better than everything I'd imagined."

She stilled her teeth mid-chatter.

Breathe, Claire, breathe . . .

"I know," Jakob said after a moment.

"Look, I've got a pretty limited window on account of work right now, but I can be there with you in less than ten minutes? Awesome . . . perfect! I'll see you then, Callie."

Callie?

Callie Granger?

Stifling the gasp she could barely contain, Claire covered her mouth and the plume of breath exiting it and stared, unseeing, at *her Jakob,* as Diane was so fond of saying.

Was it possible?

Had the friendship between the grieving single mother and the man her late father had loved like a son blossomed into something romantic?

No. There was no way Jakob —

Like a TV screen that had sprung to life, her mind's eye lit on one moment and then another, glimpses of Jakob and Callie together: sitting on a park bench by the gazebo looking at papers, walking down the sidewalk, riding off together in her car . . .

She'd never thought anything of it. Just assumed Jakob was looking after the daughter of a deceased yet still treasured friend, helping Callie heal in much the same way he'd helped Claire . . .

Jerking back, her thoughts skipped ahead to the previous night and the moment his screen had lit up. Before his hand had come down over the phone, she'd seen the first letter in the caller's name.

Had *C* been for Callie?

Was that why he'd silenced the call? Turned the phone over on the console between them? Because he and Callie had grown into something more?

No.

No.

No.

Jakob Fisher wasn't that guy. He was honest, kind, sweet, and loving. And he loved her. She knew this. Aunt Diane knew this. Bill knew this. Everyone knew this.

She wasn't sure what she did. Maybe she released all of her baseless tension through an audible breath, maybe the sway of relief she'd thought she'd imagined had, in fact, been real, or maybe the strangled sob she'd managed to ward off with a quiet yet determined laugh had carried farther than she realized, but whatever it was, it had Jakob glancing in her direction, muttering something she couldn't hear into the phone, and shoving it inside his pocket all in the span of about five seconds.

The same amount of time it took for Claire to realize the smile that had lit Jakob's face during his call — the smile he always greeted her with no matter what was going on — was now nowhere to be seen.

"Hey. How long have you been standing there?" he called, his voice devoid of its usual warmth.

Long enough, she wanted to say. *Please tell me I'm wrong,* she wanted to plead.

But she didn't. The pain in her heart at that moment was simply too great to do anything, let alone speak. Instead, she lifted the gallon of milk into the air and then tucked it back inside her arm.

"Ahhh. An evening run to the store?"

"Aunt Diane is making cookies. Chocolate chip." She waited for a knowing smile or a dimple-accompanied request to save him some, but it never came.

Instead, he pulled his hands from his pockets, fisted them to his lips, and blew. "Well, I probably should let you go then. Before the cookies get cold."

"No, really . . . It's okay. I'm sure Aunt Diane won't be putting them in the oven until I get home." She heard the tremble in her voice and did her best to disguise it behind a shiver that had nothing whatsoever to do with the outside temperature. "You talked to Annie, right?"

"I did. Thank you for that. That was huge."

"Do you think Abe did it?"

He shrugged. "I just don't know."

"Have you talked to him?"

"The second Annie left."

"And?"

"He said Mary and Daniel asked him to come to the house."

"But he's been banned."

"Exactly."

She considered his words, found that they led her back to Annie. "So then why did he run when Annie and Henry and the other kids came caroling?"

"He says he didn't want to get his parents in trouble for speaking to him."

"So he's saying he'd just gotten there? As Annie and Henry were pulling up?"

Jakob's nod was slow and protracted. "That's what he says . . ."

"Wow."

"And it gets better. Abe had a bid in for the same project out in Breeze Point."

She stared up at him. "The assisted-living place that Samuel was going after?"

"And Daniel got? Yeah, same one."

It was a lot to take in, a lot to digest. Before Mary's letter to Ruth, she'd have been over the moon at Jakob's news. "I —"

"Claire? I hate to cut this short, but I still have a lot of work to do inside before I can even think of calling it a night." Turning, he paused his hand on the station's doorknob and glanced back at her. "Since it will probably be late, let's just skip tonight's call, okay? I'm sure you could use the sleep with all the stuff I know you've been juggling for One Heavenly Night, and . . . I . . . I don't want to risk waking you if this" — he pointed inside — "goes real late."

Oh, how she wanted to argue, to remind him it was never too late for their good night call ritual. But she couldn't.

He wasn't going back inside to work.

He was going back inside to wait until she drove away.

And then he was going out to Callie Granger's house.

She could drive out there and wait, verify what she already knew thanks to the call he'd cut short because of Claire, but what was the point? No, what she needed more than anything at that moment was to be alone. To think. To feel. To cry.

Mustering a smile past the tears he was too far away to see anyway, Claire nodded. "Yeah, sure. That's fine. We can catch up tomorrow."

She'd just turned into the driveway of the inn when she knew she couldn't go home. Not yet, anyway. Her thoughts were far too jumbled, and her tears way too close to the surface to be able to hide what had just happened from anyone. And while the thought of crying into Aunt Diane's shoulder held true appeal, she wasn't ready to admit the unthinkable aloud just yet.

Still, she suspected the strain in her voice, coupled with the dance of the headlights across the front hallway from her U-turn, hadn't gone unnoticed during the rapid-fire *oh-I-just-realized-I-forgot-the-milk-so-I'll-head-into-Breeze-Point-to-get-it* phone call she'd made to Diane to give herself a little more time. If she was right, her eventual return would be met at the door with a steaming cup of hot cocoa and a ready-and-willing pair of ears. If she was wrong, she'd simply offer to put the cookies in the oven and use the time in the kitchen to get herself together.

Turning left, she headed back toward Lighted Way, her gloved fingers gripped around the steering wheel so tightly, she wasn't sure where one stopped and the other began. For a moment, maybe two, she considered driving out to Esther's and trying to lose herself in Baby Sarah's sweet coos and infectious smiles, but a glance at the dashboard clock killed that thought. Annie, too, was likely settled in for the night, going over the day with her dat while they played some sort of game at their kitchen table.

She felt the asphalt change over to cobblestones beneath the tires and immediately turned to look at the police station. Sure enough, a glimpse at the department's rear parking lot between breaks in the buildings yielded an empty spot to go with Jakob's darkened office window. Swallowing against the unwelcome tightness in her throat, she continued on, passing Glorious Books, Heavenly Toy Factory, and Taste of Heaven(ly). When she reached the front of Gussmann's, she slowed just enough to afford a peek at the second-floor windows behind which Jakob lived. They, like the one denoting his office, were bathed in a darkness she both expected and dreaded to see all at the same time.

Somehow she made herself continue down the road despite the very real pull to park behind Al's and wait for Jakob to return. But she was a stronger person now than she'd ever been, thanks, in part, to Jakob himself. She wanted to be that person, with or without him. One way or the other.

Sitting in a car, lying in wait for him to return, wasn't strength; it was desperation. Strength was what she needed. Strength would help determine her next course of action.

And just like that, she knew where she needed to go — a place where time seemed to stand still yet hope never seemed out of reach.

Soon, the ping of gravel against the bottom of the car welcomed her into the Amish countryside, and with it, some of the tension in her shoulders and her chest began to ebb. Out here, with the hustle and bustle of the English world behind her, she could feel her worries slowing and her thoughts clearing.

Even at night, when the only real light came from her own headlights, she could still make out the farmhouses and fences of the people she'd come to call friends, whether they were simply the type who returned her wave when she was out walking, or invited her into their home for a piece of pie and a glass of fresh cow's milk.

She didn't need to read the names on the mailboxes she passed. She knew them by heart and in order: King, Lapp, Stoltzfus, Lehman, Beiler, Miller.

Just beyond the first of the Millers' properties, she turned left, the limited gravel of the main road disappearing in favor of dirt. Ruts, caused by a few early snowfalls and unsettled temperatures, mandated she slow her pace, and she obliged. When the road came to a fork, she meandered to the right until, a few curves and one covered bridge later, she reached the top of the hill and pulled off the road, her high beams bouncing across the leafless trees before coming to rest on the only place she wanted to be at that moment.

With a twist of her wrist, she cut the engine and stared out at the familiar landscape still illuminated by the headlights. There was something about this spot that allowed her to breathe and to think, two things she desperately needed in that moment. The only thing missing from the equation, though, was —

Movement just beyond the scope of her lights had her reaching for, and then discarding, her keys once again. Surprised, she looked to her right and to her left, but there was no sign of the horse and buggy that went with the face now turned in her direction. Nor was there any sign of a second person sitting on the rock.

Reaching into the glove compartment, Claire grabbed hold of the flashlight Diane kept behind the owner's manual and stepped from the car, her gaze riveted on the tall form rising to his feet in response.

"It's just me — Claire," she called as she shifted the path of the light away from Benjamin Miller's eyes. "I didn't see your buggy, so I thought I was alone."

"I did not bring my buggy."

She cast the flashlight down at the ground, but when it came time to actually pick her way around the upended trees and smaller-size rocks between them, his hand, calloused and steady, was there to help. Slowly they made their way back to the rock on which he'd been sitting when she'd pulled up, the peace she'd been in dire need of mere moments earlier suddenly lapping at the edges of her being.

When she was settled on the same rock on which they'd stargazed together nearly eighteen months earlier, he took the flashlight from her hands, switched it off, and pointed up at the sky. "I think the night's stars are enough light."

Scooting over, she waited for him to sit beside her and then cocked her chin up until all she could see were the stars twinkling above like steadfast beacons in a storm. "Oh, Ben, they're so beautiful."

"Yah."

She took a moment to find the few constellations she could pick out and then lowered her focus back to the blue-eyed

255

man in the broad-brimmed straw hat. Even in the limited light, she could make out the dark brown hair visible beneath the inside edges of the hat.

"I'm sorry if I'm interrupting something. I can find another spot closer to town, if I am."

"You are never an interruption," he said, his voice hushed yet firm. "I am just surprised to see you here at night."

Digging her hands into her pockets, she lifted her shoulders in line with her cheeks and kept them there as a buffer against the slight breeze that was always present in this spot, no matter the time of year. "I wasn't ready to go home, and I didn't want to just keep driving."

"Have you not been home yet?" he asked.

She shook her head.

"Did you have dinner with Jakob in town?"

Aware of the dread slowly climbing its way back up her throat, she returned her gaze to the sky. "No."

"By yourself? In your office at Heavenly Treasures?"

Again, she shook her head, her voice, when it finally emerged, seeming far away even to her own ears. "I was there later than normal, but no, I didn't eat there or anywhere else yet. I . . . I'm not hungry."

She could feel him studying her, maybe even weighing a question or two, but in the end, a comforting silence fell between them as he, too, looked up at the sky, his gentle breath calming her own. "So you walked here? In the dark?" she finally asked.

"I walked. But" — he tilted his own head back even more — "it was not dark."

"Is everything okay? With you and Rebeccah?"

His gaze lowered to meet hers, a slow smile spreading across his mouth. "Yah. It is good."

Nodding, she glanced ahead, to the valley below, the starlight above helping to pick out the outline of Ben's house, not far from that of his parents'. "Just wanting some quiet time, then?"

"Yah."

She scooted to the edge of the rock and stood, the calm his presence had managed to find inside her slipping behind sadness. "Then I should go. So you can think or stargaze or —"

"No. Please stay." He stopped her forward motion with a quick hand and then waved her back. "It has been too long."

He was right.

It had been too long.

Too long since they'd exchanged more than a wave or a few friendly words in passing . . .

Too long since they'd connected the way they did when they were here, talking about life and dreams and hopes . . .

Pulling her knees up and under her chin, Claire wrapped her arms around her shins and gave in to the smile his friendship demanded. "Have you figured out what to give Rebeccah yet?"

"I have thought of many things I can make, like you suggested — a chest like the one Jakob had me build for you, a table for her sewing machine, even a rocking chair. But Emma's home is not Rebeccah's home. Her home is in upstate New York, where she will return soon."

Claire drew back. "Rebeccah is leaving Heavenly?"

"It has been six months since Wayne died. Henry needs less help on the farm every day, and Emma is finding her way with the rest of the children. Rebeccah does not think it will be long before Emma will be okay with her leaving."

"Will *you* be okay with her leaving?" she asked.

It was clear he tried to maintain his smile, but it was every bit as clear it was a losing battle. "If she leaves, it will be God's will."

"No. If she leaves, it will be because you didn't follow your heart."

His eyebrows arched toward his hat. "I do not understand."

"Yes, you do. *In here.*" She pointed to her chest. "Rebeccah makes you happy, Ben. We can all see it — me, Esther, Eli, Annie, Mr. Glick, Al, everyone. It's why that gorgeous smile showed up on your face the second I mentioned her name, and why it disappeared when I asked if you'd be okay with her leaving. You *love* her, Ben. You know this."

She didn't need a flashlight, her car's headlights, or even the starlight she did have to know Ben's cheeks were flushed. She could tell by his shorter breaths, the fidgeting of his fingers, and the way he returned his gaze to the sky while he tried to recover. Eventually, though, he spoke, his words husky. "Yah, I love her."

"So make her that chest, or that sewing machine, or that rocker, and give her a home to put it in — a home she can share with you as her husband."

"I did that once. Many years ago. With Elizabeth. It lasted only weeks."

She found his hand in the dark and covered it with a squeeze. "And that was awful,

I'm sure. But Elizabeth's death was a long time ago, Ben. It's okay to love someone again after all these years. Rebeccah being here, and you two meeting and growing close the way you are, *that* is God's will."

Seconds turned to minutes as they sat there together, side by side, two friends who'd once hovered at the edge of something else yet settled on something deeper. In their silence, she could almost hear him thinking, processing.

"Perhaps you are right," he finally said.

"I am." She retrieved her hand and, instead, linked it through his arm. "In fact, I suspect the thought of getting married and spending the rest of her life with you will be the best Christmas gift you could ever give her."

The smile was back, claiming his eyes as well as his entire face. "Thank you, Claire. You are a good friend."

"So are you." With her cheek pressed against his sleeve, she looked into the valley again. "The two of you would stay here, right? In Heavenly?"

"Yah. If she will have me."

"Oh, she'll have you, I'm sure." It felt good to laugh, to savor the cool air against her exposed cheek, to shed her own worries and fears in favor of someone else's happiness. "Maybe One Heavenly Night will be just the place and time to ask her."

"That is not the Amish way."

"It could be."

He cleared his throat and then turned so he was facing her rather than his home. "So why did *you* come here tonight?"

And just like that, the lightness that came with the moment, and the distraction his presence had provided, disappeared, taking with it her laugh and her smile in rapid succession. "Nothing . . . special. I . . . I guess I just wanted a little fresh air after being cooped up all day."

"That is why you sit on your aunt's porch each night," Ben reminded her. *"After* you have *eaten dinner."*

"I had a lot to do at work." She closed her eyes against the memory of Mary's letter to Ruth. The doubt it had stirred in her heart for her friend was painful enough all on its own without admitting it aloud to the woman's brother. No, right now she needed Ben, needed his closeness and his friendship.

"Is it Jakob?" he asked, his voice cutting through the darkness like a blade.

Oh, how she wanted to say no. To assure him, as well as herself, that everything with the detective was as wonderful as ever. But she couldn't.

"Claire?"

Aware of the tears building behind her eyes, she nodded once — fast — and then looked back up at the sky. "Do you remember the very first time we sat out here and I made a wish on the brightest star?"

"You made two wishes. One was to live a simple life surrounded by love and family; the other was for us to figure out who was doing those things to Shoo Fly Bake Shoppe."

Stunned, she dropped her eyes to his. "You remember them?"

"Yah."

"Wow," she whispered.

"Both came true."

She started to speak but stopped so her heart could bask in the truth of his words a little longer.

"You have many people who love you, Claire."

"Thank you."

"And the problems at Shoo Fly were fixed."

"They *were . . .*" Then, not wanting the inflection in her voice to take them in a direction she wasn't prepared to go, she continued on, pointing his attention back to the sky and the brightest star she could find.

"If I were to make another wish, it would be for happiness to last forever."

"And it can't?"

The tightness in her throat was back. So, too, were the tears she refused to give an inch. "If I close my eyes to reality, it could. But I don't want to pretend. With anything. I wasted too many years of my life pretending I was happy when I wasn't, and it ate away at my confidence and my sense of self-worth. I won't go back there. Not again."

His answering silence seemed to echo through the bare branches, reminding her she was outside on a cold December night, wearing a jacket designed for style more than warmth. Yet before she could even shiver, his arm was around her shoulders, pulling her in for an awkward yet sweet side hug. "It is as you said about me and Rebeccah — that everyone sees how I am happy with her. It is the same for you and Jakob — everyone knows how happy you are with him."

"Because I was . . . *am.* That's not the issue here."

"Then what is?"

It was so tempting to tell him, to share everything she'd heard and seen on Lighted Way not more than thirty minutes earlier, but she couldn't. It was all too new, too raw, to share aloud just yet. Besides, she'd come here, to this spot, to get her head together and make a game plan, not to fall apart.

"The issue," she said, squaring her shoulders, "is that I'm stronger now. Smarter. I don't sit back and wonder about things anymore. If I want to know something, I find it out. If I can change something, I change it. If I can't, I put my efforts toward something I can. And that little voice inside my head? It's there for a reason, and I should listen to it. I just need to remember all of that and *keep on plugging away,* as Aunt Diane likes to say."

The silence returned, only this time, instead of looking up at the stars, Ben kept his eyes on Claire. After several beats, the skin around his eyes crinkled with a slow, knowing smile. "Even if I had not seen you since that first time on this rock, I would know your first wish had come true."

Her gaze, which had wandered back to the stars, shot back to his, waiting.

"It is clear that you are surrounded by love and family," he said.

"It is?"

"Yah. You are different now than you were back then."

Intrigued, she, too, turned her body to face him. "Different? Different how?"

"It is as you just said. You are stronger now. But you do not have to say that for me to know it. It is in how you carry yourself now. It is how your smile, when you are happy, is not just here" — he pointed to her mouth — "anymore. It is *here*" — he gestured first toward her eyes and then toward her chest — "*and here* now, too. And that is good."

She tried his words on for size and realized they fit. Perfectly. "Love and family makes all the difference, doesn't it?"

"Your aunt Diane is a good woman. I am glad you have her."

"I am, too. That woman has been a blessing to me for as long as I can remember. She is why I found my way here when everything fell apart. But she's not my only family here in Heavenly, not anymore."

His brow furrowed. "Oh? I did not know you had more kin here now."

"Kin? No. Aunt Diane is my only blood relation in this town. The rest of my blood family is scattered across the country. But blood isn't the only definer of family, not for me, anyway. It's also about being there through the ups and downs — lending an ear, a voice, a tissue, a hand, a cheer of encouragement. You've shown me that, as have Esther and Eli, Harold and Al, Annie

265

and Bill, and on and on. So yeah, that wish absolutely came true, and then some."

"You did not say Jakob."

Startled, she rewound through the names she'd shared in her head, and as she reached the last one, shame came knocking. Because no matter what was going on with him now, Jakob had played an enormous part in getting her to where she was at that moment. "You are right," she admitted, her voice suddenly choked with an avalanche of both gratitude and pain. "Jakob has been, and done, all of those things for me — and so much more. And I will be forever grateful to him for that."

She looked up at the stars one last time and then slid off the rock and onto her feet. "I think it's high time I left you to your own thoughts, don't you?"

"I am glad you came," he protested. "I have missed time like this with you."

"I have always believed that God puts certain people in your life at certain times. In my mind, I've always thought of those people as being His angels on the ground." She met and held his gaze. "That was you tonight, Ben."

CHAPTER 17

She let herself in through the back door and hung the car keys on the hook above the catch-all table in the small entryway that doubled as a mudroom. Here, like everywhere else in the inn, there was a place and an order to everything. Hooks for keys, open shelves for shoes and boots, a medium-size umbrella stand, a mail holder for both outgoing and incoming letters and parcels, and a spot where she and Diane left notes for each other when needed.

Slipping out of her coat, she glanced down at the powder blue note waiting for her on the table, Diane's calligraphy-like penmanship filling it from top to bottom.

Claire,
There is a bowl of beef stew wrapped and waiting for you in the refrigerator in the event you didn't eat. I saved a roll for you, too. Bill also made sure to set

aside two cookies for you, and those are on the counter. If you need me, and I happen to be asleep when you get in, knock on my door.

I love you.

Diane

"You'll be awake," she whispered, grinning. "You always are."

She hung her coat at her spot on the rack, heel-toed off her ankle boots, and carried the still-cold milk into the kitchen and over to the fridge. Sure enough, on the top shelf where the milk was supposed to go was a bowl of stew, just as the note had promised. And for the first time since her lunchtime visit from Annie, she felt as if she could actually eat.

Part of that, she knew, was her time outdoors with Ben — the fresh (albeit cold) air and peaceful surroundings working their usual magic on her body. But part of it, too, was simply taking a step back and forcing herself to look at things with a level head.

Ruth Miller wasn't a killer. She knew this, believed it with everything she was. But that wasn't all she knew. She also knew Ruth wasn't a liar. It wasn't in the girl's makeup to weave a story or turn on theatrics.

So as upsetting as that letter from Mary

had been, if Ruth said she'd never noticed the yellow envelope, then it was true. Someone else must have spotted it in the stack and opened it without Ruth knowing.

Claire swapped the milk for the stew and carried the bowl over to the microwave on the opposite side of the room. While her dinner heated up, she located the roll and butter, grabbed all necessary utensils from the drawer, and set them at her usual spot on the counter. A pad of paper and a pen from the telephone drawer rounded out her setting.

Soon, with her piping-hot stew at her elbow, she turned her attention to what she knew so far, stopping every few bites to jot notes.

Who opened the letter?

It was a fair question. So, too, was the answer she hated writing down.

Samuel.

Really, aside from Ruth, Samuel was the only other one that made sense. The letter holder had been given to both of them as a wedding gift. Which meant that both had access to it in the buggy and after they'd gotten home.

How long, by buggy and by foot, would it take to get from Ruth and Samuel's home back to the Esch farm? When did Ruth and Samuel leave (with their gift) in relation to the time of death? Would there have been enough time for them to get home, for Samuel to read the letter, and then to go back?

She pulled her bowl back in front of her and took a few more bites, her thoughts flocking to Samuel Yoder, a man she really didn't know all that well. Yes, she'd sat beside him at many business owners' meetings, and yes, he, too, had gotten on board with the One Heavenly Night plan the moment she verbalized it aloud for the first time, but what did she really know beyond the fact that he seemed nice?

"Not a lot," she murmured into the empty kitchen.

Then again, Ruth had married him. That alone should say something, shouldn't it?

Nodding at her silent question, she took another bite of stew and pulled her thoughts back to Ruth, who was shy, yes, but she was smart. Shoo Fly hadn't turned into the success it was simply because Ruth could bake a mean pie. Had that helped? Sure. But it was Ruth's instincts and her ability to read her customers that had been the real magic in her success. Someone who could do that was surely capable of spotting the kind of traits a killer would possess, right?

"Unless Samuel simply snapped out of desperation," she mused.

Pushing the bowl back off to the side, she grabbed her pen and the pad and began to write again.

How bad is Yoder's really hurting?
How bad is Shoo Fly really hurting?
Was Samuel in debt before the wedding?

She hovered her pen above the last question and considered crossing it out. The Amish weren't the type to get in debt. In fact, according to Aunt Diane, when the Amish got married and purchased their first house, they almost always had the kind of money socked aside to make a significant down payment.

But maybe Samuel was the exception since he owned a business? Shrugging, she let the question stand as she moved on to the next line.

If not Samuel, if not Ruth, then who?

She tried to think back to the cases Jakob

had shared with her during their time together — petty theft cases, insurance fraud, and murder. Looking at possible motives in relation to means had been a big help in many of those cases.

Pulling in a breath, she flipped the page over and slowly, line by line, wrote down the motives for murder she remembered Jakob sharing with her on more than one occasion, stopping after each one to add any possible tie to the Esch murders.

Hate crime. (They're Amish . . . could that be why?)

Robbery gone wrong. (Jakob said nothing was missing!)

Mob/gang/murder for hire/initiation. (No!)

Jealousy/obsession. (Samuel jealous of Daniel's success?)

Crime of passion. (Samuel's anger?)

Money/greed. (Assisted-living deal?)

She wasn't sure she had them all, but it was a place to start. Next came all possible means she could come up with in relation to Mary and Daniel Esch. Jakob had told her there was no sign of forced entry. Yes, a window had been left open to the elements, but it was unlocked, not broken. There was also nothing to indicate the couple had tried to get away, thus making it seem as if their killer was no stranger . . .

Ruth and Samuel.
An employee.
A neighbor.
A family member . . .

Jerking upright, Claire's spoon clattered onto the linoleum at her feet. Ruth and Samuel weren't the only suspects anymore. Abe was now, too, thanks to Annie.

Daniel winning the bid for Breeze Point didn't just hurt Ruth and Samuel. It hurt Abe, too. Only with Abe, it wasn't just about losing work. It was about something much deeper.

Her focus zipped back to the paper and the last two motives she'd noted.

Crime of passion. (Samuel's anger?)
Money/greed. (Assisted-living deal?)

Since a crime of passion could be anger based, didn't it stand to reason that Abe's name belonged on that line, as well as the last one, every bit as much as Samuel's? After all, based on what Tommy Warren had told her in the barn, Abe had been treated unfairly. Many times. Surely such treatment had created some good old-fashioned resentment and bitterness . . .

It made sense. A lot of sense, actually.

Add in the fact that Annie saw Abe running from the home as she and Henry arrived and, well, it was almost a no-brainer.

Grabbing the roll and her knife, she slit it open, slathered the inside with more butter than was probably prudent, and took a bite, the excitement mounting in the back of her head pushing its way to the forefront along with the early stages of a plan . . .

CHAPTER 18

In the daylight, the Chupp farm wasn't much different than most of the farms in Heavenly's Amish country. It had the same sparsely graveled driveway, the same German-style bank barn, the same dark green shades hanging in the farmhouse's second-floor windows, the same bike rack filled with scooter bikes, and the same hustle and bustle happening between house and barn that was as much a part of the Amish morning as a hearty breakfast.

It was only to the practiced eye of those who called Heavenly home, though, that the differences tied to this particular morning were so clear. Today, the field behind the barn that played host to grazing cows in the warmer weather resembled the kind of parking lot one might see at an outdoor concert pavilion. Only instead of rows and rows of cars, there were several lines of horseless buggies parked one behind the other. Off to the right and under a large white tent were dozens and dozens of horses, the day's frigid cold temperatures mandating the heavy blankets many, if not all, of them sported. Even from her own parking spot on the road, she could see the animals' breath dotting the air inside the tent.

Claire knew, from the handful of Amish funerals she'd attended to date, that the service would start soon, followed by the burial and a meal. Since she was a trusted Englisher with ties to Bishop Hershberger's daughter, her presence, while initially eyebrow-raising, wouldn't be unwelcomed, and for that she was glad.

Glancing at the dashboard clock, she picked up her phone and dialed the shop.

"Good morning, this is Heavenly Treasures, how can I help you?"

"You sound like a pro," Claire said, grinning.

Bill's laugh, strong and hardy, filled her ear. "I'm a quick study, I guess. And you, my dear, are what I imagine first-time parents are like when they leave their baby for the very first time."

"A first-time parent who is feeling way more guilt than worry," she corrected.

His laughter ceased. "Hey. I told you. I'm good with this. Really. Not only is it a way for me to help you out a little, it'll also give me a chance to see — firsthand — if owning a specialty shop in Heavenly is something I'd enjoy."

"Like you'd give up your travel agency in . . ." She stopped, sat up tall, and wandered her eyes back down the very road she'd taken to get to the Chupp farm. "Wait. Are you saying what I hope you're saying?"

"If you think I'm saying what I'm saying, then yeah, I'm saying what you hope I'm saying."

It was her turn to laugh. "Okay, that just made my head hurt."

"I can handle this, Claire — really," Bill said, his calm and reassuring presence on full auditory display. "Getting here when I did has given me plenty of time to figure out where everything is before I have to open. So just do what you need to do, find out what you need to find out, and I'll text you or call Diane if I run into any major issues."

"You're sure?"

"I'm sure. Oh, hey, Harold stopped by a few minutes ago and mentioned a tour bus that's due to arrive on Lighted Way around eleven thirty. He said that was a good thing because their likely first stop will be Taste of

Heaven(ly), thereby buying me a little more time before their arrival here."

Groaning, she dropped her head back against the seat. "Ugh."

"I've got this, Claire," he repeated. "Even if they get here earlier than expected."

Pulling in a breath, she held it, counted to ten in her head, and then released it along with the impossible notion of being in two places at one time. "Okay. Thank you."

"You're welcome, kiddo. See you soon." And then he was gone, the silence left in his wake leading her gaze across the street once again.

In just the time span she'd been on the phone — four, maybe five minutes — more buggies had arrived in the field, each one unhitched from its horse and left to wait until it was time for the long procession out to the cemetery. Mourners in black winter coats and head coverings — brimmed hats for the men, kapps for the women and girls — made their way up the driveway, the men splintering off to stand beside the barn, the women heading up to the house.

A flash of light drew her eyes to the rearview mirror and the morning sun glinting off the side panel of an approaching minivan. Like the others she'd seen turn into the driveway so far, it slowed to a crawl as it passed by, the driver clearly assessing the proper place for car traffic in relation to buggy traffic. Even with the tint on the windows, which made it impossible to see inside the minivan, she knew, when it stopped, that the side door would slide open and Amish would come flooding out, the drive to that particular farm, or the number of people needed to transport, simply too great to use a buggy.

She watched the minivan pull into the driveway, hesitate behind the line of other Amish taxis unloading their occupants, and then turn, slowly, into the field of buggies before parking, finally, in the far corner. Seconds turned to minutes as the side door remained closed, prompting her to look again at the dashboard clock: 7:45.

Grabbing her purse and keys, she stepped onto the road, locked the door, and made her way up the driveway, noting the continued arrival of more Amish as the service loomed closer. The men stood off to one corner of the yard, talking among themselves. The women, she knew, were in the Chupp home, where they'd remain for about another five minutes or so. At that time, they'd go into the barn and take their seats. Shortly after that, the men would begin filing in — ministers and older men first, followed by younger married men, and finally unbaptized boys. They, too, would take their seats, opposite the women and girls. In the center, between the gender-divided sections, Mary and Daniel would lie in death's repose in simple, unadorned open pine caskets.

She also knew there would be two sermons — a shorter one of about twenty minutes in length, and a longer one lasting about an hour. The Amish around her would sing from a special hymnbook that had no musical notes, just lines of text to which an almost chant-like tune — some lasting for as long as nearly thirty minutes — had been handed down across many generations.

At the completion of the three-hour service, the minister would recite Mary's and Daniel's names and say a prayer while the Amish and their guests walked past the deceased for one last look before the caskets were transported out to the wagons tasked with taking them to the cemetery.

While the family and others who wished to do so attended the burial, Claire and everyone else would remain behind at the Chupps' to visit over a meal. She couldn't say for sure, but she suspected Esther and Eli would stay behind rather than go to the cemetery on account of Sarah's size and the outdoor temperature. If they did, she would sit with them. If not, she'd find someone else. Either way, she hoped the more relaxed atmosphere surrounding the meal would provide an opportunity or two to learn more about Daniel and Mary's son and, perhaps, speak with him directly.

Even without using the notes she'd jotted down in the kitchen last night, Claire knew what she wanted to ask, what she wanted to know. She'd only gone over it a dozen times in her bed while trying to keep her thoughts from straying to the nightly call with Jakob that wasn't —

"It's Claire, right? From the other night?"

She stopped, mid-step, and turned toward the voice, the dark hair and eyes, coupled with the ill-fitting English suit and cheap dress shoes from the first night of the viewing, sending her limited theatrical ability into full-test mode.

"Yes, and you're Abe . . ."

His long, narrow chin dipped nearly to the collar of his shirt with his slow, labored nod.

"How are you holding up?" she asked, touching his arm.

"I'm not sure how to answer that other than I think I'm still in shock a little. I wasn't ready for this. I wanted Dat to see

Trish and I together, as adults, and I wanted them both to meet the baby when he's born."

Turning toward the field he'd just exited, Abe extended his hand to a hesitant yet pretty blonde in a simple black maternity dress heading in their direction. Behind her, by no more than a few feet, was a pair of familiar faces Claire recognized at once.

"Trish, I want you to meet someone." Abe pulled the pregnant woman closer and then released her hand in favor of draping an arm across her shoulder. "This is Claire — Claire Weatherly."

Trish's cat-green eyes widened between long, dark lashes. "Wait, this is the one you were telling me about last night, right? The one involved with the cop who invited you to the station yesterday so he could check on how you were doing?"

Check on him? Is that what Abe called being questioned in the double murder of his estranged parents?

If Trish caught the flush that preceded Abe's nod, she gave no indication. But Claire caught it. Before she could respond with anything intentionally yet subtly probing, though, Trish retraced her steps just far enough to accompany the slower-moving pair the rest of the way. "Mom, Tommy, this is Claire. She's —"

"I know Claire, dear." Nancy Warren sidled into the center of their makeshift circle, her own muted blue-green eyes crackling to life. "She owns that cute little gift shop on Lighted Way, and her aunt owns Sleep Heavenly."

"The bed-and-breakfast? Oooh, I have always wanted to know what it's like inside there. It looks so pretty from the outside," Trish gushed.

"It is. The parlor is my favorite room in the house." Claire glanced to her left, noted the Amish women entering the barn in groups, and hiked her purse farther onto her shoulder. "It looks like they'll be starting soon. Are you heading in?"

Stiffening, Abe followed Claire's gaze to the barn. "Is Jakob here yet?"

"I . . . I don't know that he's coming," she said, her words sticking in her throat.

"He said he was. Said he'd sit with me outside the barn."

Tommy snorted. "Ah, the two disgraces, sitting side by side, where no one has to look at them . . . How welcoming."

"Tom, please," Abe protested on an exhale. "They're my family. I need to be here."

"*We*'re your family, dude — Trishy, me, and Maw. Have been since the day the rest of them relegated you to being treated like *that.*" Tommy pointed at the single bench positioned outside the large barn doors.

"Tom, please," he repeated.

Shooting his hands into the air, Tommy took a temporary step backward. "Okay, okay, I'm done. Your call, your life. But Trish isn't sitting outside, in her condition, in this cold. It isn't gonna happen."

Abe pulled a face. "I had no intention of letting her sit outside, Tom." Gritting his teeth, he turned back to Claire, searching. "If it's not too much trouble, would you mind letting Trish and everyone sit with you? That way they know *someone*?"

"Goodness gracious, Abe Esch, I've been shuttling Amish around for decades in this town." Nancy planted her hands on her hips. "Why, I'm betting there isn't a single person in that barn right now that I haven't had in my van at some point in all those years. You don't need to be pushing us off on Claire like some sort of —"

"You'd be doing me a favor, actually," Claire said, hooking her thumb in the direction of the barn while slanting an understanding smile in Abe's direction. "But we really should get inside before the men go in."

"She's right." Abe pulled his wife in for a

quick hug. "I'll be fine."

"You'll freeze," Trish protested.

His broad shoulders rose and fell beneath his own dark coat. "I'll be fine. I promise. I'm just grateful Bishop Hershberger is allowing this at all."

"You're grateful he's making you sit outside on a bench all by yourself?" Tommy spat through clenched teeth. "Like some kind of diseased dog? Are you kidding? Are you even hearing yourself right —"

"He *won't* be alone."

Startled, Claire looked up as Jakob, dressed in a dark woolen coat over a navy blazer and khaki-colored dress pants, strode into place beside Abe, his strong, capable hand coming down on the young man's shoulder in a show of something that looked a lot more like understanding and quiet solidarity than suspicion.

"Jakob," Abe said, glancing at his wife. "You made it . . . Like you said yesterday when we talked . . . at the station . . ."

"I did." He reached into the front pocket of his dress coat, pulled out two thick pairs of department-issued gloves, and handed one to Abe. "I'm thinking we might want to put these on, don't you? Might help keep the feeling in our fingers a little longer . . ."

"Wow, yeah, thanks."

"My pleasure." Then, leaning forward, he whispered a kiss across Claire's forehead, his breath warm against her skin. "In case you're wondering, he asked me to keep our talk from his wife in light of her condition. So I'm honoring that for the time being. Also, I stopped by the shop on the way just now and Bill said you were already here. If I'd known you were coming, I'd have offered to stop by and pick you up so you didn't have to borrow Diane's car."

Claire knew she should say something, anything, but in the end, she simply turned and led Abe's wife and her family across the driveway and into the barn.

She found Esther the second she stepped off the cafeteria-style line with her turkey sandwich and piece of chocolate pie. The new mother was seated at a table not far from the Chupps' back door, gazing down at the bundled mound nestled inside the crook of her arm.

"Would you like some company?" Claire asked, bypassing her friend's look of surprise in favor of the sleeping infant she couldn't ignore if she tried. "Because I'd gladly trade you my sandwich *and* this pie for a chance to hold that sweet little girl for a while."

Esther's quiet laugh drifted upward, stealing a smile from Claire as it did. "You do not have to give me your food to hold Sarah."

"I know. But I'm guessing you didn't get anything for yourself on account of letting her sleep, yes?"

"There will be time to eat later," Esther said, looking back down at her baby. "When she is awake."

"When she's awake, you'll be too busy engaging her to eat then, either."

Esther's cheeks flushed with the truth. "Yah . . ."

"So let me have her, and you" — she set her plate down in front of Esther — "have this."

"But when will *you* eat?"

"When I have to give her back to you because she's not mine to keep." Lowering herself onto the bench, Claire worked her fingers between the baby and Esther's sleeve and slowly, carefully, pulled the baby to her chest. "Oh, Little One," she whispered. "You make all the bad things just disappear, don't you?"

Esther pulled her hand back from the sandwich to peer at Claire, worry donning lines across her otherwise smooth forehead. "What bad things?"

Claire lifted her gaze just shy of Esther's

before dropping it back down to Sarah. "Nothing in particular. Not really. It's just stuff like this, *here* — stuff that shouldn't be."

"He will know soon. Do not worry."

"He?" Claire asked, looking up.

"My uncle."

It took every ounce of energy she could muster not to crane her neck around in search of Jakob, but she succeeded. "What will he know?"

"Who did this awful thing to Mary and Daniel."

"You're not upset that he questioned Ruth?"

"Eli is not happy. Ruth is his twin sister. But I tell him it will not last. Soon, Jakob will know. Because of you."

"Me?" she echoed, necessitating a quick bounce of her arms to keep Sarah contentedly sleeping. "What are you talking about?"

"Ruth told me of your visit yesterday. The questions you asked. She told me you want to help my uncle find the truth. That is why I say Jakob will know soon. Because you will see that he does."

"I'm trying, Esther, I really am, but . . ." She gazed down at the baby. "What happens if Eli and Ben can't forgive Jakob for talking to Ruth about this in the first place?

What you guys have managed to build behind closed doors means the world to him."

"Ben does not know — Ruth does not want him to know. And Eli? He will be fine, in time. I will see to it that he is." Esther stopped, took a bite of her sandwich, and released a tiny moan of pleasure. "Mmm . . . Did you hear my stomach during the service?"

"No . . ."

"It sounded like yours would when you would open the window by the alley and the smells from Ruth's baking would come into the shop. I tried to use Sarah to cover the noise, but I do not think it worked, since Hannah had to hide a smile." Esther took a second and third bite and then rested the remaining food back on the plate. "I had hoped you would come into the barn sooner so you could sit near me, but you did not."

"I'm sorry. I would have liked that, too, but I thought it best to sit with Nancy and her kids. So they'd feel a little less out of place, I guess."

Esther scrunched her nose up tight. "*Everyone* here knows Nancy and her children. When we do not want to take our buggies to the doctor or a store, Nancy is one who takes us. Even when I was little,

Mamm and Dat would pay Nancy to take us places we had to go. It is that way for many here today."

Dividing her attention between mother and baby, Claire soaked up her friend's words, the journey they'd taken her on bringing her up short. "Wait. You're twenty-three now, right?"

"Twenty-four."

"Twenty-four," she repeated, casually taking in the tables to their left and right while her thoughts wandered in a different direction altogether. "So does that mean you grew up with Mary and Daniel's children?"

"Mary and Daniel had many that are much older than I am. But Greta and Abe, they were only a few years older."

Bingo.

"Are you friends with them?" she asked, only to realize her mistake in conjunction with Abe's banning. "I mean, with Greta, anyway?"

Poking at a piece of turkey overhanging the edge of her sandwich, Esther lowered her chin to the top of her coat and her voice to a volume Claire had to strain to hear. "She was a few years older than I was in school, so she was always with the older girls. But Abe was my friend. He was kind and he was gentle, and we would share

cookies from our lunch pails at recess sometimes."

Kind . . .

Gentle . . .

"Were you surprised when he left the
church after being baptized?" Claire asked.

"I was surprised it got to that."

"Meaning?"

"The old bishop . . . He did not see."
Then, as if fearing she'd crossed some sort
of invisible line, Esther sat up tall and
reached for her sandwich, her voice still
hushed. "It was nice to see Abe today, even
if I could only see a little bit of his face and
his hair through the crack of the barn door."

"I would imagine such treatment might
anger Abe."

Esther shrugged. "Abe was not one to
anger. It was not his way."

"Perhaps his way is different now that he
is English."

Glancing down at her sandwich, Esther
seemed to consider Claire's words. "Perhaps
you are right."

"But you don't think so?" she prodded.

"I do not believe Abe's heart would
change simply because he is no longer
Amish."

The baby stirred in Claire's arms but did
not wake. "So you don't think less of him?

For leaving?"

"I think it is sad. He worked hard, tried hard." Esther looked beyond Claire toward the barn. "But still, I am glad he was here."

"Bishop Hershberger allowed him to come. He sat with Jakob on a bench outside the barn."

"I am sorry Jakob could not be inside with you. But it was for the best today."

"Today?" she asked, following Esther's gaze to a plump Amish woman exiting the house with a plate of sandwiches in one hand and a basket of fruit in the other.

Esther lowered her sandwich back to the plate. "The Chupps do not think well of my uncle. If it was not for the bishop, he would not have been allowed on the property."

"Jakob has been to Amish funerals before. The Amish just turn their backs."

"That is not enough for Lloyd and Greta," Esther said, her voice barely more than a whisper. "They are very strict to the Ordnung."

Claire glanced back at their host and took a moment to really soak her in — the black coat, the matching winter covering atop her kapp, the sullen lines around her mouth and eyes so unlike that of either of her parents. "Then it must kill her that her brother left after baptism."

"It was Mary who was sad, not Greta." Esther's eyes led her on a brief tour of their surroundings before settling on a tall, lanky man in a black hat and black coat, standing, arms crossed, in a circle of Amish men, his eyes darting around the grounds while clearly hanging on every word his brethren were speaking. "For Greta and Lloyd Chupp, it is not enough to just turn backs to those under the ban. For them, it is as if those like Abe and Jakob are dead."

"But they're not dead," Claire protested. "They're right here. In the same town."

Shrugging, Esther retrieved her sandwich. "That is why I am glad my uncle did not sit inside the barn today, even if it meant he could not sit with you as he would want to."

The words, their meaning, the naiveté behind them, were like a punch to the stomach. "It was . . . fine. It was better this way."

Esther stopped, mid-chew. "It was *better*? To have Jakob outside?"

Uh-oh.

"With Abe," she rushed to add. It wasn't the whole truth, of course, but she wasn't ready to wiggle that loose tooth just yet. Besides, she was there to learn what she could about the one suspect who could bump Ruth and Samuel off the list completely, not engage in the kind of conversation that would have her bawling in no time. "So what about now?" she asked. "Do you ever see him anymore? Now that he's English?"

"No. I have not seen him since he left. I see only Greta now."

Again, Claire's gaze returned to the food table and the woman who'd lost both her parents to a senseless act of violence. "I've never heard you mention her before today . . ."

"I see her on Sundays when there is church in our district, but that is the only time. Eli does not think well of the Chupps."

"Is it because of their strictness?"

Like a periscope rising from the ocean's waters, Esther straightened her shoulders and her neck; scanned the tables, the yard, and the farmhouse doorway; and then pushed the plate and its pie in front of Claire. "Lloyd and Greta like to make problems where there are none. That is why Eli does not speak when Lloyd is near, why he will only stand near him when others — like Benjamin — are there, too. He says when others are near, Lloyd cannot say things were said that were not said, or say things were done that were not done.

"Perhaps if Abe had done that, too, he

would have been in the barn today with Mary and Daniel instead of sitting on a bench, trying to see them for the last time through the crack of a door."

CHAPTER 19

Claire was halfway down the driveway when she spotted the twenty-something pacing back and forth behind the barn, smoking a cigarette as if his life depended on it. That voice in her head, the one that knew she should have been back at the shop an hour ago, told her to keep walking — to make her way to the bottom of the driveway . . . to cross the street . . . to get in the car.

But it was the other voice, the one dictated by her own endless curiosity that won in the end, pulling her off her intended path and putting her square onto the one Tommy Warren was practically wearing into the ground.

"So how is Abe holding up?" she asked, stepping around the corner of the barn.

Startled, Tommy stopped, took an elongated drag on his cigarette, and then dropped it onto the ground, toeing it into smithereens. "I don't know. I offered to go out to the cemetery with him after the caskets were in the ground, but he opted to follow behind the procession with that cop you're dating."

"But everyone from the procession came back thirty minutes ago. At least."

"Everyone except Abe and your cop."

It was on the tip of her tongue to correct his choice of pronoun in relation to talk of Jakob, but she wasn't there yet. In time, yes, but not yet. Instead, she peered around the edge of the barn toward the tables and chairs still inhabited by more people than one might expect, considering the gathering clouds and dropping temperature. Sure enough, the search she'd refused to make prior to that moment yielded no sign of Jakob or Abe. "They sat outside on that bench for three hours. Maybe they drove into town to grab a bite to eat where it was warm."

"Abe wouldn't do that without checking in first." Tommy pulled a pack of cigarettes from his pocket, fished out the last smoke, and let it dangle between his lips while he retrieved his lighter. "*Especially* when he knows we're waiting here for him," he corrected, thumbing the needed flame to life.

Nodding, she traveled her gaze toward the field beyond, the stark brown of the harvested earth stirring a listlessness inside her. "I love this time of year for the holidays, but it always seems kind of wrong when the fields look like this. They're supposed to be lush and green and filled with promise."

Tommy's answering laugh echoed around them. "You haven't been out here before, have you?"

"I'm in Amish country all the time."

"Nah, I'm talking here" — he pointed his now-lit cigarette at the ground — "at Chupp's."

"I was here the other night, same as you, remember? For the viewing?"

"I meant during the day."

"Then no."

"I figured as much. Because that field right there" — he led her eyes back to the field with his chin — "won't look any different come spring."

"Why not?"

"Because Lloyd farms like he does everything else."

"Meaning?"

"He doesn't. He just waits for the magic wand to do it for him."

It was her turn to laugh. "As if."

"Exactly. But folks feel bad for Greta, so they buy her jams and jellies, and throw just enough odd jobs in Lloyd's direction so that they don't have to sell or move . . . yet." He took a quick drag of nicotine, his jaw tensing. "But Abe? The one who works like a dog all the time? Who still, even now, won't speak ill about any of them? Yeah, *he*'s the one who's made to sit on a bench in thirty-degree weather for three hours to mourn people who turned their back on him . . . And the kicker? *He does it!*"

It was a frustration and an anger she knew every bit as well as the tightness moving its way up her throat. "I struggle with the whole banning thing, too. All the time. But it's what Abe knows, what he was raised to believe. Like Jakob."

"Yeah, well, if you ask me, Abe's too good for all of them."

"You and Abe are really close, aren't you?"

"We are. Trishy, too. Been that way for years." He inhaled hard, exhaled harder. "Maw said it was like we filled the hole our dad left in our hearts with Abe."

"Did you?"

He flicked some ash onto the ground and then took another drag. "I don't know. Seems like psychobabble to me. We were just kids from very different worlds having fun together. I mean, going to Abe's house was like going to Disneyland for me and Trishy. We'd be outside for hours; chasing barn cats, jumping into hay, and running for what seemed like miles without having to watch for cars. It was fun, you know?"

"Always the three of you?"

"When we were little, yeah. Then, when we got a little older, it was more just Abe and me for a while. Trishy was always smarter than me, more driven. She had all these big ideas for her life. So while she was off doing things, I was sticking like glue to what I knew."

"Meaning Abe?"

Tommy nodded. "Abe was driven, too. But he knew I had nothing — not the grades, not the drive, not the anything."

Claire leaned against the aging wood at her back. "I don't believe that. Everyone is good at something. It's just a matter of finding what that something is."

"You sound like Maw." He took another, longer drag and then resumed his trek from one corner of the barn to the other, his pace a little calmer, a little slower. "Abe is the one who helped me find it."

"You mean the thing you're good at?"

Tommy nodded.

"In cabinetry, right?" she prodded.

Tommy reached the corner farthest from Claire and then spun back around. "More or less. He talked Daniel into letting me hang around them while they worked. And little by little, I got the hang of what they were doing and how I could fit."

"And how was that?"

"At first, it was about trying to make things run more smoothly. Like getting them the right tools when they asked for them instead of just handing them whatever was closest and slowing the process down, like Lloyd was always doing. And then actually retaining what they told me from one day to the next." He flicked a line of ash onto the ground next to his boot, curled the remaining cigarette inside his thumb, and held his palm up, revealing what looked to be faded paint nestled in the lines of his hand. "One day, I stayed late because I had nothing else to do. I knew one of the orders needed to be painted and Lloyd wasn't gonna get it done in time, so I picked up a brush and did it myself. Daniel thought I did a good job and had me paint another set, too. Back then, I just painted everything whatever color Daniel told me to use. A customer wanted white cabinets, I gave them white. They wanted green, I gave them green. But as Abe began to get more creative with the design of the cabinets, I started getting more creative with the paint brush.

"We had a good thing going," he said,

tossing the cigarette onto the ground. "Until Abe started getting shunned for stuff he wasn't doing."

Bingo . . .

"And he just took that?" Claire prodded. "He didn't argue? Didn't plead his case?"

"He tried, but the lies kept coming."

"And that's when he started actually doing the things he was accused of doing? The drinking and stuff?"

"Yep."

"So Abe just gave up?" she argued.

"When Daniel found him doing the very thing Abe had denied doing for so long, yeah, he gave up. And it was a free fall from there." Tommy reached into his pocket, looked inside the empty cigarette pack, and shoved it back inside, disappointed. "Until Maw got ahold of him and he finally sobered up."

"You said something the other night, about him getting to talk to Mary at some point?"

Tommy's shrug was limp at best. "All I know is they talked and he put everything out on the table for her — the shunnings he hadn't earned, the way they affected him, and why, ultimately, he left."

"What did she say?"

"I don't know. He didn't tell me."

"But you two are best friends . . ."

"No doubt. But he knew how I felt about them and how riled up I got anytime he tried to see their point. Drove me nuts."

"So he shared no real specifics from their conversation? No actual words?"

"I know he went ahead and told her he'd been dabbling in cabinet work again, and that he and I were going to bid that Breeze Point job as Abe's Custom Woodworking." Tommy stared out over the open field, his eyes hooded. "Turns out that was a big mistake. He told his mamm, she told Daniel, and — wham! — we were undercut by the *newly resurrected* Esch Cabinetry, only now they were calling themselves Esch Custom Woodworking. Cruel all on its own, sure, but magnified a thousandfold when you stop to consider the fact they were now hurting Abe's unborn son, too."

Abe's unborn son . . .

That was it. The missing piece — the moment the present and the past had collided with such force the misjudged son Esther had called kind and gentle had finally snapped.

A chill like nothing she'd ever felt before reverberated deep inside her core. Everything he was saying, everything she was hearing, pointed to Abe as the —

"Oh . . . hey . . . are you cold?" Before she could speak, before she could even nod, Tommy shoved his hand into his coat pocket, felt around, and pulled out a single folded black glove, his brow furrowed in confusion. "Okay, well, I'm not sure where I left the other one, but here . . . take this. At least one of your hands will be warm."

Looking back, Claire wasn't entirely sure how she'd managed to extricate herself from behind the Chupps' barn without arousing Tommy's suspicions. She had a vague recollection of faking an incoming text and then saying she had to get back to the shop, but considering her current mental state and the way her lungs were protesting her sudden need to run, rather than walk, to her car, it was more than a little possible she'd just up and took off.

Either way, she was less than ten strides from her car and no more than a mile — tops — from an answer she both wanted and didn't want all at the same time. If she was right, Abe hadn't killed his parents. That, in and of itself, was a victory when everything besides the killing pointed to him as a good and decent guy. But if she was right for the reason she suspected, it just meant Abe was about to be saddled with even more pain than he already knew.

Slowing to a walk, she made a visual sweep of the field across the street, her mind's eye making short work of the few buggies that remained. In warmer months, the people who had assembled for Daniel and Mary's funeral service might have lingered even longer over food and conversation. But today, the frigid temperature and impending winter storm had mourners beginning to flock to their buggies. She wished she could tell one buggy from the next the way the Amish were so often able to do, but even without that ability, she was fairly certain Annie's was not one of the ones that remained. That meant the teen was either at her house with her bishop father or, perhaps, relieving Bill from his temporary duties at Heavenly Treasures.

"Whoa! Don't take another step . . . You're *not* getting away this time, beautiful lady . . ."

She stopped, squeezed her eyes closed against the traitorous flutter in her chest, and then slowly turned, her eyes meeting Jakob's through his open passenger side window. "Oh . . . hey."

"I tried to find you when I got back from the cemetery, but Esther was under the impression you'd already left."

"Esther spoke to you?"

He shrugged. "Not in words, no. But after my second or third trek around the house, she caught my attention with a well-timed cough and a pointed glance in this direction. But just as I was heading out to find you, I saw an opportunity to talk to Eli and I took it."

"Uh-oh. How'd that go?"

"About what you'd expect at first. He stood there, looking across the fields, steam practically coming out of his ears. But I talked him through my job as a detective and why I can't cut corners. Ever. I also told him I don't believe Ruth had anything to do with this."

She felt her body sag against the car in relief. "And Samuel? What about him? Are you ready to cross him off your list, too?"

"Barring some explosive evidence I'm not privy to at this moment, yeah. He's essentially off already, anyway."

Tucking her hand into her jacket's front left pocket, she fingered her phone, her thoughts zeroing in on the picture of Ruth's letter she'd yet to share with Jakob. She knew she should show him, but in light of the item in her other pocket, she opted to hold off just a little longer.

"I know I should take his name off the

board completely, but the second I do that, I'm down to Abe," Jakob continued. "A guy who was spotted at the scene, had a contentious past with the victims, and had been beaten out by one of them for a job he both wanted and needed. He is, in a word, *perfect* for the crime."

"You don't seem too happy about that . . ."

His gaze traveled off her face and onto the road in front of them. "I like the guy. I don't *want* it to be him."

It was on the tip of her tongue to tell him it wasn't, but to do so would open herself up to questions she wasn't ready to answer. Not yet, anyway. Besides, on the off chance she was confusing the whole glove thing with something she'd read in one of Aunt Diane's paperback mystery novels, it was best to wait.

"But . . ." He waved away the rest of his sentence and, instead, rested his head against the back of his seat. "Fortunately for me, Eli's immediate focus is his sister. So when I said I didn't believe she had any involvement in the murders, the anger he was harboring for me seemed to drain right out of him."

"I'm glad." And she was. Because no matter what was going on between her and

Jakob, she wanted better for him than Abe had had. She wanted him to know that he still mattered to his family even when the rules they abided by in life told them he shouldn't. Everyone deserved that. Navigating life without that certainty was simply unfathomable to her.

"Hey, I'm really sorry about bailing on our call last night, but it couldn't be helped."

She felt her eyebrow rise at his wording. *It couldn't be helped?* Really?

"Needless to say, when I finally got into bed, I spent the next hour or so staring at the wall, wishing it was next week and . . ." He sat up straight. "Anyway, I better get back to the office. Maybe, with any luck, something's come in on the tip line or from some misplaced crime scene report that'll let me go after someone — *anyone* — other than Abe Esch for these murders."

Deep down inside, even knowing Abe's suspect status was good for Ruth and Samuel, she realized she hadn't really wanted it to be him, either. Yes, she'd gone looking for dirt on him, but it hadn't felt right. After all, Abe had picked himself up off the ground . . . He was married . . . He had a baby on the way . . . He had people who loved and believed in him no matter what . . . And Esther had always liked him . . . Guys like that weren't supposed to be killers. They were supposed to be happy.

But as she slipped her hand into her right pocket alongside Tommy Warren's mateless leather glove, she knew Abe's happiness was about to be shaken to the core.

CHAPTER 20

Annie was staring up at the ornament tree when Claire stepped back into the shop, her cheeks and hands cold from her brief trip into the alley. "If I could actually feel my fingers *and* you weren't Amish, I'd take a picture of you right now," she said, leaning against the open doorway. "You've got the Christmas glow I love to see on people at this time of year."

"I sometimes wish Dat and I could have a tree like this. The lights and the ornaments are so pretty." Annie reached up, tilted a newly arrived ornament bearing the Heavenly, Pennsylvania, name toward her for a closer look, and then let it dangle back down into place. "But it is not the Amish way."

"You get to have one here, though, right?"

"Yah."

Claire pushed away from the wall to right an overturned novelty sign and then joined

310

Annie by the tree. "I swung by your house when I left the funeral to see if you were there, but your dat said you'd come here."

Annie drew back in surprise. "You stopped at my house?"

"I did. I wanted to show you something."

"I'm sorry I was not there to greet you."

"It's okay, kiddo. Honestly, knowing you the way that I do, I should've realized you'd be here . . ."

"Yah. It is a busy time at the shop. I did not want you to work alone anymore."

A quick inspection of the tree's lowest branches had her removing a few doubled-up ornaments and spreading them around more evenly. "Bill was a godsend offering to man the shop so I could go to the funeral service today."

"He was dusting the counter when I came in," Annie said. "And he was whistling."

She had to laugh at the note of surprise in the teen's voice. "That's Bill for you. Nothing ever seems to rattle him."

"So he is gone now?"

"Yup, he's gone," Claire said. "Just walked him out myself."

Nodding, Annie took one last look at the tree and then turned and headed toward the register. "I will get to work on the clipboard. Perhaps if it stays quiet like it is right now, I can get everything on the day's list done."

"There is no list," she said, following in the girl's footsteps. "Not today."

"What about yesterday's list? When I wasn't here, either?" Annie reached across the top of the counter and plucked the clipboard from its nail. "I can do some of those things."

"I kept it light while you were gone. I figured any quiet windows of time would go toward festival prep. Or at least, that was the plan . . ."

Annie's brow furrowed as she scanned the various displays and sections around the shop. "You did not have to restock?"

"Oh, I restocked, alright. During those so-called quiet windows I thought I'd have more of."

Shame dove Annie's gaze to the floor. "I am sorry, Claire. I know it is a busy time for you with the shop, and the festival, and all of your decorating."

"Hey . . . hey . . ." Claire hooked a finger underneath the girl's chin and nudged it upward. "Life happens, kiddo. No one could have predicted Mary's and Daniel's deaths."

"*One* could."

Claire looked over her shoulder, took in the light foot traffic along the sidewalk, and then guided Annie over to the stools. "We need to talk . . . It's important."

"Have — have I done something wrong?" Annie asked, aborting her plans to sit. "Because I can stay later or come in earlier to make up for what I have missed these past few days."

Pressing her finger to Annie's lips, she shook her head. "Shhh . . . You're fine. Great, even." She dropped her hand to her side and, when Annie was situated on a stool, rocked back on her heels and used the counter for support. "I need to ask you about the night you went Christmas caroling and found Mary and Daniel."

"I did not like that night," Annie whispered.

"I know. But for now I want to ask specifically about something I think you might have said when you called me from the Esch farm."

"Did I say something wrong?"

"No. I'm just not sure if what I'm remembering came from you that night, or if I've been reading too many of those cozy mysteries my aunt has all over the house."

At Annie's blatant confusion, she moved on. "You were telling me about that moment when you and Henry first noticed the window was open and how you thought that

313

was odd because of how cold it was out-side."

"It was very cold that night," Annie said, shivering at the memory.

"You said you looked inside . . ."

"Henry got the lantern from his buggy."

"Yes. And do you remember what you saw when he shined it up to the window?"

Annie's shoulders sagged just before her whole body shuddered at the memory. "We saw Mary and Daniel lying on the floor."

Claire stepped in beside Annie and draped an arm across her shoulders. "But you saw other things first, right? Before you actually saw *them*?"

"Yah. I saw a chair — it was on its side. And there was a dish next to it. Chicken and potatoes were on the floor."

It was her turn to sag. "And that was it? You didn't see anything else?"

"That is all."

So it was back to Abe again. Only now, thanks to her conversation with Tommy, all the stray pieces of the puzzle suddenly slid right into place . . .

"I really need to stop reading before bed. I think my brain takes stuff from these stories and merges it in with my day's re-ality sometimes." She gave Annie a quick squeeze and then wandered back to the counter. "I thought you'd said something about a glove and —"

"Yah. There was a glove — a worker's glove. It was on the ground outside the window."

She spun back to Annie. "Just one?"

"Yah."

"And you say it was a worker's glove?"

"Yah."

"What do you mean by a worker's glove?"

"Because it is one an Englisher would wear — like your Jakob or Mr. Glick." Annie smoothed her basic dress across her lap, her head cocked in thought. "He must have dropped one when he was picking up a cabinet or something."

"Did you show the glove to Jakob when he came to the scene?"

"No, I was not worried about a glove when Jakob came."

"Did Henry?"

Annie pulled a face. "I know only that when Henry went inside, I held the glove for him. Later, when Jakob and the other police were on the way and we were waiting in his buggy, I set it on his seat. I do not remember him showing it to Jakob, but it was not important."

Au contraire . . .

"Do you think you'd remember the glove

315

if you saw it?" she asked.

"I think so." Annie's face grew pinched. "Did Jakob lose a glove? Is that why you are asking such things?"

"No, I came across one that I think might be its match. It is in the pocket of my . . ."

The rest of her sentence faded from her lips as the front door jingled and Jakob stepped inside, breathing against his fisted hands. He swept his gaze across the room, its trademark sparkle igniting when he spotted Claire. "I thought it was cold earlier, out at Chupp's, but it's even colder now."

"I will leave you two alone for a few minutes," Annie said, slipping down off the stool. "I will see if it is as I remember."

And then the teen was gone, her simple black lace-up boots making nary a sound as she made her way toward the back hallway, her quick glance and single nod in Jakob's direction an improvement.

"I didn't mean for Annie to leave."

"She . . ." Claire swallowed. "She needed to check something in back for me."

He dropped his fingers to the top edge of his jacket and unzipped it to the bottom. "According to the guy from Channel Five, we're looking at close to a foot of snow tonight."

"Oh . . . wow . . . that's a lot."

She could feel him watching her as she returned the clipboard to its nail, waiting, no doubt, for a bigger, more Claire-like reaction to his weather report, but she had nothing.

"Claire? Is everything okay? You seem upset. Troubled. Is something going on I don't know about?"

She paused her hands on the edge of Annie's stool, closed her eyes to a silent count of ten, and then opened them to find Jakob studying her closely from the other side of the counter. "I'm pretty sure I'm the one that should be asking you that last question."

"I'm not upset," he said, closing the gap between them. "A little preoccupied with this case right now, but I'm not —"

"That's not the question I was referring to." In a different time, and a different place, she might have marveled at how calm she sounded, but in the moment, it was more about wanting to keep her voice down for Annie's benefit than anything else.

He pulled up about a foot from the counter, the quick side-to-side of his eyes a clear indication he was thinking. "Then what question are you . . . wait. There's not anything going on with me that —"

"Claire?"

Forcing a smile to her face and a lightness to her voice, she held Jakob's gaze for another moment and then turned toward Annie. "Yes, kiddo? What's up?"

"It is the same."

"What is?"

Annie pulled her hand from behind her back and opened it to reveal a neatly folded piece of black leather. "Your glove. I think it is just like the one we found outside Mary and Daniel's the night we went caroling."

The thudding in her chest was back.

So, too, was Jakob's voice, his words thundering across the room. "You saw a glove at the scene?" In a flash he was by Annie's side, his gaze ricocheting between Annie, Claire, and the glove. "Why didn't I know this?"

"It — it was just dropped."

"Where?" he barked.

"On the way to the window," Annie said, her voice trembling.

Jakob's jaw tightened. "The window the killer may have used to get inside the house?"

"I . . . I . . ." Annie backed into the wall. "I do not understand."

"This is it? The one you found?"

"I . . . I think so. Perhaps Henry will know for certain."

"Henry knew about this, too?"

Claire rushed forward, putting herself between the detective and the frightened teen. "She and Henry clearly didn't realize what they had, Jakob. It was an honest mistake."

He turned angry eyes her way. "And you? You've had this in your possession this whole time and you didn't say anything?"

"No!" She plucked the glove from Annie's shaking hand and held it inside her own. "Today, after the meal at Lloyd and Greta Chupp's, I was speaking with someone behind the barn. He saw that I was cold and he offered me his gloves. Only, when he reached into his pocket, there was only one. Something about his surprise and the way he patted his coat looking for the other one tickled a memory of something Annie said when she called me from the scene. It was so out of left field I actually began to think I was crazy, that she hadn't mentioned a glove at all. So I asked her just now — right before you came in."

"Who gave it to you, Claire?"

"Tommy Warren."

The name pushed him back a step. "Tommy Warren?"

"Yes."

Palming his mouth, he stared at the glove

in Claire's hand. "Where is the other one?" he rasped, looking up. "The one that was dropped?"

Claire led his troubled gaze back to the girl cowering against the wall. "Annie, sweetie? Do you know what happened to the glove you found that night?"

"I set it on Henry's buggy seat, but I do not know where it is now. Perhaps Henry will know . . ."

CHAPTER 21

The click of the chief's door at the end of the hall drifted into the room and brought Claire to her feet. She'd tried to talk to Jakob on the ride out to the Stutzman farm, but between his calls to dispatch and the questions he kept firing at Annie in the back seat, there hadn't been an opportunity.

The talk with Henry had been extensive, the bewildered teenager's initial shrug in reaction to Jakob's inquiry about the glove quickly bowing to the answers he couldn't seem to give fast enough.

Yes, he'd picked up a glove on the way over to Daniel and Mary's window . . .

Yes, he'd handed it to Annie when he saw the tipped-over chair and the spilled food . . .

No, he hadn't thought to show it to Jakob that night — why would he? It was just a glove someone had dropped. Daniel and Mary were dead . . .

He didn't even remember finding it until they'd gotten back into the buggy after they'd been released and he saw it on the seat . . .

And finally, yes, he was pretty sure it was still in his buggy somewhere — perhaps underneath the horse blanket he'd used to keep Annie warm on the ride to and from Sleep Heavenly later that same night . . .

Claire and Annie had followed Jakob and Henry out to the barn and waited while Henry searched the immaculate interior of his late father's buggy. When he got to the checkered horse blanket he kept folded on the floor in front of the back seat, he pulled it out and, with Annie's help, opened it, fold by fold, until, on the last fold, a blur of black leather and stitching fell onto the hay-strewn ground at his feet.

Even from her spot some six or seven feet away she'd known, in an instant, it was a perfect match to the one clutched in Jakob's hand. The size, the stitching, the wear pattern, all of it . . .

And as she'd stood there, staring, yet another snippet from yet another seemingly inconsequential conversation came flooding back, rooting her feet to the barn floor.

"The day Abe left that farm for good was the last time I stepped foot on that farm or his

sister's. Maw says I should forgive, that a job is a job. But I'd sooner riffle through a garbage can for food than make so much as a penny driving the likes of any of them around."

It was a comment she knew Jakob would want to hear, but there simply hadn't been time. Yet.

Now, using the precious seconds she had before her first sighting of him in more than twenty minutes, she wiped her hands against her dress slacks and took in a steadying breath.

"Hey," he said, breezing into the room with a folder in one hand and her phone in the other. "Sorry to leave you alone in here for so long, but the chief wanted to see the gloves, and then I had to talk him off the notion of filing charges against Henry and Annie."

"Charges?" she echoed with a gasp. "For what?"

He elbowed his chair away from the desk enough to sit, his gaze pinning hers with a look she couldn't quite identify. "He wanted tampering with evidence."

"Henry and Annie didn't tamper with evidence! They didn't know that glove *was* evidence."

"It was found at the scene — steps away from the point of entry. It was evidence."

323

He dropped the folder and pen onto the desk and himself into the chair. "They should have said something."

"Annie *did.*"

"*To me,*" he added. "Not you."

Recovering the answering gape of her mouth, she teed her hands in the air. "Those two kids didn't realize that glove was evidence, Jakob. You heard them! They just thought someone lost a glove under the tree when they were picking up a delivery for Daniel."

"You could have some charges, too, Claire. For obstructing a case. Twice."

She dropped her hands to her side. "Look, I know I should have shown you Mary's letter to Ruth as soon as I read it yesterday, but I . . . I froze. I was afraid it was evidence against Ruth, and I didn't want it to be. But I was going to tell you — I *did* tell you."

"Yeah, *thirty minutes ago,* on the car ride back from Henry's . . ." He handed her back her phone.

"I'm sorry. I really am." She took a fortifying breath and pressed on, her head reeling. "In terms of this thing with Tommy, I didn't even remember Annie mentioning the glove until this afternoon, and when I did, I thought there was a chance I was confusing it with something I'd read in a book."

"Again, you didn't come to me . . ."

"And if I had, and it really was something I'd read? That wouldn't have been a waste of your time?" She leaned forward, braced her hands on the edge of the desk so her eyes were level with his. "I literally found out, not more than two minutes before you walked into my shop this afternoon, that Annie had, in fact, mentioned finding a lost glove the night they found the bodies. And you were there when she came out and told me she thought the one I had was a match to the one she'd found!"

He looked down at the closed folder as a weighted silence fell between them, the only discernible sound in the room coming from the rhythmic tick tick of his wall clock. Finally, he held up his hands in surrender. "I'm sorry. I get it. I really do. I get that you wanted to process the letter, maybe even figure out who'd seen it all on your own. But you can't do that, Claire. It's my job to follow the evidence."

"I know. I'm sorry."

Dropping his forearms onto his desk, he met and held her gaze. "You would have called me about the glove if I hadn't shown up when I did, right?"

Would she have? She wasn't sure.

She might have gone out to Henry's on

her own . . .

She might have —

No.

"Yes. I would have called," she said, reclaiming the chair opposite his. "It would have been with a heavy heart, but I'd have called you."

Relief chased the question from his eyes and he dropped back against his chair, his fingers finding and kneading his temples on a long, labored sigh. "Heavy, why?"

"Because Abe just lost his parents . . . and Tommy is his family, too . . ."

"I know."

She, too, leaned back in her chair. "He told me he hasn't stepped foot on the Esch farm since the day Abe left."

Jakob's laugh held no humor. "His missing glove says otherwise."

"Abe is like a brother to him," she sighed. "He loves Abe. Why would he kill the guy's parents?"

"*Because* he loves him, that's why."

"I don't get it." But even as she said the words, she knew they weren't true. She didn't want to get it, but she did.

Tommy loved Abe so much, the thought that Daniel and Mary could intentionally set out to hurt him again via a bid no one saw coming had likely stirred his anger to

326

such a boiling point he'd exacted revenge.

"By killing them, Tommy just hurt Abe more. How could he not see that?" she asked.

"He was blinded by his anger to the point where he wasn't able to see the irony of what he was about to do." Sliding his hands between his head and the back of the chair, he looked up at the ceiling, his voice cloaked with sadness. "That's the way it is with most crimes of passion. They make little to no sense to anyone but the one perpetrating the crime. It's sad on so many levels."

"So what now? You arrest him?"

"We bring him in for questioning."

"When?" she asked.

"He's on his way as we speak. Two of my cops are bringing him in."

"Oh." She knew she should be happy the case was closed, that justice would be served, but somehow, it felt like a hollow victory.

"You okay?"

She wanted to say yes, but she couldn't. Tommy's questioning and inevitable arrest would mean heartache not only for Abe but also for Trish and Nancy — good people who'd opened their hearts and their home to Abe and given him a family when his own had turned their backs on him.

It would also mean Jakob would be free to have the conversation she knew was necessary yet she dreaded all the same. She wanted Jakob in her life, she wanted the future she thought they were building toward. But she couldn't want it enough for the both of them. She'd been there and done that once before, and she knew she deserved better.

"Claire?"

Reaching down, she picked her purse up off the floor, hiked it onto her shoulder, and stood. "I should head out. You've got a big evening ahead of you."

"Whoa, whoa, whoa." He lurched forward and onto his feet, the chair creaking with his exit. "Slow down a minute. They're not here yet."

"They will be. And I need to go home." She squeezed her eyes closed in time with a quick swallow. "I need to prepare."

She'd felt Bill and her aunt watching her off and on throughout the evening meal, but with four other people seated around them talking about the snatches of Amish life they'd observed while exploring Heavenly that day, neither had been able to ask anything on a personal level.

When dinner was over and cleanup began,

she'd flitted back and forth between the dining room and the kitchen so often, there'd been little time for anything beyond a few *thank-yous* and a smattering of *don't forgets* before Tom and Debbie Steele from Room 3 were knocking on the open kitchen doorway asking Diane and Bill to join them in a game of cards.

Now, a good ninety minutes later, she could still hear pockets of laughter intermingled with an occasional cry of victory, and she was glad. Maybe next week, when the festival and her breakup with Jakob were behind her, she'd be ready to unleash a few tears onto Diane's shoulder, but for now, she needed to keep a tight rein on her emotions lest she fall apart. Her fellow shopkeepers up and down Lighted Way were counting on her, as were any residents who may have circled the big day on their home calendars.

Pressing her forehead against the cool glass, Claire watched the lazy, drifting snowflakes begin to pick up speed, first shielding and then covering the sidewalk from view. If it kept up at the current rate, she'd be getting up earlier than normal to help shovel the front walkway in preparation for checkout. If it continued into the morning and beyond, Heavenly Treasures might just have to close for the day.

It was a thought that would normally leave her giddy.

But now there was only dread.

With busyness came distraction. With quiet came time to think and —

"Nope. Not going there," she murmured, turning back to her bed and the scads of to-do lists spread across the quilt Esther had given her on her last birthday. By all accounts, everything was ready to go for next week — everyone that needed to be confirmed, was confirmed. Every detail was finalized. Every volunteer scheduled for their post and their hour. Barring any unforeseen complications, One Heavenly Night was looking good. Real good.

She ran her finger down the master list one more time, stopping on the last entry: Ruth's Christmas cookies . . .

As much as she hated the thought of Abe's face when he learned his best friend had killed his parents, there was a positive in the case being over, for it meant that Ruth could finally tell Samuel about the baby.

She gave in to the smile that came with the notion of Sarah and her new baby cousin growing up together and playing with each other after church and during visits to each other's homes. It was everything she'd wanted for her own children one day — children that would have been related by blood to Esther and Sarah if Jakob —

Sinking down onto the bed, she scooped up her phone and scrolled through her pictures, the moments and people she loved most in the world either there or somehow related to the ones who were.

There was Aunt Diane in the kitchen rolling out dough for Christmas cookies . . .

There was Harold Glick, mid-dance, celebrating the way his window display had come together for the holidays . . .

There was Ben's horse and buggy in the alley with a stack of Ruth's pie boxes on the front seat . . .

Jakob on the front porch, grinning back at her over his shoulder . . .

Jakob and her cuddled together on the sofa in Aunt Diane's parlor, smiling up at the phone for what ended up being yet another blurry attempt at a selfie . . .

Jakob —

She scrolled right and came to a stop on Mary's letter to Ruth, the uneven writing and the fears it had stirred in her heart stopping her breath for a beat. But it was okay. Ruth and Samuel were innocent. They hadn't murdered the elderly couple. Tommy Warren had . . .

She touched her fingers to the screen, pulling the letter into easy reading range.

Dear Ruth,

I know you will not think too kindly of me by the time you finish reading this letter, but the Bible says, "These are the things that ye shall do; speak ye every man the truth to his neighbor." That is why I must tell the truth.

By the time you read this, you will know that Samuel's bid for the Breeze Point job did not win. You will also learn that the one Daniel put in for Esch did. Many, including Samuel, will think it is because his was better, and that is truth. But it is also truth that it was a better bid because we made sure it was so. For many years Esch was good and strong because of him — his work, his name.

I know it was wrong. I know there will be confusion and disappointment and pain, but that is what forgiveness is for. That is what I must remind myself, too. You cannot change what you have done. You can only change what you do. That is what Daniel and I are doing.

You and Samuel are young. You have each other. There will be many years to fix the mistakes I pray you do not make with your loved ones.

From,
Mary Esch

It was hard not to laugh at the irony of Mary's last sentence, the woman's justification for stealing the bid the exact opposite of what, in fact, happened. Mary hadn't fixed the mistakes she and Daniel had made in regard to their loved one. No, they'd only made it worse. And now that same son was without his best friend — the one person in his life who actually did see him for the upstanding young man he'd always been.

The vibration of her phone sent her gaze back down to the device in time to see Jakob's name pop up across Mary's letter. She debated letting it go to voice mail, but in the end, she picked it up.

"Hi, Jakob."

"Hi, yourself. I'm sitting here, at my desk, picturing you sitting on your window seat watching the snow. Am I right?"

"No."

He waited through her silence, and then, when it became apparent she wasn't going to elaborate, he moved on, his tone taking on the fatigue she knew he had to be feeling. "So I just had my guys take Tommy back home."

She tightened her grip on the phone. "You didn't arrest him? Why?"

"Because he gave me no reason to believe he wasn't telling the truth. And trust me, I grilled him for" — she heard him move away from the phone and then return less than a second later — "five hours. Asked him the same series of questions a dozen or more different ways and nothing he said changed. He is adamant that he hasn't stepped foot on Esch land in six years. In fact, until yesterday's viewing and today's funeral, he hasn't stepped foot on Chupp's property, either."

"He said something about that to me that night in the barn, when you and Abe were in the house viewing the bodies."

"Could've been a ruse, of course, but considering he wasn't even on my radar when he said that to you, it's a little less likely." Again, it sounded like he moved the phone for a moment, but this time, instead of silence, she heard papers rustling in the background. "Anyway, I sent a few of the cops out to different farms — Hershberger's, Miller's, Stutzman's, Chupp's, and Lapp's. Had them ask if Tommy Warren ever drove them anywhere . . . If they knew who else he drove . . . That sort of thing . . .

Pretty much everyone has been transported by Tommy somewhere over the past few months. Except Chupp. Derek said that when he stopped out there, he spoke to the wife, Greta. Said she's never been driven by Tommy, just Nancy.

"So then I called Nancy and asked if she keeps records of her drop-offs and pickups. She reminded me she doesn't have to because Amish taxis aren't regulated by the state the way normal taxis are, but she does just the same. Says it's a way for her to keep track of her days."

"Okay . . ."

"She faxed me her log from the day Abe submitted his bid until the day of the murders. And assuming it's all accurate, Tommy's name shows up a lot. Just never in conjunction with Esch or Chupp."

"But his glove was outside the victims' home," she reminded. "There's no getting around that."

"And he didn't try to. When I told him it was there, he stared at me like I had two heads. There was no posturing, no blinking, no buying time. Said he couldn't explain it, even demanded to see the glove when I first mentioned it as being the reason I'd brought him in. But when I showed him the one we found, he said it was his. No doubt. Even turned it inside out to show me the label where he'd written his initials in Sharpie."

"Wow."

"Wow is right. So I asked him when he remembers wearing them last. He said it was probably on one of the taxi runs he made for his mom. That in the winter, when he's waiting for her van to get up to a bearable temperature inside, touching the steering wheel without gloves is like holding ice cubes in your bare hands."

He exhaled into the phone, his frustration over the case evident. "So then he goes on to tell me how much he pitied Daniel and Mary for believing Lloyd's rantings and ravings over their son. Even admitted how much he hated the fact Abe and Mary sat down together. He said she didn't deserve a kid like Abe. But he said it was Abe's decision and that getting to tell her the truth after all these years had been good for him."

"But it didn't change anything, right?" she prodded. "Abe was still persona non grata as far as his parents were concerned."

"He left the church, Claire. He knew it wasn't going to change their ability to have a relationship with him in the open. He just wanted them to know the truth; he wanted them to know Lloyd had lied about him to the bishop, that he was a good and honest man with a wife and a baby on the way, and that he was going to try and make a go of the trade Daniel taught him — a trade he wanted to share with his own son one day."

"I wish his words could've mattered on some level," she said. "I wish Mary and Daniel hadn't reopened their business out of left field the way they did . . ."

She pulled the phone from her ear, switched the call to speaker, and tapped her way back into Mary's letter, the woman's cryptic words seeming to leap off the screen.

For many years Esch was good and strong because of him — his work, his name.

I know it was wrong. I know there will be confusion and disappointment and pain, but that is what forgiveness is for. That is what I must remind myself, too. You cannot change what you have done. You can only change what you do. That is what Daniel and I are doing.

You and Samuel are young. You have each other. There will be many years to fix the mistakes I pray you do not make with your loved ones.

Wait.
Was it possible?
Had Daniel's seemingly out-of-left-field

bid been *for* Abe instead of *against* Abe? A way to give him the name he'd lost through lies? And if it was, how did that change —

"Claire?"

"What if Abe was telling the truth?" she said, gathering her thoughts together. "What if Mary and Daniel *did* ask him to come to their house that last night? What if they were going to tell him he could have the company? That they'd won the bid *for* him? That they *wanted* him to build under the Esch name?"

The utter silence in her ear told her everything she needed to know in that moment. Jakob was processing her words, running them through the detective part of his brain.

She, on the other hand, needed to keep talking it out. For herself. "I mean, if you reread Ruth's letter from *that* perspective, it reads very differently."

The paper shuffling was back. Then, "Oh, Claire . . ."

"It doesn't mean Tommy or Abe didn't do it," she said. "Because if we're right, and Daniel and Mary bid and won the job for their son, they never got to tell him that. All they would have known was they didn't win and that Daniel did."

"Abe didn't kill his parents," Jakob said.

"I know this with everything I am."

"And Tommy says he wasn't on that farm that night, and you're inclined to believe that, too, right?" she prodded.

"Right."

"So if Tommy wasn't on the Esch farm that night or any other night, then how did his glove happen to get dropped outside the very window the killer likely used — or pretended to use — to kill Daniel and Mary?"

She heard Jakob draw in a breath, could picture him following it up with a palm to his mouth as he took in her words. But she didn't need him to say anything. Her question had been rhetorical and he knew it.

After a few deep breaths (his) and a few last glances at the letter (hers), his voice returned in her ear. "You interested in making a drive? I can get the department's snow beast."

"Snow beast?"

"The black SUV that sits out back in the parking lot . . . It does snow like nobody's business."

"I'll be out front in twenty minutes."

CHAPTER 22

Foot by foot and, at times, inch by inch, they made their way down Aunt Diane's driveway, the mounting snow promising a difficult drive. Between them on the long bench seat were the hats, gloves, and scarves she'd secured from the inn's front hall closet after jotting a note for her aunt.

Claire had considered stepping into the parlor and sharing her plans aloud, but all that would have done was dull her aunt's fun. The note, when it was found, would tell Diane everything she needed to know . . .

"So I'm not going to be stopping at stop signs unless I have to. The less stopping we do, the less chance we have of getting stuck. Same goes for slowing down at all. Once I find the quickest yet safest pace possible, I'll try to keep it there." Jakob glanced her way. "Sound good?"

"Sounds good."

At the bottom of the driveway, he turned left onto the main road, his wipers working furiously against the speed and volume of the falling snow. The plows she knew would start coming through the streets as the storm wound down were nowhere to be seen. The winds the forecasters had predicted were starting to gust, drifting snow, shaking power lines, and decreasing visibility with each sudden burst. Ahead of them, in the flake-covered beams of the SUV's headlights, the snow was relentless.

"So that paper there" — he nudged his chin and her gaze to the open bench space between them — "that's the list Nancy faxed me this evening. I highlighted all of the runs Tommy made for his mom in the three weeks leading up to the murders. That'll be our road map of sorts tonight."

Lifting the computer printout onto her lap, she strained to make out the four distinct columns barely visible in the limited light from the dashboard. The first column showed the date, the second showed the customer's name, the third showed the destination and whether it was expected to be a quick or lengthy stop, and the fourth showed either Nancy or Tommy as the driver.

"And after you and I got off the phone, I

decided to call out to Abe's place."

"Oh?" Claire said, sliding the printout back onto the seat.

"Yeah. I wanted to hear him tell me about his conversation with Mary again. The one that Nancy Warren helped arrange."

She glanced Jakob's way. "Do you think he held something back?"

"No. I just needed to hear it again, see if something struck me differently." He tightened his grip on the steering wheel as the tires adjusted to the change from snow-topped pavement to snow-topped cobblestones. "He told her he was getting back into cabinetry. That working with his hands in a trade he learned from Daniel made him feel closer to them somehow. He told her about the baby on the way and that it was going to be a boy. He told her that one day, maybe his son would work beside him just as Abe had once done with Daniel."

"He told her what he was going to call his company, right?"

"He did. He told her he was going with Abe's Custom Woodworking and that he was getting ready to bid on his first big job."

"The Breeze Point job . . ."

"The Breeze Point job," Jakob repeated, nodding. "He said he even showed her the calculations he used to come up with his bid."

"So she knew his bid."

"Yup." Stripes of light from the lanterns they passed lit and then shadowed his face. "Abe said she was surprised he still did all his calculating with paper and pencil when he lived the life of an Englisher."

"A life they essentially ran him into," she mused.

Again, Jakob nodded. "Funny thing is, I know Abe misses the life. It's there in the way he opts for paper and pencil instead of computers, and in the simple way he dresses, and even in his beard."

"Lots of guys wear beards."

"But the length he's got? It's about what you'd expect for an Amish man who's been married for the same amount of time Abe has been married to his wife, Trish."

Claire took a moment to look over at Heavenly Treasures as they passed and then redirected her sights to Lighted Way as a whole. Sure enough, the almost Dickens-like shopping area seemed to stand even a little taller in the snow. But as quick as the thought came, it was pushed to the side by the very reason they were on the road in the first place.

"I'm curious," she said, returning her

focus to the man behind the steering wheel. "What was Mary's reaction when Abe blamed his repeated shunnings on Lloyd? Did she listen? Did she argue? What?"

"She left."

Claire stared at Jakob. "She just up and walked out?"

"Pretty much."

"She didn't say anything?"

"She didn't . . . no. Not according to Abe, anyway."

"That had to have infuriated him, no?"

Jakob met her eye for a second, maybe two. "It's why, along with his presence at the scene on the night of the crime, he fit as our perpetrator. On paper, at least. Daniel and Mary were devout Amish. Abe was under the ban. They wouldn't have invited him to their home. It just wouldn't have happened. But to answer your question without having been there when he and Mary spoke, no, I don't think it did infuriate him."

"Why on earth not?"

"Because her reaction wasn't any different than it had been when it happened. There was no change, no big thing to get angry about."

She sat with his words for a few moments as they left Lighted Way and ventured out into the countryside, where the dark roads merged seamlessly with the dark homes and fields. "A few seconds ago you said *Mary* didn't say anything when she left. Did *Abe*?"

"When she was on her way out to Nancy's car to go home, he stepped outside after her and told her Greta knew."

"His sister?" she said on a gasp.

"Yup."

"Wait. So Greta knew Abe wasn't drinking —"

"At the time . . ."

She waved his assertion away. "I get that. I know he eventually started doing the things he was being falsely accused of but . . ." Pausing, she gathered her thoughts as cohesively as possible. "You're saying Greta knew her husband was lying to the bishop about her own brother?"

"That's what Abe says."

"And — and she . . . she let it happen?" she sputtered.

"She and Lloyd were newly married. Lloyd was related to the bishop. I think she was afraid to speak against them. Add in the fact it might sour her parents' feelings for her new husband and I think it makes perfect sense." Jakob slowed the SUV enough to take the left just beyond Benjamin's farm, but still they fishtailed. "Hold on, Claire, it's getting pretty treacherous out here."

She strained to make out the road in their headlights, but it was becoming more and more difficult to know where it was in relation to the land on either side. As if reading her mind, he pointed out the elevated snow on either side of them and how it denoted the presence of fences.

"Anyway," he said, getting back to their conversation, "in Greta's defense, she was with Lloyd when Abe was caught *really* drinking a few months later. So *if* she'd had any thought of speaking up on her brother's behalf, I'm sure it went out the window then."

It was a lot to take in, a lot to process, but still, she tried, her thoughts rewinding and fast-forwarding, again and again. A glance at Jakob showed he, too, was deep in thought. They rode that way past a few farms until another slip of the tires snapped them both back to the present.

"The ME confirmed it was death by suffocation, right?" she asked, fidgeting with the edge of the printout.

"Yes."

"With pillows?"

"Yes."

"Then I would imagine, with them both

being in their mid-eighties, that it wouldn't have taken a whole lot of strength to hold a pillow on their faces until they stopped struggling —" She sat up straight. "Wait. Why didn't the second one run while the first one was being smothered?"

Carefully, while still keeping a tight hold on the steering wheel, Jakob stretched the fingers of first his right and then his left hand. "Mary had two sizable bumps to the head — one in back like Daniel had, and one to the side of her forehead that Daniel didn't have. The ME thinks both preceded death.

"That finding leads me to believe the killer knocked them both down, got to work on Daniel, and then had to knock Mary down a second time before he was able to get the pillow on her."

She took a moment to see the scene, as Jakob described, his pronoun usage giving her pause. "You said 'he' — 'before he was able to get the pillow on her' . . . Have you ruled out the notion the killer could be a female? Because Mary and Daniel were both pretty frail."

"No, I haven't ruled anything or anyone out, officially. Except Nancy."

"But Nancy had to have had some anger toward Mary and Daniel herself, wouldn't she? She clearly regards Abe as a second son . . . Abe and Tommy losing the bid to Daniel hurt her son *and* her daughter, too . . ." The more she spoke, the more she found herself warming to the idea of Nancy as the killer. Only —

Sighing, she nixed her own idea aloud. "Planting her son's glove at the murder scene would hurt Tommy . . ."

"She also had an airtight alibi for the time frame in which the murder took place. She and Trishy were at a wedding shower in Philly."

"Ugh! Ugh! Ugh!"

His answering laugh was short lived. "Welcome to my past few days. If I wasn't hitting a dead end like we just did, then my own internal radar was messing with the others on my list."

"It's so frustrating," she whispered. Stilling her fingers on the corner of the printout, she pulled it onto her lap and then pointed down at her purse. "If I keep it angled down so as not to blind you, could I use the light on my phone to look at this list? Because whoever Nancy drove after Tommy's last run is the first farm we should visit."

"Whoever *Nancy* drove? I don't understand . . ."

"Because the last time he had both gloves

for certain was the last time he drove. That means, if he left one of the gloves in the car, it would have been there the next time Nancy drove."

He hit the brakes so hard and so fast, she bumped her head against the dashboard in the ensuing fishtail. Popping the gearshift into park, he slid across the seat, cupped her cheeks with his hands, and inspected her point of impact with nothing but sheer horror on his face. "Claire, I'm so sorry. I wasn't thinking, I just heard what you said and —"

She stopped his words with a gloved finger. "I should have waited to bend for my phone until you gave me the go-ahead."

"Are you okay? You hit the dash pretty hard."

"I'm fine."

"Am I blurry? Do you have a headache?"

"I'm fine, really."

"You might not be saying that in an hour."

"Then we should probably get back to things, yes?"

He looked as if he was about to protest, but when she plucked her phone from her purse and hit the flashlight feature, he followed her finger down to Nancy's printout. Slowly, and then with gathering speed, she led them down the page to the last highlighted entry, their individual gasps at the sight of the name merging into one.

The cold snowflakes felt good on her forehead as they trudged, side by side, through the last few feet of light from the SUV. He'd tried a few times to back out of the ditch, but there just hadn't been enough traction to get the job done. Instead, Jakob had wrapped a scarf around her shoulders, secured it in front of her face, and kissed her head just before he pulled her hat down around her ears.

"Your phone is fully charged, right?" he asked yet again.

"As charged as it was when you asked back at the car, not that it matters out here — in the middle of nowhere — all that much."

"Sorry. I guess I'm just wishing I'd stuck to my guns and made you sit in the car while I went inside. Alone."

"And I'm glad you didn't." When they reached what he said was the driveway, they turned out of the headlight's beams and kept walking, the benches and tables of earlier either covered by snow or loaded into the bench wagon she could see sitting in front of the barn. Beyond that, in the limited light from the waning moon, she could just make out the exterior lines of the darkened farmhouse. "Are we going to knock and wake them up?"

"*I* am. You're going to stay out of sight. In case there's trouble."

She wanted to argue, but she let it go. Jakob was the cop, not Claire. And really, right or wrong, she wanted to savor the feeling of being cared for and worried about for just a little while longer.

A sound not unlike glass shattering set Jakob into a run through the nearly calf-high snow. She tried to keep up, but his long legs and strength had her following behind in his indents. As they rounded the bend in the drive that gave them a straight shot to the house, he turned around, pointed her toward the tree Ruth had stood behind three days earlier, and when Claire stopped, he began to run again, his body disappearing into the darkness as a shout, followed by a woman's scream, floated into the night.

Soon, glass was shattering again, followed by another shout, another scream. Reaching into her pocket for her phone, Claire looked up in time to see a quick flash . . . and then Jakob . . . and then the orange glow of fire lighting her way across the snow.

She was almost to the door when he

grabbed her by the waist and pulled her back, their bodies tumbling off the porch and onto the snow as the second floor melded into the first, the flames hungrily eating everything in their path. "Jakob . . . Jakob . . ." she shrieked, rolling off him and onto her knees. "I thought you were inside, I thought I lost —"

It was his turn to silence her words, pulling her close while he worked to catch his breath enough to speak. "I'm here. I'm here."

She looked back at the fire, pulled off her scarf, and tucked it into Jakob's hands. "Hold this. I can use it to pull you away. It's getting too hot, the fire too big."

"No, no, I can move. I'm fine." He sat up, scanned the area around them, and then, cupping his hands along the sides of his mouth, he began to shout. "Hey! I'm here — I'm up front! I've got her!"

"Who are you talking . . ." His eyes led hers toward the side yard in time to see Tommy Warren step into the fire's light, his arm wrapped tightly around Greta Chupp.

CHAPTER 23

It was nearly two in the morning when Jakob ushered Claire into his apartment over Gussmann's and shut out the rest of the world with a turn of the deadbolt. "I am so sorry I can't get you back to the inn right now. If I'd thought about it when the fellas first brought us back here, I'd have taken you home then, before we got even more snow."

"I wasn't ready to go home then," she said, slipping out of her coat and draping it across his waiting arm. "Way too much adrenaline pumping."

He hung her coat inside the closet and then led the way into the tiny yet comfortable living room she could maneuver around in the dark, if necessary. The couch off to their left was overstuffed, the blanket draped across its top perfect for burrowing under on movie nights. The end table next to the far side of the couch contained a coaster, a small candy dish, and a single hardback book — the latest Andrew Grant thriller Jakob had purchased at Glorious Books the previous month. To her right was the fireplace, its mantel boasting the framed black-and-white photograph of winter's Lighted Way — the gift she'd given Jakob the day they'd met.

"I'd offer to make a fire, but I'm thinking we've had more than our share for the night?"

Nodding, she flopped onto the corner of the couch. "Do you think it's out yet?" she asked.

"There's a chance it's moved to the barn, but the fire chief thinks it'll go out on its own before it gets there." He pointed into the kitchen, his eyes lighting on hers. "Popcorn? Something to drink? Or do you just want to go to sleep?"

"Popcorn works."

"Coming right up."

Seconds later, she heard the cabinet, and then the microwave, opening and closing — the familiarity of the routine both comforting and heartbreaking all at the same time. It was time to get everything out in the open, she knew that. But for just a few more minutes she wanted to pretend they were the team they'd once been — the team she thought they'd be forever . . .

Drifting her head back against the couch, she looked up at the ceiling while she steadied her breath. "So that's it? The case is closed? Lloyd Chupp killed Mary and Daniel?"

"That's right. And if we hadn't shown up when we did, Greta Chupp would be the one dead, instead of Lloyd, and Tommy would likely be under arrest — all orchestrated by Lloyd."

"He was that bitter?"

She didn't need to see Jakob to know he was nodding. The momentary pause in his answer was a good enough indication.

"He wanted what Abe had with Daniel when he and Greta first got married. But Daniel didn't take too well to Lloyd's laziness. When Lloyd learned Daniel was thinking about turning the cabinetry business over to Abe, Lloyd got angry. Thought it should be his, as Greta's husband. That's when he started making up those stories about Abe with the hope it would destroy the boy's relationship with his father."

"And he was right."

"Sadly, yes. But instead of turning the business over to him when Abe left, Daniel just closed it down. Lloyd was furious, of course, but it was tempered by the fact Abe was out of the picture."

When the popping from the kitchen slowed, she heard the microwave open and the buttery treat being poured into the cream-colored bowl they always used. The sound of the refrigerator opening meant he was pouring two glasses of milk — one for her and one for himself. When he was done, he'd load everything onto a small tray, grab a few napkins, and carry it back into the living room.

She knew this because it was what he did — what they did together.

"Over the years, Lloyd tried to get Daniel to let him open the company back up so he could run it . . . usually after he'd tried some other way to make money and he messed that up," Jakob said. "But Daniel wouldn't budge. Said Esch Cabinetry was done."

"Then Abe and Mary had that talk, and Mary walked out on him when he brought up the lies," Claire mused.

"She did. But remember, he told her Greta knew the truth."

Greta . . .

She cleared a spot on the coffee table for the tray, and then pulled the popcorn bowl onto her lap when he sat down. "Mary asked her, didn't she?"

"She did. And Greta told her the truth." He plucked out a few fluffy pieces and popped them, one at a time, onto his tongue. "Mary, in turn, told Daniel, and that's when they decided to make things right — or as right as they could when Abe had left the church after baptism. Since Mary knew Abe's bid, and Daniel could guesstimate what Samuel's might be, they were able to put one in that would still make money yet virtually ensure they got it. They asked Abe to come out to the farm that last night because, I believe, they wanted to tell him Esch Custom Woodworking — and the accepted bid — was his."

" 'You cannot change what you have done. You can only change what you do. That is what Daniel and I are doing,' " she recited by memory from Ruth's letter. "Wow. It was right there. In that letter."

"If you're seeing through the right glasses, it is. When you look at it with something entirely different in your head, it doesn't read the same."

"So I take it Lloyd found out? About Daniel reopening the company for Abe?"

"He sure did, and that's when he snapped. His jealousy of Abe got the best of him. So he killed Daniel and Mary before they could tell Abe. And he decided to try and frame

Tommy for the crime with the glove — as yet another way to push back at Abe for being liked and trusted in a way Lloyd had never been." Jakob took a few more pieces of popcorn and then laced his fingers behind his head. "But then we didn't see the glove, and we learned Abe had been out there, and, well, it wasn't the end of the world for Lloyd if Abe ended up going down for the crime, after all. Same end result, you know?"

"And what about Ruth's letter? Who read it?"

"We don't think anyone did. We think Mary just didn't seal it when she slipped it inside the box."

"Wow."

"I know. And tonight? Those noises we heard when I left you by the tree? That was Tommy confronting Lloyd because he'd figured it out, too."

"It was his mom's forms that they faxed to you, wasn't it?" she prodded.

"It was. He saw them sitting on the fax and he looked through them. And just like you did, he realized his glove was likely left in the car after his last run. Out of curiosity, he looked to see who his mom drove next, and when he saw Lloyd's name, the wheels began to turn."

"But how did he get out there before we did? Especially in this snow?"

"He borrowed a neighbor's snowmobile. Parked it far enough away that Chupp wouldn't hear him coming. When he got inside and confronted Lloyd with what he suspected, Lloyd actually threatened to kill Greta and pin it on Tommy. Lloyd and Tommy fought, the kerosene lantern got knocked over, Lloyd pushed Greta, and she fell into a table, which, in turn, knocked a candle onto the spilled kerosene. Tommy grabbed her and ran . . . straight into me. By then the flames were everywhere and I knew we had to get out. We were heading out the back when I heard you screaming my name. I was afraid you were going to go inside after me."

"Because I was."

Transferring the popcorn bowl from her lap to the tray, he gathered her hands in his own and brought them to his lips. "I thank God I heard you calling my name, because I'd be lost without you."

A week ago, it was the kind of statement that would have melted her heart. But it wasn't a week ago . . . It was now.

And now she knew differently.

"Why didn't you tell me about Callie?" she asked, reclaiming her hands.

He froze in place. "Callie?"

"Callie Granger. The woman whose calls you haven't wanted me to see or hear . . . The woman you were heading out to see last night but pretended you weren't . . ."

Covering his face with his hand, he tilted his chin until his head was practically parallel with the ceiling, his silence thwarted only by the slow thud of her heart.

"Jakob?"

"Oh, Claire . . ."

"That's it? That's all you have to say?"

"It's all I can say. For now."

"Can or will?"

"Please, Claire, I need you to be patient."

She looked beyond him to the window, the snow falling steadily outside showing no sign of letting up. But she had her feet and she had boots. That was enough to get her where she needed to go — where she'd be welcomed with outstretched arms.

Rising to her feet, she headed toward the door, the sadness she felt overwhelming but not insurmountable. "I'm going home now."

"Home?" he echoed, pushing off the couch. "Claire, you can't leave now. It's still snowing, remember? And we need to talk about this."

"You're going to tell me what's going on?"

"No, I can't. I . . . I just can't. Not yet.

Not this way."

She opened her mouth to argue, to point out there was no right time or right way to break a person's heart, but instead, she yanked open the door and stepped outside.

"Claire, please. I don't want you out in this."

"I'll be fine." And she would. She'd come back from heartbreak before, and one way or the other, she'd do it again. "I'm glad you're okay, I'm glad your case is closed. And I'm glad you came into my life when you did. You helped me become stronger and to have faith in my worth. That's why I know I'll get through this. In time. I just wish, with all my heart, I didn't have to."

CHAPTER 24

It didn't matter where Claire stood, or in what direction she looked. Lighted Way's first annual One Heavenly Night was everything she'd dared to imagine and a whole lot more.

To her right, standing inside the gazebo, singing their hearts out for the crowd who'd assembled around them, were Annie and Henry and their fellow youth group members. It was hard to know, exactly, if their rosy cheeks were from the cold or from the pleasure of sharing their songs with so many people, but if she had to guess, she'd say both.

Beyond the gazebo, at the western end of Lighted Way, couples — both young and old — were eagerly awaiting their turn on the horse-drawn sleigh that looked as if it had come straight from the pages of a story-book.

Across the street, but closer to where she

stood, she marveled at the crowd beginning to form for the next Living Nativity. Already they'd shared the story of Christ's birth twice, with the smiles and laughter the animals stirred giving way, both times, to the quiet oohs and ahhs when Joseph (Eli) and Mary (Esther) held the Christ child (a bundled-up Sarah) inside the manger. Maybe, if she was in the right place at the right time, she could sneak in a cuddle with Sarah before the night was over.

To her left, just past Glick's Tools 'n More, families and teenagers sat around the bonfire, roasting chestnuts and cooking s'mores while Al shared facts about various Christmas celebrations around the world. When the stories were funny, there was laughter; when they weren't, there was mesmerized silence.

Inside the otherwise vacant building to the left of the police station, Santa held court in his elaborate red cushioned chair, listening to the wishes of each and every English child who'd witnessed his arrival atop the town's shiny new red firetruck several hours earlier. Beside him, she knew, was the large red basket Esther's mother, Martha, had made at Claire's request. Inside the basket were the Christmas cookies Ruth had made and Claire had replenished three times already — the "North Pole" treats almost as big a hit as Santa himself.

Almost.

But the best part of all was that everywhere she looked, people were smiling and laughing, speaking and listening, and learning about one another. Amish spoke to Amish, English spoke to English, and in some cases they came together — to listen, to marvel, to smile, to laugh, to make a memory — their commonality in that moment a shared faith and a shared home base.

Sweeping her gaze back through the various stations, she spotted Aunt Diane and Bill. They were standing, arm in arm, at the gazebo steps, singing along with Annie and her friends. She rose up on tiptoe as she looked back toward the nativity, spotting Ben's cows, Eli's sheep, and even Samuel's goat, Gussy. As the laughter turned to quiet gasps, she rose up even higher and grinned at the sight of her best friend gazing down at Sarah with such love it was impossible to look away. One day she'd have that. And if she didn't, she was grateful God had guided her to a place where she could know Esther and Eli, Ruth and Samuel, Ben and —

She darted her gaze back toward the bonfire, across to the storefront where she could just make out Santa with his big bulging stomach, and back to the alley where Benjamin so often parked. Somewhere, tucked away in a quiet corner, her sweet friend was daring to love again by asking for Rebeccah's hand in marriage. She didn't need to see him or hear her response to know what it would be. Benjamin Miller was a keeper, plain and simple. And Rebeccah complemented him perfectly.

Somewhere, too, she hoped Ruth was telling a more relaxed Samuel about the baby they would soon have, the knowledge that he'd be doing some contract work with Esch Custom Woodworking on the Breeze Point project surely enabling him to embrace the news and his sweet wife.

"Claire?"

She turned toward the voice she still dreamed about every night as she was drifting off to sleep and gave in to the smile she couldn't hold back even if she tried. No matter what had happened between them, she still loved Jakob Fisher. Always would. After all, that's what true love was — steadfast and never ending.

"It came out pretty good, didn't it?" she asked, grinning.

"The festival? It's incredible. In fact, I'd go so far as to say it's *almost* perfect."

She felt her smile falter. "Almost?"

He brought his eyes back on hers and held them there. "Almost."

"Is there an issue I don't know about?"

"It's not an issue, exactly. It's more of an explanation, followed by a question. Then, depending on the answer, this night will, in fact, jump all the way to perfect."

"Jakob, I don't understand what —"

He pointed to the bench just a few feet beyond Heavenly Treasures. "Can we sit?"

"I don't think that's such a good idea. I've done everything I can to keep myself together to this point because I had to. For this festival and everyone here tonight. But Jakob? I'm holding on by a thread right now, and I can't afford to let go until it's —"

"Please?"

She looked back toward the bonfire, across to Santa, down toward the nativity, but there was nothing and no one that seemed to demand her attention at that moment. Shrugging, she let him guide her to the bench, her gaze falling on a thin manila folder. "Uh-oh, someone left something behind."

"No, it wasn't left behind. It's there because I put it there. For you. For us."

"For us?"

Taking her hand, he gently walked her backward until she had to sit. "You have no idea how many times I started to pick up the phone to call you these last few days. Or how badly I wanted to chase after you that night instead of staying in the shadows watching to make sure you made it back to the inn safely."

"You followed me home? In the snow-storm?"

"I followed you as far as there" — he pointed to the building on the opposite side of the street — "and then I watched until you turned up your aunt's driveway."

"Why?"

"Because it was snowing. Because you were upset. Because I needed to know you were safe. Because . . ." He stopped, shook his head, and then squatted down on the ground in front of her. "Claire, there is no Callie."

Again, he shook his head. "I mean, there is *a Callie*, of course. But there is no Callie *for me*. Never has been, never will be. There's only you."

She stared at him. "But I heard you, the other night, the things you said, the way you told me you had to go back inside to work even though you'd just told Callie you were coming out to see her."

"Remember Mary's letter to Ruth? How it sounded one way because that's what we took it to mean? But once we stepped back, without those preconceived notions, it sounded very different?"

"Yes . . ."

"Well, I think that's what happened the other night, when you heard me on the phone. Probably because I acted like a caught fool the few times she called when you were around."

She felt her knee begin to bounce and tried to stop it with her hand. "But you said you got her picture and that it was gorgeous," she said, her voice shaking. "You said it was everything you both wanted and that it was a million times better than you'd imagined."

"Because the picture *was* gorgeous, it *was* a million times better than I could have imagined, and" — he grabbed her hand, and together, they stopped her shaking knee — "it *is* everything *we* — as in you and me, not me and Callie — both want."

Leaving her hand in place, he reached across the bench, plucked the folder from its resting spot, and set it atop her hand — opened.

"All those evenings we started to watch a movie at my place only to shut it off and daydream about our future together? The kitchen you want, the workshop I'd like, the patio we need to entertain all our friends? It's all right *here.*" He pointed at the picture of a cottage-style house that sparked a sense of familiarity she couldn't place at the moment. "That's why Callie was calling, why she was sending me pictures, why I was going out to see her that night . . . She does part-time work as a Realtor, and I asked her to keep a lookout for me — for us."

"For us?" she rasped, looking from the picture to Jakob and back again.

"For us."

Her head was spinning so fast she didn't know what to say, what to think.

"This place was actually the old guest house for what is now Sleep Heavenly. It was sold off probably a decade before your aunt bought the inn."

Casting her eyes back down at the paper, she noted the similar windows, the similar porch railing, the similar gingerbread styling around the eaves. "This is behind the tree line in the back of Aunt Diane's property, isn't it?"

His mouth spread wide in a smile. "It is. And I wanted to tell you the other night when you were at my place, but it wasn't a done deal yet and you walked out so fast, I didn't know what to do. I wanted to stop you, wanted to tell you about all of this right then and there, but I didn't want to do it that way. I wanted to do it *here* . . . tonight. I wanted it to be special."

"I . . . I don't know what to say."

His smile widened still farther, calling into play the dimples she so loved. "That's okay because I haven't gotten to the question part."

"The question part?"

He held up his index finger, resituated his squat into a full-out bended-knee pose, and reached into his pocket to reveal a small brown leather jewelry box. Then, with hands that were both strong and a little shaky, he opened the box, removed the ring from inside, and gently coaxed her tear-splattered hand away from her mouth. "Claire Weatherly, would you do me the great honor of becoming my wife?"

"Your *wife*?" she echoed.

"My wife."

"Oh yes, yes, yes — a million times yes!"

Jumping to his feet, Jakob pulled her up and off the bench as applause broke out around them. She didn't need to look to know her Heavenly family was there; she could feel their presence, their love, their happiness.

He drew her close, his breath warm on her ear. "*Now* this night is perfect."

ABOUT THE AUTHOR

While spending a rainy afternoon at a friend's house as a child, **Laura Bradford** fell in love with writing over a stack of blank paper, a box of crayons, and a freshly sharpened number-two pencil. From that moment forward, she never wanted to do or be anything else. Today, Laura is the national bestselling author of the Amish Mysteries, including *Just Plain Murder* and *A Churn for the Worse.* She is also the author of the Emergency Desert Squad Mysteries, and, as Elizabeth Lynn Casey, she wrote the Southern Sewing Circle Mysteries.

The employees of Thorndike Press hope you have enjoyed this Large Print book. All our Thorndike, Wheeler, and Kennebec Large Print titles are designed for easy reading, and all our books are made to last. Other Thorndike Press Large Print books are available at your library, through selected bookstores, or directly from us.

For information about titles, please call:
  (800) 223-1244

or visit our website at:
  gale.com/thorndike

To share your comments, please write:
  Publisher
  Thorndike Press
  10 Water St., Suite 310
  Waterville, ME 04901